NINE INCH BRIDE

BOOK ONE

AN

EPIPHANY

ON

WALL STREET

by _anonym

Copyright 2014 anonym

Author Networks 2nd Edition*

ISBN: 978-0-9853897-8-9 (paperback)
ISBN: 978-0-9853897-6-5 (ePub)
ISBN: 978-0-9853897-9-6 (Kindle)

[*Book one was originally published under the title Conundrum © 2012.]

Readers are Saying

"A slight jaunt into the future, nicely done, and destined to become a classic."

". . . nothing contained in its text is very far from what exists today. A question of degree, only—or perhaps, some would say, a question only of what is publicly known."

"Begins with a riot of imaginative storytelling where non-fiction thought leaders leave off—Noam Chomsky and Chris Hedges come to mind."

"As the title character revels in and reviles the language on which she depends, she becomes in her singularity a metaphor for humankind."

". . . fills a void as the literary answer to *Atlas Shrugged*."

"Beautifully written . . . a delicious, literate satire which repays close attention."

"A well thought out dystopian novel, where 'Revolutionary meets Wall Street' in a bonfire of corporate culture . . . extraordinarily insightful."

Prologue to the Series

Some saw the hand of God in the unfolding of events I will relate, divinity at work, as did we for a while in wonder at our victories. But we were in truth no more nor less than instruments in the music of our times.

I set my story down for Sahar, and for the history we made, as democracy again takes root in the American soul and reaches arms to the sky. I knew her as no other did, and I write to tell you before I die what really happened in America.

Certainly she was a gift, and we played as gods and lovers, but forgiveness, no, I do not ask for it, nor for accolades or myths.

Our fateful first meeting begins my tale. Whether I am believed or not, my work is done in telling.

CHAPTER 1

What goes up must come down

I stood on the World Trade plaza facing the setting sun, low in its winter angle, gilding the building facades. The air was mild for the late season. A light breeze blew in from a shimmering amber bay.

The heel of one foot had come free of its confines and rested on the rim of my shoe, my weight on the odd leg, like a lame donkey. My suit jacket was opened, tie looped from the collar, shirt soiled with sweat, unbuttoned. I might have been mugged to judge from the mask of bewildered rage compressed upon my face.

I had avoided the plaza for years. Now as the swollen drama of the day subsided, I stood in silence as if rooted in the hallowed ground. The bare expression jangled my nerves. Why is the ground of the dead 'hallowed' and not the ground of the living? What was really memorialized here? An implosion of architectural arrogance, obscene in its scale? A desperate feat of arms hurled against it? Failure and humiliation? Grandeur?

My life had collapsed with the market this afternoon, and wet eyes made a blur of the horizon. My drama could not be exaggerated, I believed, as I stood fists clenched, a battle-ground of hot serrated thoughts that resolved to one certainty: I was ruined. The edifice of my life was a wreck. My implosion would have no memorial.

Broke and in debt, I felt stripped naked standing there. I had been blindsided by a crash for the second time in my 28 years. This time I was leveraged out, every cent of my own and every cent I could borrow on margin I had put to work with the calm confidence of the Wall Street professional that I was. My vanity now seemed to have come full circle with a smoldering vengeance.

The World Trade Tower's shadow, crawling inexorably along the plaza stones in the failing sun, seemed like my flung-down soul. My eyes were locked in a blind stare, and within the mind's eye arose a vision of reason and order, an incarnation of justice and faith, hard work, reasoned risk, and a well-deserved payoff—mine—crushed like the lives here memorialized.

Memorialized. Bile rose in my throat at the word. The machine that is time would not stop to remember me. The world would toil on insensate. Fallen and disgraced in the coliseum of finance, I had no sanctuary. The towers of avarice all around would not nod for my reprieve. All thumbs were down.

I waited for rage, pent up and compounded, to come hurtling back at the glass and steel spire, which seemed poised to implode under its overweening mass, poised to hammer down all sense and sensibility in its footprint. I waited for the spire to collapse in a rage of smoking jetsam like the Twin Towers, my bloodied corpse among the splintered bone and pulp like so much landfill trash. I willed it, to no avail.

It was not yet dark, the sun a sliver of blaze across the river, when the plaza began to fill around me. Well packaged flesh and bone straggled through the obedient doors of the surrounding buildings as the elevator banks regurgitated their cargo. Faces passed around me, sullen, drained, bitter, silent. The gaps between them gradually closed until a steady throng of workers marched past me in the gathering dark.

My stomach clenched at the sight of them in the anxious twilight. In a sudden intuition they seemed to me like a swarm of cannibal appetites, of teeth and clutches and blows that did not bite or claw or beat upon me only because I'd been reduced to a ghost. I was cold, and shivered convulsively, certain I bore witness as one who was not there.

In the February dark beneath the bare Tower, my isolation grew until I had to fight the urge to walk along with them, to trudge in unison with the rush hour throng, to insist on my kinship in their hurt this terrible day. Like them, I too would have a home for the night before my life was uprooted.

I stood my ground and attempted to square my shoulders, fidgeted, demanded control of my body, my mind, my life, and fidgeted again. There was more truth in the cold night air than in any consolation. I lost the thread of my thoughts, clutched my jacket closed, and found my thoughts again, repellent thoughts.

For those left with the stake, the buy-in of a lifetime awaited, one in which I would have no share. I fairly seethed in envy, pitied and despised myself.

An algorithm of trading maneuvers, complete but for chimerical x, calculated themselves with a will of their own and died in stark remembrance: my account was a black hole, a vortex from which no light escaped.

Memorialized. "Damn," I cursed explosively aloud, stamping my heel back in its sheath. "Damn it all."

~

I dreamed restlessly of a lava slide, a hissing, molten slurry of fire and char that crawled avariciously toward me, my back to a wall of stone with no escape. I dreamed a low music, a bird sound, mechanical and incongruous, banal in the terror of my predicament, a melodic hoax mocking my final moment. The music grew louder as the lava's breath, a searing stink of sulfur, overcame me. At the last second, breathless and gagging, I was hoisted up and out of the inferno as if by angels.

I dimly recognized the sound as the persistent chime of the Net-box, its refrain like the laughter of a loon. Someone was calling me, I cogitated horizontally, unable to open my eyelids. Banality dropped into place like a ton of lead. I remembered the cause of this reluctance to open my eyes was the whiskey I drank the night before. Sweat from my brow ran into the eye closest the damp pillow. Squinting with the other one, I was unable to make out the blinking ID display across the room and croaked to the bedside transceiver, "Show caller."

It was Robbie, a fellow trader at the fund with whom I had an honest if teasing friendship. "Answer," I said and raised myself on one arm to greet the pallid face filling the monitor. "Hey, fatso," I rasped feebly. The gap in his front teeth showed through fleshy lips. The close-up view cropped out his thinning hair.

"They get around to canning you, pretty boy?"

"What… What time is it?" I sat up and rubbed my eyes with my knuckles, my squinted eyes jousting with the light. "Can who?"

"You, that's who. They canned me last night. The vid was playing Wagner when I walked in the door." There was a silence.

"I haven't heard anything." I was alert now. "Show my face," I commanded and the lens eye found my voice and framed my head and shoulders. I regarded the thumbnail display of myself with dismay as the sleep-disheveled head stared back at me bleary-eyed. I knew the worst already.

"Half the equity and all of the index crew, everyone who got hammered is getting axed, and that includes you, hotshot." There was a long pause as my mind chased its grieving neural networks.

"Everyone?" I asked.

"Yeah." His face seemed to be hurting, tense and reddened, his eyes liquid like he had been crying, or soon would be. I had not seen this expression on his face before.

"Just like that?" I managed to say, succumbing to the communion of misery. He did not answer for a while.

"Two weeks base and collect your box at the door," he added as an afterword to his own sunken thoughts. He was pulling me down, down.

"Gets worse," he said, finding his voice again. "They're doing the same thing over at the big four. I called Neil. He's out, and you know what that means for you."

Neil was one of the better performers at Finchley's, a small boutique fund, just as Rob and I were at Mercantile Hedge, a larger though less prestigious operation. Robbie's point was that Neil was the son of Texon's CEO. If anyone had protection, it was Neil. Or me, the me of the day before yesterday, top gun and rising star who shot skeet with the company owner and dated his granddaughter, the me that seemed to have been vacuumed out of my hulk like an abortion. The silence dragged on as the implications settled into plain truth, until both of us were embarrassed.

"I was leveraged out." My voice broke unexpectedly. "The margins..."

"See you in line at burn court."

Robbie was pulling me to tears and I had to get off the phone. "Let me go, Robbie," I rasped. "Call you later."

"Sure. Gonna look into a chauffeur's license. I can't make the rent."

I gazed unseeing at the Netbox screen after the departure chime, waiting for the tears. I regarded the flat monitor existentially as if for the first time. It seemed like a botched prosthetic head, then like a ghoulish paw waiting for the right moment to slam my soft, deserving skull.

I fell back into bed as an incoming call was announced with its bird-like sound, musical and mocking. It was exactly 8:00 A.M. I shut my eyes, grasping in dark certainty for illusions, but the sound was irrefutable in its logic. I knew I could no more resist it than close my ears.

"ID caller." It was the boss. "Preview," I gasped, and the screen filled with the PR photo of his earnest face. I lay unmoving, head on pillow, and did not volunteer mine. "Answer." It was a recording over the still image. The ritual words were spoken in a voice to which there was no appeal. For this I was grateful. We were the first casualties in a crash, always. There would be no reprieve.

With the fade-out of the message, I shut my eyes. I felt dirty and sapped. I'd been over and over the numbers and there was no way out. Eighteen calendar days until the next rent. Ruinous penalties by March 2nd, and five days later, the Marshal would arrive with papers and the police.

"News wall," I finally spoke. The left wall pixilated into a commentator in front of the stock exchange. An analyst and fund manager were discussing the market "holiday" the exchange had decreed. Channel after channel the news was the same, until reality had finally blunted itself on my consciousness.

Speculation was rampant. One commentator showed a who's who list of folks with the cash to take advantage of absurdly punished sectors, recession-proof cherry picks at disaster discount. Another provided a history of technical oversight reforms put in place to insure such panic declines would not overwhelm the hapless reforms of a decade ago.

Too big to fail had failed again, but the market was out of whack with fundamentals, the pundits reassured viewers. The President and Fed Chairman would hold a joint press conference on money supply and bailout. Twice the dual meaning of the Chinese word weiji, crisis and opportunity, was noted. Total Security Theorem, which ruled Net trade and commerce, was the only stock left standing.

Nearly everyone owned some token of stock through a mutual fund, from the apprentice just out of school to a janitor nearing retirement. The latter probably would not live long enough to recoup what was lost in a single day. Capital flows would freeze and consumer demoralization would harden into layoffs and unemployment in every sector. The middle class had been bamboozled, again.

Empire City, the world's financial capital, home of Wall Street and Freedom Tower, would be stricken with an exodus of the freshly fallen. I was one insignificant piece of the pain. There was nothing consoling in this realization.

I swung my legs off the bed and got to my feet, making for the terrace, swiping a robe from the chair on the way. The glass door slid apart a bare second before my face collided with it, a game of chicken I played out of habit. I pulled the robe around me in the cold and leaned out over Second Avenue, 27 stories below.

There was far less traffic than usual, but I half expected to see the streets deserted. An exceptional number of police drones were sprinkled among the passenger cars and taxis, and there were few pedestrians for a morning rush hour, but otherwise the city seemed indifferent. The sun shone brilliantly from behind my building, illuminating a silent sky of azure. To either side of my balcony, the blue silhouette of shadowed structures invaded the pale sky. Soot-grayed remnants of snow still lined the upper ledges, and a north wind, accelerated in the channels of the City canyon, rustled through winter-killed roof gardens below.

On buildings before me to the west, the sun glinted splendidly on glass, beyond a bright azure sky. The sound of shattering glass forced my glance to the left and upward. Across the street, several stories higher than my perch, a window had exploded outward. A dark suit emerged among its lattice and shards, astonishingly it was a man, his arms swinging at the air above the avenue as his legs, which had propelled him out and clear, were still pumping at a run. His arc was brief.

He plummeted akimbo in breathless silence as time stretched on, and smacked the sidewalk concrete audibly from where I stood high on the terrace. His face seemed to emerge from the pavement itself. An ink stain spread from beneath his skull.

There were screams from the street. A woman walking a tiny dog on a leash heaved her breakfast into the gutter. Windows opened in the canyon, heads surveying in all directions. Sirens dopplered closer. The smashed body attracted a small crowd. Some turned and fled, nauseous when they made sense of the pulp in its suit and tie. A shoe lay empty beside the foot in a proper black sock.

Police and ambulance vehicles arrived together a few moments later, the responders emerging briskly to survey the scene. Heads conferred briefly, the police entering the building while the EMS slid a body bag under the remains with some difficulty. They had him cleared away in minutes. Even the dispersed brains and the shoe had disappeared, a misshapen shadow of blood on the pavement all that remained. A crew member paced the area, and bent over, retrieving some indiscernible thing. Then the okay was given to hose off the walkway, and the shadow disappeared under a parked car. The ambulance drove off, its siren silent.

The wind had picked up. I turned back inside, less cold than sick at heart. I shivered and shook as the door thud shut behind me. I glared around at the impertinence of the furnished room, agitated but oddly inspired. I could feel myself punching through glass, hurling into the air with the might of rage and resolve. I could feel the jumper's splat in my bones.

What would I think in those timeless seconds going down? What regret would share the terror as I flailed in space, the ground rushing up to smash me?

There's always time for suicide, I said aloud defensively, intending no joke, and collapsed into a chair, face in hands as my stomach churned in a roller coaster of emotions. There were less showy ways out. I stood up again. I sat down. I got up. I stood there then sat, deflating into the chair. I knew I had to act, and quickly, only to find myself defeated by the futility of action.

Why did I have to go out there and witness this man's frantic rush to death? I felt nothing for him, but could not deny I was thrilled with the grandness of his gesture. I was guilty and ashamed. Consciousness seemed unbearable.

I groped for any random thought that did not end in the man's splat and remembered, incongruously, that Keira should be back from her latest Mediterranean jaunt. She would be staying at the Old Man's estate in the Catskills. Twenty-three days in all before the uniformed man with a badge and a gun knocked at the door. I had to do something.

I stood up and sternly admonished myself to "get the fuck out of here." It was a reassuring sound, the solid and convincing "uck" of it, full of vacant finality. I went to the vid and commanded the mirror view. Brushing my hair with my hands and looking my reflection in the eye I had a eureka moment. "Take a vacation with Keira," I said wonderingly aloud. "Take an extended vacation, indefinite if possible." I had see-sawed wildly into hope.

"Keira, Keira, Keira," I said, and rehearsed in my mind on the way to the shower how this might work. "Medium, hot," I said, and the nozzles obeyed. I lathered my hopes to life, rinsed my doubts away, and dried myself critically in the mirror. Beautiful Keira, I thought. Old Man Wellingham, her grandfather, tycoon of tycoons, was set against us, and the reason *du jour* was her extravagance—two week's allowance lavished on me in the form of a shiny new Porsche for my birthday some months ago. That had her doting granddaddy choking with disapproval, though he was antagonistic from the minute he had learned of us.

Her extravagant gift was now all I had to pay off the margin call on my trading account. I had to sell it, and fast. Default on the call would cost me my trading license, as would bankruptcy. I'd be stigmatized for a decade. My degree in finance, for which I bore half a million in debt, would be rendered worthless in the meltdown. The trap that had sprung on me was nearly perfect.

Keira was pliable, but each angle of approach seemed to end in stalemate, except one, which I reasoned would have to be called an elopement. There was no other way to persuade her. Of course, I should marry her. They'd never cut her off completely, and two could live very nicely on a fraction of her allowance. "What more do you want out of life?" I demanded aloud.

Granddaddy could squeeze her father, force him to draw her down to subsistence levels. Even at that there were countries where the exchange rate would make us care-free. Damn the license, I could still trade my own account and do that from anywhere. She might go for it. In time her father would find a way to get around the Old Man. In time they'd accept us, even the Old Man. He would at least die eventually, thank God.

I could love her. Maybe I was the only one who really could. She was brisk, alert, spirited. She gave meaning to the word vivacious. She was also boundlessly self-centered. We seemed to agree on that one thing: she always came first. She was bitter about the scars across her belly from her father's stupid accident, and she had a hateful streak because of it, but she also had a wonderfully deep sensual responsiveness in her favor. She was a Stradivarius really, so finely tuned to sexual touch. "All in all," I said aloud, confronting my mirror image. "Show me one unattached soul who wouldn't think you an idiot not to marry her."

Or at least try. I strove to convince myself that this was still just the first morning of my fallen state and I had yet to formally gauge my prospects. The jumping man might just have my nerves jangled, I reasoned. I had twenty-three days for a miracle to reveal itself, while I clawed at every angle to make one happen—or down, down, down I'd go.

I pondered, searching for a flaw in the trap, until the what-ifs beat themselves senseless one against the other and only the extremes were left standing: I could join my mashed friend in a body bag or marry a modestly bitchy, oversexed, mega-heiress. And I had best get a move on if it was going to be the latter.

For now, I decided, it's still a game and I am still a player in it. As long as there was an option, I had to try it. "Concierge!" I commanded, now frantic to act. The transmission light flickered. "Car at the front door please," I said to the corridor wall on my way out of the apartment.

"Door," I said to its range flicker, and went out into the landing hall. An elevator stood empty. I'd have my choice of rides. "To the lobby, 'Valkyries,' window view, slow."

"Ride of the Valkyries" stormed in surround sound as the walls beamed in my slow descent from cameras outside, as if the elevator were glass enclosed, gliding smoothly down the outside of the building. Vertigo gave way to a childish delight, the forgone safety of home and the impending, perilous bottom lost to a moment of rhapsody.

I fairly beamed as I exited, greeting the concierge at her desk with a smile and a wink. The immaculate cream Porsche stood directly in front of me, engine running, door opened, the cockpit beckoning. I dropped in and shut the door with a solidly gratifying thunk.

"Top down," I ordered, eyes lingering over the seductive controls. I revved the engine in idle, reckoning this would be our last drive.

* * *

CHAPTER 2

Takes two to tango

The road was smooth and the traffic light, orderly and efficient, a stark contrast to the Manhattan of old movies, where foul-belching dinosaurs roared deafeningly along pot-holed streets jammed with cars, their exhaust fumes stoically endured by pedestrians assembled at the crosswalks.

Electric-only zones had been established, and air in the Island City felt clean, at least when the wind came from the ocean or the Catskills. Since the City had been privatized, all commercial traffic stopped in the boroughs, and bridge and tunnel rail depots dotted the East River shores. The odor of fossil fuels only reached us when the wind blew in from the industrial Jersey shore across the Hudson to the west.

Residents were given preference in the private car quota set for the City, so for the better part of the day, driving along the canyon streets was actually pleasant. The uptown drive took me through the heart of its architectural splendor, an eclectic chaos of angular glass and steel monoliths, pyramids and spires. All around me stood the aspiration of mankind and the temples of our undoing.

Pedestrian zones on the West Side were graced with low, ivy-clad stone and brick buildings, embracing whole neighborhoods of colorful antique residences, quaint shops, and private gardens enclosed in wrought iron.

The Old Man profited at every turn from beautification mandates the City Board imposed, like clinging vines. The Board required solar installations, feeding profits to Solar Skin Technology, one of the Old Man's myriad holdings under Green Con. Everything relating to nature was a Green Con product, from the soil in the tree pots to the walls and levees holding the sea back from flooding the lower island.

As Chairman of the Board of Empire City, virtually every profit center was his treasure, from raspberries to real estate; and what he did not own outright, he had a share in. There were pieces of sidewalk he owned, the property demarcated with a line of brass inlaid in the concrete and duly noted in a small corner plaque embedded in the sidewalk.

I knew Keira would be at the Old Man's estate or at home in Connecticut if he drove her crazy at the guesthouse. The Old Man had forbidden her the City to punish her for the Porsche under me. I was already the cause of considerable frustration to her and, under the circumstances, she could not overlook a dive in my financial condition or the gaping void in my financial prospects.

That void changed everything. My liabilities as a mate had grown like warts. I was an imposter in these credit card clothes and gifted sports car. Approaching the GW Bridge gate, where I waited in line beside a panorama of the great City sparkling in the sunlight to the south, I felt ashamed. I was an orphan from the sticks who made good, heading down, down, down. Dark pessimism returned and I flushed with anger at these mood swings against which I seemed to have no defense.

I had to keep my spirits buoyant. It was a matter of survival. I could not face these people in this crippled state of mind. I spoke for jazz guitar, very loud, heater on, and let the windows down as well.

The gate scanners on the Jersey side of the bridge uploaded identity, ownership, insurance, residency, and travel data from the vehicle while debiting the toll, and I left a brief rip with the tires in departing, the plaintive yelp noted by more than one person in uniform. But I was not speeding, and I knew such behavior by the youthful and privileged was common at the gate.

I called Keira.

"Two hours, Keira," I said to the mic in the dashboard. "What are you wearing?" Since picture phone had proved a form of intoxication, an active car monitor would be regarded as akin to drunken driving.

"I'm trying on little black dresses," came the reply. "You sound like the top's down."

"Yes."

"Well don't get a ticket. I'm barely unpacked."

I took the car out of gear and revved.

"Vroom to you too. Oh, no. Grandpa is headed this way. He hasn't given me a proper greeting yet. Oh, please God, don't let him stay long. Got to go-oh," she sang.

She would have had the outer wall in camera mode, projecting its image to the inner wall as if no wall were there, and seen her grandfather coming. It dawned on me that I was the cause of his sudden visit. He had probably picked up the call on his surveillance. There would be no getting around him in any event.

He would know already that I was ruined, and have a sadistic feast on my guts. On the other side of the ledger, I expected she'd like nothing more than to get the hell out of there, anywhere.

That was all I had to do, get her out of his clutches, and then let her decide. It was a long shot getting her out, however, and would take all the balls I could muster.

Instead, I was unraveling by the minute. My head could not overcome the hollow of misgivings in my heart. I shivered and flushed in a sweat. I pulled the mirror to me and confirmed a dangerous reddening at the fringes of the eye. "Damn it all," I yelled as I thumped the wheel and came to a stop in the break-down lane.

There was no turning back now, I persuaded myself, breathing consciously for calm, "Re-lax, re-lax…" I breathed. "Don't be a cry baby, Kenny," I teased, a lingering and effective memory from an amalgam of surrogate mothers.

There was no point in thinking about anything. I'd get past him or I wouldn't. She would come with me or not, but if I let myself mull like this, I had no chance. I revved the motor and popped the Porsche in gear, leaving a long squealing burn to match my inner friction.

I drove two hours more, slowly regaining my composure as I prayed for wit and calm sufficient to the undertaking. I drove until the roads became narrow, winding, unpredictable. There were no more reassuring embankments, and railings seemed placed only where someone likely had perished before. The road canted sharply up and leftward one moment, the next steeply down and right, winding all the while like my emotions, a dangerous ravine on either side. The winter air was fragrant with conifer, the heater bathed me in warmth. I felt my sensitivities were on the mend taking note of these things.

It seemed like any other day at the village, a snow-clad daydream morning. The quiet storefronts were arrayed in colorful distinction exactly as I remembered. Up the creek road to the Old Man's estate, my determination simmered in the cold.

At the entrance the guard nodded as car and station exchanged data, and the majestic wrought iron gate swung open to a spacious uphill roadscape sentineled by lofty well-spaced pines. Beyond the tree-lined drive were rolling meadows blanketed in white and dotted with inviting stands of perfectly groomed conifers.

I passed the caretaker's house, smoke swirling from the chimney top. In front, Pedro was at work on a huge log with a primitive set of hand tools. I waved and pulled over. "Good to see you, Pedro."

"*Que pasa, Amigo,*" he said. "*La señorita?*"

I nodded. "What are you making there?"

"Boss wants a totem pole."

"A what?" I asked, thinking I must have misunderstood.

"Totem pole. Eskimo, like this." He unrolled and held up a photo poster of an Aleutian totem pole, one frozen grimace atop another—pain, laughter, rage, fear, and wonder in ascending order. I saw my face in each of them in turn.

"He likes to make up work for me in the slow season. This totem, he says, is a gift to the god of good fortune."

"What good fortune?"

"He does not tell me, but of course, it is making money. I can tell from his hand clapping."

"He's in a good mood?" That could mean a clean getaway if Keira was game.

"Oh, yes, a very good mood. Juanita burnt his lunch and he did not even curse her."

Wonderful, I thought. I might get through today after all.

"Even the crocodile is happy sometimes," he added.

"Thanks, Pedro. Keira is at the guesthouse?"

"Last I knew." A shotgun boomed in the distance. "He is shooting the clays."

He would know I was here already, I thought. The guard would have beeped him. Boom went the gun again.

"How long will that keep him busy?" I asked.

"Another hour, maybe less," Pedro replied knowingly. "Then Miss Prentice helps him to ski."

"Is she the latest?" A widower, conjecture about his affairs was a staple of gossip, unlikely as they were at his age.

"*No sé, pero la señorita...*" He outlined an hourglass with both hands.

"Ha, I'll bet." The Old Man surrounded himself with attractive women and had two beauties on his staff, a petite redhead in her early thirties who handled his technology and a lanky Russian brunette in her late twenties who spoke five languages and handled the phone. As far as anyone knew, he never bedded either of them, or any of the itinerant beauties decorating the manor from time to time, though he acted as if he had them all in turns in a show of virility belied by his seventy-six years.

"You have your wood to cut," he said nodding toward the guesthouse with a grin. "Go. She is waiting."

"Thanks, Pedro." I eased into gear and waved good-bye. Seconds later I was careening down the lane, the rancorous engine announcing my arrival. I came to a skidding swerve in front of the guesthouse she had to herself, throwing up a spray of snow. A good entrance, I thought, taking in the face of the dark log and stone cottage, its solidity belying the pixel wall she would be looking out as if it were glass. I grinned in spite of myself and bounded the snow toward the steps thinking, a blessed hour long island of reprieve. Dismissing the idea of knocking, I swung the door open.

Keira was seated on the high step of the sunken floor, her elbow on her knee and looking absently out at the Porsche, a wood fire crackling in the stone fireplace. She was alone and barefoot in a skimpy black dress, one leg half tucked under her, the other exposed high on the thigh. Her slender ankle hung over the edge of the step, toe pointed to the floor. The dark chestnut hair was cut to expose the back of her neck but hung nearly to her shoulders in front, framing her small face and blue eyes in a tunnel as she turned to beam a smile at me. She blushed and looked back outside.

I stooped to nuzzle her right temple with my left cheek, hands firmly below her bare narrow shoulders. She turned to me and we kissed. It was too brief and her posture spoke of distraction.

"Are you okay?" I asked, and swung down beside her.

"Exhausted." She looked me directly in the eye. "He told me again to say it's over between us, and he said it was the last time he would tell me." She looked away.

I kissed her ear at the nexus of her neck and cheek, then her neck behind the ear and below, then the corner of her mouth. She turned and I kissed her thin lips, briefly, over and over, until she warmed, extending a leg out from under her and leaning into the kiss. I broke to find the nexus on the other side of her neck, kissing the hollow there all the more lovely for the wisp of dark hair curving down across her cheek.

"Ummph," she uttered, stirring and moving her head back, but I kissed her mouth again before she could find words. She was as aroused as I, and the kiss melted into a languorous dream with a volition of its own.

"Ken, he was here for twenty minutes," she managed to gasp. "Which is more than I can bear."

I moved my hip into hers and brushed my hand down her shoulder, the other taking her head. I kissed her eyes, her right temple, the side of her head above the ear.

"He said you were 'morally adrift' and I shouldn't waste more time on you."

"Takes one to know one," I murmured.

"He said you missed your calling, that should have been a porn star." I chuckled along with her, nuzzling her neck.

"He said he wished you'd hurry up and get rich so you'd turn a lighter shade of green."

"Ha," I laughed, surprised.

"He said…" I stopped her words with a kiss, my left had taking her rib cage while the other reached around her back, pressing her bosom firmly against me. Her arms reached out and returned the embrace, and we kissed gradually harder until she moved her head back and put it on my chest.

"But then he said you would never amount to anything because you're a slave to sensuality."

"At the moment, I'd have to agree," I managed to whisper, then started in again on the hollow below her ear.

"So am I," she said, and I pulled her to the floor as we kissed again, caressing her face and neck with my left hand until it came to rest just above her breast. She was breathing heavily between kisses, and I swung my knee between her legs, pressing upward as my hand caressed the nipple beneath her dress. She groaned faintly and I wedged my knee up tighter into her crotch, hitching her dress up, coaxing her wetness. I watched her thighs tighten over my leg and realized I was fully hard, and craved her.

She had no panties on, and she smiled as the realization illumined my face. The room seemed to float. I took her hand and stroked the length of her arm until her hand was at my waist, then guided her to feel my hardness. She held me tenderly through my pants. Then her hand closed and imparted a gentle tug as I reached behind her and found the rear most part of her wetness.

Boom went the Old Man's gun far away.

My cock found her labia of its own, pressing its way inside until it filled her with a moan. I stroked her within, and she lost volition, clutching at me with her thighs while I was deepest in her. I stroked her again until she made a crescendo of song, stiffened all around me and convulsed into orgasm, the tenor of her voice breathless as if in disbelief.

The gun boomed in the distance and I kissed her upper mouth. Her head arched back, her flared nostrils black holes, unbearably mysterious, and let my semen shoot inside her with a gasp, brow to brow until pulsing, I was spent.

We lay together drowsing in a light embrace. It was only minutes but seemed longer, and I could not help the clarity of mind that made lying there awkward and uncomfortable. Trading algorithms danced in my head, and I stirred from the bed of her body.

She was coming around too, her eyes alive with thought long before she spoke.

"He said you were broke, lost it all in this crash." She distanced her head to look at me. "He said you don't even have a job anymore."

"The car's gone." I zipped my pants and started for the door, legs buckling as if a little drunk. I leaned outside, the draft of the door blowing snow powder into my face from the awning. I saw the tracks leading off toward the manor. Boom, came the well carried sound of the old man's shotgun. I turned back, closing the door, awhirl with questions. Boom. The sound was plainly

audible through the real glass panel wall, which faced in the direction of the range and the afternoon sun.

She had hitched down her skirt and was sitting up on the raised
floor, her arms drawn together around her knees and her forehead resting on them. The sweep of her hair concealed her face.
Through a glass window on another side of the house, I spotted
the Porsche top a hill and disappear toward the manor house.
What the hell, I thought.

I returned to her and she stopped me with a raised palm and the
plaintive words, "Ken, I... I lied about the car." Boom.

"Lied?"

"I didn't want you to worry. It's not paid off."

"It's not..." Suddenly it became clear. "You were making pay-
ments? You said it was two weeks allowance." Boom.

"It was," she said. She began to cry. I sat beside her and took her
shoulders. "I spent ahead though," she confessed "And he made
my father cut off the payment." Boom. "I can't cover much of
anything anymore. I had to leave London and come here. His
bank holds title."

"He's repossessing it?" She turned to face me. Her tear-reddened
face nodded, then shook, and she shrugged. She looked down. I
was silent, waiting.

"He just told me, Ken."

I was already cold with new calculations of my ruin. With no
way to cover the margin, my career was over, like it or not, even
if the market were to bounce back tomorrow. Elopement was
now my one and only hope.

"Keira, let's go away. Let's get out of here."

"It's true then? You're broke?" Boom.

I calculated possible answers in the heartbeat allowed, and said, "The job is gone. There's nothing to hold me here. We can call a car and take the first plane to a sunny place where the exchange rate is good."

"I can't. How… Oh, the hell with it. Let's go. I am so sick of it all." In the quiet that ensued she barely whispered, "Do you love me, Ken?"

I took all of her in. "Yes," I said. "I love you, Keira." Boom. Her face brightened through the tears and we moved into each other as if magnetized. I realized for the first time that, God help me, I did love her.

"I'll make the call," I said as I rose and moved toward the Netbox across the room. "Car service from this location. Voice only, call," I requested hastily. Boom. "Hello. How soon can you have a town car here for the Albany Airport?"

"Less than an hour, sir," came the reply. A square of light appeared on the monitor and I realized I had no way to pay.

"Here, take this," she said, reaching into her handbag and extracting a chit card. I took it with a queasy feeling and touched it to the monitor. Boom.

"Have the driver call this number at the gate," I told the dispatcher.

"Yes, sir. Thank you for riding with Country Manor."

I estimated the time to Kennedy International and considered where to take her from there. "How about Belize?"

"It's so hot and humid. He had a lot to say to me," she added ominously without moving, her eyes now dry and clear.

"More of the same?" I asked, my attempt at nonchalance a failure.

"No. He took a call while he was here, something about politics. You know, make the hemisphere safe...for democracy and whatever. He got himself in a huff over that call, then started in on you." Boom.

I was attentive. He often railed about governments in South America, and God help me, penniless as I was, I could not stop myself from thinking there might be a tip somewhere in it that I could trade on.

"I don't know. Some kind of shell," she said reading my face. "In Brazil maybe. I don't remember. I was completely browbeaten by then."

"Did he mention any names?"

"Just mentioned some shell." Boom. "You talk to him, if it's important. He told me he will never let you have me."

"He can't keep us apart and he knows it."

"He knows no such thing." Boom. "He said you don't know the first thing about marriage or money. He said you didn't properly understand the superiority of our ethos, his I mean, whatever that means. He gave me such a headache."

She paused, remembering. "He said you should have been born British. Then you'd know what it meant to be hopelessly middle class, but being American you thought your looks and wisecracks earned you a place at the table."

"He's illegitimate, the bastard."

"He couldn't help it, and his parents, my great-grandparents by the way, did marry."

"Five years and two mistresses later, the way I hear it."

"Please respect grandma's memory, and it isn't as though he hates you personally. I know you don't hate him." Boom.

"Oh, really?"

"There is no time when I'm staying here, time just stops," she said abandoning the subject. "I no sooner arrive than the boredom drives me—" She grasped her hair and released it immediately, extending her arms and fingers then clutching her hair again. Perhaps there was no word for it, and the compressed screeching sound she made next was a new one in the human vocabulary.

"He called you a looter, and your claim to being more than a financial halfwit was... What did he call it?"

"Baseless?" Boom.

"Yes, that was it, and then something about compensation for being an orphan. He went on and on."

"What else?"

"You care more about every word out of his incessant mouth than anything I ever have to say."

"Keira, you know that's not true."

"Isn't it? You light up around him even while he plays the cat with your mousy little ears, and you both enjoy it. None of his rants come close to the ones he has about you."

"What else did he say?"

"See how you are?" she observed. "Don't let me get in the way of you two. He said if you weren't such a good shot, he'd never have let you set foot around here." Boom.

"What did he say about the shell, Keira."

"Nicky something. Nick Cough, sounded like to me."

"Nick Cough?"

"Kelly. Kelly Nickoff. That was it, I think. He said it so fast the name didn't even sound American." She offered. "It was Kellee's then the rest."

"Kelleeznickoff. Kalis… Kalashnikov?"

"Sounded more like Kaleeznikoff. Is it a shell?"

"Jesus."

Basic infantry weapons had evolved little over many decades, though leaps were made in telemetry optics and programmable rounds. The Gen III Kalashnikov chambered the pricey high-tech rounds, which I remembered from one of Neil's rants, applied the new optics-fed telemetry before and after the shot. The new specialized bullets could be controlled to air burst for fragmentation behind the target and there were incendiary and poison gas versions.

"He said he'd rather you were religious than greedy. At least then you would have some respect for power. He accused you of voting Democrat. That's not true, is it?"

I thought she was joking at first, but the look on her face indicated she was not. All that separated us returned with that one question. The world of which she was a creature, would always be, that no lovemaking could bridge, was the reason I'd lose her. I closed my eyes to ward off a full-scale invasion of doubt.

I sat beside her, taking her hand. "He's serious this time," she said facing me.

"Are you, Keira?"

"Let's go before I change my mind." She got up purposefully but halted within a few steps and began pacing the sunken floor. "You know, he'll punish my father unless I am cut off completely."

"Your father is still his son, and still your father. He'll get you what you need."

"Not for long. Grandpa has ears everywhere. Nothing gets past him. The whole place is on high alert, by the way. Don't ask me why. Every call in or out is probably bugged. He'll know about us leaving."

"Listen," I said. We listened together. There was only silence.

We looked at each other with the same urgent thought, as if seeing each other for the last time. When had the booming stopped? A heartbeat later the perimeter alert chimed and a golf cart came into view outside the pixel wall, swerved off the dry roadway, and came fishtailing across the snow, making directly for the front door.

The great Avery Wellingham clambered out of the cart like a young man, bounced up the steps, and rapped on the door with a knockedy-knock-knock, knock-knock. Then he let himself in. The tall and broad patrician, wearing his shooting jacket unbuttoned and a feathered cap, stepped inside and closed the door behind him. He doffed the hat to show a full head of well-groomed grey hair. He was plainly in good spirits.

"Keira," he said in his gruff voice, nodding. "Welcome to Grand Manor, son," he said, using the word to needle my orphanhood as he always did, his wide grin filled with falseness. He soaked us in, one then the other and back again. "Ugh!" he said and the grin faded. "I see you two have been busy." Then, brightening for show, he winked. "Don't waste any time, do you, sonny?"

Keira adjusted what she guessed was awry with her hair and dress, but it was her face that gave her away, her features flushed and her exercised lips thickened. She sat primly down on the raised floor, huddling her knees in her arms. Then her forehead went down atop them.

"Neither do you, Avery," I said politely, knowing how my use of his first name irked him. "A pleasure to see you again. We were just talking about you. It seems my car has wandered off into your pastures."

"Well, it's not such a big place. I'm sure it'll turn up."

"A big day yesterday. I trust you didn't fare too badly," I said, figuring I'd let him get his crowing in.

"Ha, rode that to town," he chuckled. "Best day in years."

"Saw it coming?"

"Well, let's just say Santa Claus had a little prescient for me," he said, chuckling at his pun and clasping his hands together. I thought of Pedro hacking out the evil face of the totem pole with hammer and wood chisel.

"Take it on the chin, son?" he inquired, his tone indicating he was sure of it. Rather than let him sweat me though, I lied.

"Oh, I had a hedge on the side that buffered me pretty well. I thought I'd take a long vacation, though."

"Ha," he said. "Too bad about the job, kid. But you know I have a majority stake in Merchant, and I agreed with the CEO's decision regarding the cuts. It wouldn't do to have them show partiality." He nearly burst out laughing at this to leave no doubt as to its falsehood.

The bastard had likely seen to my firing. "I was looking for something new anyway," I deflected. "It seems so is Keira. We're thinking Brazil."

Keira shook her head from side to side without removing her brow from her knee. My glance went back from her to catch his reaction, which was swept with a lopsided smile.

"It seems Keira is having second thoughts. Aren't you, dear?"

"Rio sounds wonderful," she said tonelessly without lifting her head.

Despite her non-affirmation, it seemed a cloud had lifted from the Old Man's brow as he teased out some meaning from her tone.

"Rio is nice this time of year, but with all the kidnapping, poverty, rape and murder in the news down there, hardly the place to take my precious granddaughter."

Keira lifted and dropped her brow on her knees, hiding her head lower.

"Well, no sense wasting a beautiful day. How about a few rounds, son, as long as you're out here."

"I'd be delighted, but I have a plane to catch." He wanted to pry us apart, I figured, to work on me as he had been working on her, but gloves off. I wouldn't give him the chance. The hired car would come and we'd get in it. The last time he stopped a car she had called for in an effort to get away from him, Keira threw a bona fide fit, ranting and screaming as if kidnapped. The whole show followed: an ambulance, therapy for hostage trauma, a prescription for confinement anxiety. She punished him the best she knew how, with his own weakness for her.

"Two perfect scores this week. One just now. Naw, I think you don't have it in you anymore, and you are all shook up about yesterday. Well, maybe I can make it worth your while. Say, best of three gets you a brand new cream-colored Porsche."

"Avery, I already own one."

"Not free and clear, you don't."

"Yes, as soon as I wire in the overdue balance. I had no idea there was anything owed."

"Ah, yes, your little hedge. Well, let's say then I'll double whatever you made with it yesterday." He was enjoying himself.

"I'm flattered, Avery, but that would be quite a lot. I could hardly take such advantage of you."

Keira turned her head enough to allow a wide eye to peer at me through falling locks. I knew she wanted him out badly enough for me to go with him, and my debts were tugging at my forebrain too. I could name the amount but never prove it, and double zero was zero, if he could prove that. Keira had no way of knowing that, if he wanted to, the Old Man could indeed prove it.

"Less than an hour," he coaxed. "If we run late, I'll fly you to Kennedy myself." He had a small strip at the north end of his property where he leased a supersonic jump Lear with pilot and crew on call.

"Very tempting, Avery, but I haven't seen Keira in so long. Forgive me for passing." We'd take the hired limo I decided, and leave while we could, the hell with the damned car. Make him play the cheapskate with her allowance. Her head raised a little and dropped down to its sunken position, and then she raised it upright.

"Go. Please. Both of you."

"Well, the lady has spoken," Avery said, seizing the opportunity, and strode to the door, holding it open. "I'll have him back in no time, dear."

I shot her a look, but there was no way out of it now.

"Call you in forty-five minutes," I said, fishing out my Puck and tapping in auto-dial.

"Have fu-uhn," she sang, the song filled with a dark tone.

He closed the door behind us and extended an arm toward the electric cart. "Dirt before the broom," he said with a pretense of jocularity.

I turned on him. "I don't mind a breath of fresh air, but we haven't settled the terms."

"You didn't make a dime yesterday. You lost your fool shirt. You want terms? How about I let you walk out of here on two legs?"

"Ah, the gangsta routine today is that it, Avery?"

He was plainly livid. "You want the terms: You win, you drive out of here with title to the car. I win, you never see her again."

"Mmmm. Let's tell Keira what she's worth." I started back toward the door and he grabbed my arm.

"Don't think I won't have you stopped. She can bawl all she wants. I'll give her a sedative and you'll be on your way with nothing."

"You really don't care about her, do you?"

"I care for her more than you'll ever know."

"So what is the problem?"

"With you? Get in I'll tell you." He slid into the driver's seat of the waiting golf cart.

Looking at him sitting there, patting the seat beside him in a droll approximation of earnestness, it occurred to me he might actually "disappear" me as easily as the Porsche.

"Okay, look. If you win, you get the car back, free and clear, and you can take off with her. I win, no car and I get to boot your wise ass. Then you can take her if she still wants to go."

I got in, saying nothing. There was no way to tell if he was lying, and neither she nor I was in a position to refuse the cash the car represented. I should keep him where I could see him in any event, I thought.

"Strict rules on loading," I said over the whir of acceleration and the crunch of the snow. He chuckled, regarded me sidelong, then belly laughed, barely steering the cart, which fishtailed left and right in the snow.

"Why, thank you, son. Unfortunately, splattering your brains this afternoon would be inconvenient."

"You have a ski lesson at 2:30," a voice emanated from his wrist case. "Tell Miss Prentice I'll be delayed an hour. Keep her entertained."

"You've had calls." It was the lithesome Russian.

"Have the Porsche brought to the range," I called over to his wrist.

"I'll take them later, Sheila. Thank you. Please tell security to bring the Porsche to the range. Off."

I thought of weiji, the Chinese word for crisis that did not necessarily spell opportunity.

Minutes later we pulled up to the range, a combination skeet, trap, rifle, and pistol range backed by a semi-circular hillock with woods beyond, the snowy ground strewn with bits of shattered orange clays. The Porsche already sat in the parking area, top down, pretty in the sun. The skeet court was cleared of snow.

He led the way to his gun house. Inside, opposite the door, stood a transparent case of gleaming double barreled shotguns, each more ornately engraved than the next and all inlaid with gold and silver. Twin barreled side-by-sides and over/unders of every gauge, length, and choke, culminating in a row of antique masterpieces at the far end of the line. On another wall hung rifles dating back 150 years along with a few relics from the flintlock and black powder days. The third wall held a like display of handguns of various vintages, and the fourth held shelves stacked to the rafters with neatly labeled ammunition, choke tubes, carry cases, and gun cleaning supplies.

"My pride and joy." He extended his arms, hefting down a long barreled side-by-side from a ready rack near the door. "Here, take it," he offered. "I've been doing well with it." I took hold of it.

"Give it a swing," he coached. The gun was as much art as function, perfectly balanced. "Still want to use the shorty?"

I nodded and handed the side-by-side back, a marvel of handling though it was. The shorty lay atop several utility pump actions and semi-autos in various states of disrepair leaning helter-skelter in an open closet. I picked up the stubby unadorned Browning, a battered field grade with an English stock and double 24 inch barrels stacked one atop the other.

"I don't know how you can stand that thing. It swings like a twig," he said, as I opened the action for a check.

"Whippy in the wrong hands. Mathematics in mine," I claimed, resting it over my left arm. My adoptive uncle had this same make of gun, which he used for turkey hunting in Vermont. He had loaned it to me off season, and I learned to shoot skeet with it despite its many shortcomings. I never knew another shotgun and would be handicapped with a new one.

"Grab that basket of ammo," he said.

We shot the first round quickly, in silence but for shouts of "pull!" and a few impolite remarks. He'd grin, chuckle, or wink every time I pointed out where he should be standing when I prepared to take my shot—someplace I could see him and his gun out of the corner of my eye. The shooting came to me naturally, but he won the round by a shot on a technicality. I'd chipped a clay in the final station.

"Not bad for a rusty bucket," he said of me in gloating condescension.

We shot the second round more slowly, the competition growing in earnest. He led until station 7 doubles, where a clay sailed out from left and right at once and I hit each cleanly. He missed one of his, and he could not tie at the last station unless I missed my last shot. Despite his fit of coughing at the moment of release, I did not miss.

At the start of the deciding round, I put the question to him. "So, what is it, Avery? That you can't countenance my begetting beautiful, brilliant kids with your lovely granddaughter?"

"Son, I'm not going to waste words with you. I'd like you to understand she knows nothing of men but you, and that she could have her pick of bachelors, men of achievement, princes, kings, billionaires. I would like to persuade you that she deserves the chance to play the field as much as you did yourself at her age, even that you are better off without the heartache she'll bring you because, in time, she'll wake up to all the gifts she will never unwrap on account of your lousy Mick charm. You need money and a new start, not another notch in your belt. Ten years from now, you'll thank me for it."

"You asking me for a price again? I thought we were past that."

"You're a fool. And you'll lose this bet too."

"And if you lose?"

"Well, you've called my bluff. I won't put my granddaughter through another one of those tantrums, even for her own good."

"Pull," he called. Boom. The clay shattered neatly. "Pull." Boom. The low house bird was pulverized. He reloaded. "Pull." Boom and Boom. He smoked the double.

I took the station and ordered, "Pull." I dusted the high house clay as soon as it was airborne, repeating the performance with the low house and then the double clays.

There had been a skeet club near Wharton years ago, and I'd left a shelf of amateur trophies behind, then another club outside Boston before I landed the Empire City job with its residency permit, something people would, and occasionally did, kill for. Most everyone I knew found it an odd sport, especially for a scholarship egghead, but it had led to the Old Man's invitation to come out here, which was how I met Keira. In a way, we were his doing.

"Whatever my doubts about your gene pool, that's not the main thing," he continued as if discussing a cut of meat. "You're bright, good-looking, ambitious, and a good shot. What more should I want for a grandson-in-law, right?"

"Pull," he called. Boom. A technical hit, the clay splitting in two. He chipped the low house too, a technical miss, and chipped the low house again in the double release from either side.

"Pull," I called. Boom. "Pull." Boom. I reloaded. "Pull." Boom and boom. I blasted all of them neatly into orange mists.

"My question exactly, sir," I added, hoping a show of respect might mollify the man.

"Well, the list is long, son, but bottom line: there's too much at stake."

"Pull," he called. Boom. It was a hit. "Pull." Boom. Another. He was plainly relieved there would be no more doubles until station 6.

"You mean money," I said.

"Pull," I called. Boom. Smithereens.

"I could make you rich before the sun sets without giving you a dime."

"Pull," I repeated, dusting the clay.

"Why don't you then?"

"No one of mine will have to concern themselves with money to the end of time. I wish my son had your intelligence, but he apparently bumped his head one time too many when his nanny wasn't looking."

"Pull," he called. Boom. Again his string caught it late and bit off one edge, deflecting the greater part which, robbed of its momentum, sailed briefly and quickly tumbled to the ground. "Pull," he called again. Boom. A clean hit.

"Pull." Boom. "Pull." Boom. I found blasting the clays the more gratifying for the hostility welling within me.

"The thing is loyalty," he said getting back on track. "Pull." Boom. The disc fragmented. "Pull." Boom. The low house bird left a coil of smoke lingering in the air where it was intercepted.

"Pull." Boom. "You mean loyalty to you?" I asked. "Pull." Boom.

"That you ask damns you for a Democrat and a Catholic," he explained contemptuously. "Sure, to me. To my family, my empire, my class and our future."

"Pull," he commanded. Boom. He reloaded. "Pull." Boom and Boom. He nodded for emphasis as the double clays burst. "Like your illusions," he grinned. "Puff."

I ventured, with all the sincerity and respect I could muster, "Sir, I love your granddaughter and intend to marry her."

"That's very touching," he said. "I require loyalty beyond question. I have to be able to speak freely about anything at all, and I need to be able to count on understanding and cooperation."

"Like with the Kali's," I ventured noncommittally, using the friendly word for the weapon. It was the wrong answer.

"Forget whatever she told you, sonny, for your own good. Our markets are polluted with socialism in our own back yard," he charged angrily. "Take your shot."

I called weakly, "Pull." Boom. "Pull." Boom and Boom. The single and double clays disintegrated.

"You have no head for politics," he went on. "You question where you shouldn't and don't where you should, but I'm not here to edify you. You are what you are, a bounder who can't be trusted where to land; and with all that's at stake, I can't have someone I distrust at my back, turning my granddaughter against me. We makers and keepers sleep like fools, while socialism eats away at our values, delivers up servants like Pedro who talk back as they like and hangers-on like you who call me Avery without getting your face slapped.

"We're at war in the world. Every crumb of social obligation is reviewed and updated at our expense. What do these reds want now? A 30 hour work week? Universal health care? Subsidized education? It'll never be enough. Subsidized elections. Limited inheritance. They want the benefits of the civilization we create with our wealth handed out to them on a platter, as if freedom could exist apart from free enterprise. We're at war, and I don't trust you."

The twists in his palaver notwithstanding, I could not deny, even to myself, that King Wellingham was right in his quest for a more suitable heir. My heart was indeed disloyal. Truth told, I found him soulless and repellent. I would not play his Tory well and had to grope for words that would not further incite the weiji between us. If there were a silver lining to be found here, I could not discover it.

"Freedom is a much abused word," I finally managed to eke out, with as much ambivalence as I could inject, and followed up politely with, "Your shot, sir." Hang me if I'd argue with him.

"Pull," he called angrily. Boom. He reloaded. "Pull." Boom and Boom. He'd missed the first of the double and cursed under his breath.

"Pull," I ordered. Boom. I reloaded. "Pull." Boom and Boom. I killed the sailing toys, and when I turned, he was looking at the ground, his face slack, an old man contemplating the defeat at hand.

He looked up at me and smiled ironically. Then turned to take his shot. "Pull," he demanded. Boom. He did not miss again.

"Power must pass to those who can use it effectively, and that, son, is not you."

There was a hard finality to his tone. It dawned on me with a jolt that he hadn't dragged me out here for skeet or to pontificate. He got me away in order to get at her. He was just stalling me with this lord of power jibber-jabber. Would he dare drug her? Would he send five-tongued Sheila around for a friendly drink so she could slip Keira something?

He watched me look again at the time and smiled. I stared at him.

"Take your shot," he said.

"Pull." Boom. I smacked the high shot at the center line.

"Pull." Boom. He returned the favor, his last shot hitting the clay. I had the final shot in this round, and he'd tie if I missed it. It was the moment of "tooth," as Robbie would say. Bite or die.

"What the hell is that?" He was looking up, eyes shielded from the sun with his hand as if in salute.

I couldn't make it out, and then it seemed a large white bird circling in the air, wafting ever higher in an unseen gust. "Looks like a seagull," I proposed, though I knew the nearest lake of size was many miles away.

"Seagull, my ass. That's Pedro's damned model airplane."

I cupped a hand over my eyes and did indeed make out what appeared to be a miniature airplane, an antique model monoplane with imitation canopy, cockpit, and pilot, and an extravagant wingspan. "No engine?"

"He's sailing it with the engine off. Pedro," he commanded to his wrist. His voice would activate Pedro's communicator. "Pedro, pick up right now."

"*Si*, Mister Wellingham."

"I gave you work to do, and I expect you to be doing it."

"I am carving, Señor."

"Don't lie to me. I can see your damned airplane flying around out here." There was a long pause. "Pedro!"

"Sir, I try to make it come down, but the control is not working. It was just for a leettle while."

"You can kiss it good-bye, Pedro." He dropped two shells into the shotgun chambers and let them off quick fire at the plane, but the choke was wide and the long-winged renegade bird had risen out of range in the updraft.

"Please, please, Señor. Do not shoot!" came the desperate voice from the Old Man's wrist. "Please, I will order it down, and give you the totem pole if I must work night and day. Do not shoot!"

"Too late, Pedro." The Old Man cut him off and strode angrily to the gun house, emerging with the longest, heaviest gun in his collection, a side-by-side 10 gauge shotgun choked for taking down geese at long range. He broke open the action and rested the breach on his shoulder, chambers facing forward, then fumbled at loading it while walking back to the range, dropping shells without bothering to pick them up. He snapped the action shut on full chambers and swung the artillery to his right shoulder. Boom. He staggered back under the recoil, got control of it again, and pointed. Boom. It was impossible to tell if he'd hit it, but the plane suddenly changed course, breaking from its circular pattern and heading away from us, descending as it fled in slow motion against a headwind in the direction of Pedro's house.

Wellingham loaded the barrels and fired one off again, leaning forward against the recoil. The plane nosed steeply up, almost vertically until, suspended in the air, it presented a still target. Then its nose dropped and the plane plummeted vertically toward the ground just as his second shot boomed.

"Ha! Got it," he crowed with jubilation. It looked to me like he'd just been fleeced of his shot by a maneuver. The plane leveled off and circled tightly before heading again toward Pedro's. Suddenly its motor came alive and the plane surged forward into the wind, no longer descending. Wellingham reloaded the shotgun.

"Goddamn. Pedro! Pedro, do you hear me?!"

"Yes! Please do not shoot! The control is broken. I am sorry. It will come down when there is no fuel. Please, Señor. Do not shoot!"

Wellingham raised the mighty gun, marked the bird in his sights, then drew his aim off ahead of it and let one barrel off, dancing an impressive two-step to regain his footing and reacquire his aim before letting off the other. The plane flew on but erratically, apparently hit.

"Damn it! If I see that thing again I'll blow it to kingdom come," he shouted in frustration. "Well, what are you looking at? Take this." I docked the Browning into a gun rest and stepped over to relieve the old man of the heavy gun. "Fat lot of help you are," he added, rubbing his shoulder. As I took the piece with both hands my Puck sounded, calling Keira as scheduled.

"Quite the tiger, aren't you?" I offered politely, waiting for her to pick up.

"You will never understand, boy. You're a bastard bred to disloyalty. You will never be part of this family." We stood there together in silence for a moment. He seemed outwardly almost benign for a second, the irritable father-in-law that would never be. The Puck chimed without answer. Then he snarled, "Go ahead. Finish the round. You've already lost, sonny." The latter came out in a particularly sinister snarl.

I glared at him, waiting for reason to return, his and mine. The Puck rang on unanswered.

"She's gone," he added hotly. "That's right. Go ahead and take the car. Spend the night if you like. The house is empty."

"Where..."

"You will never know where. Or what or how. Just get out." He nodded once and strode off toward the electric cart.

I saw myself smashing the back of his skull with the butt of the 10 gauge, over and over, but it did not happen. I ran for the car, letting the ponderous gun fall to the ground. Door, I yelled, relieved that the voice recognition had not been erased and again when the ignition responded to my thumbprint. I left a plume of dust in the parking area, turning sharply into the road.

"She was in on it all from the start," he stabbed after me as I passed him in the cart, his laughter audible above engine fury and squealing tires.

The distance to the guesthouse went by in a heartbeat, and I spun the Porsche before the door. I slipped in the snow in my haste as I headed toward the house, stumbling forward to catch my balance, and ran on. The front door was unlocked. "Keira," I called, my temper flaring as I stepped inside. "Keira!" I tore through each room, knocking over lamps in a heedless rage. There was a sheet of stationery on the floor where we had made love. I snatched it up.

"Dearest Ken, forgive m—" was written unfinished as if scrawled in haste. What the hell, did that mean? Did she dump me, just like that? Would she take off on her own? Her best trick was to disappear without warning. Had she been conned? Did the

Old Man play her too? Could she have scrawled this drugged to sleep? Every which way, I was a damned sorry fool.

I could make no sense of what had just happened to me. I crushed the paper in my hand and stuffed it in my pocket, staggering for the door as if drunk.

Outside I noticed new tire tracks that led away across the snow, joining the road in the direction of the manor. Atop a mound in the road that meandered through the rolling grounds, a black ant grew larger as I surveyed the scene. A car was coming my way. I started for the Porsche.

She was probably at the big house with the Old Man. I burrowed holes in the snow to find traction and turned the car toward the mansion. It did not take long for a security jeep to emerge above a hill in front of me, the civilianized military patrol truck bristling with four fur-clad heads, machine guns in their hands and dogs at their sides.

I slowed and they rolled to a stop a dozen yards directly in front of me. They were quiet at first, then amused among themselves at the impasse. The leader quieted them. Perhaps they had orders not to provoke me, I reasoned. The Old Man could have me shot in the head and tell the authorities anything he wanted. If I somehow made it to the manor, there would only be more of them waiting with guns. I'd be handing them every provocation to kill me. A modicum of calm returned with the recognition that I was beaten.

Well, it was as good a day as any, wasn't it? Why not just end this heartache right now, I wondered nearly aloud, taking in the view. It was a good place to die, wasn't it? I imagined my blood on this rolling stretch of snow among perfectly manicured conifers.

I was a fool. There was nothing left for me to do there. My humiliation deepened each second I remained. I backed up into the snow and turned toward the gate. I watched them follow a discreet distance behind in the rearview.

As I passed Pedro's, he was nowhere to be seen. The unfinished totem pole grinned evilly. I checked the rearview just before the gate. The estate guards were still following me, and they probably would be halfway to the village. In the instant I turned my attention back to the road, something caught my eye, some movement in the mirror. For a moment I thought I'd glimpsed a woman's face. I slowed to a stop and looked back. It could have been a piece of windblown paper, or just a leaf, or a bit of moisture in the corner of my eye.

I drove out the wrought iron gates.

* * *

Chapter 3

To hell in a handbasket

That evening I was a trespasser in my home, a bruised and beaten vagabond with the digs to himself while the owner was away. It was Day 23 in my countdown to eviction, and the long, stressful drive back from the debacle at the estate had depleted me to the point of numbness. I sat mute in the darkness on the floor by the window, my gaze fixed on the patchwork of buildings and the twilight sky, a heartlessly deep blue, cradling a tumbler of whiskey.

~

Day 22.

I awoke before dawn and took my place by the glass dividing inside from out. The great City lay beyond. I made motions as if to commence a customary activity, over and over, only to find myself again staring numbly out the window.

All attempts at action conspired to humiliate me. I sliced open my finger quartering an orange and spilled coffee on the buffalo rug. I closed my shirt buttons wrong. I fumbled a dropped spoon a second time, tried angrily again, and in consequence of the repeated ineptitude bungled into a third demonstration of the same. A conspiracy of mishaps tore at my dilapidated ego. I imagined myself at a booting machine where every movement I made levered a wallop to my hapless butt.

Some lesson seemed to need learning, but what it was continued to elude me. I had to think and could not. My brain refused to comply. I was an animal lost in a stare.

I well knew the unspoken standards of the industry: more than four or five months on the shelf, I'd be considered defective merchandise. A recession could take years, which meant I might never get back on the gravy train again, even if I managed to cover my debts. Since Manhattan had been privatized, the stakes had risen with every passing year. For newcomers like me, salary just covered rent. My first real bonus was just a few months away when I got the axe.

Cheap digs far out in Brooklyn would be my first way-stop down. At the bottom of the spiral there was residence in some "trickle town" where trickle-down never reached. Some of these trailer parks had grown into trailer cities of the long term excommunicated. They were plagued with disease, crime, and conflagration. Those fallen from the Street had their own black market there among the millions fallen from past bubbles bursting. The poor ate the poorer in an endless struggle to survive.

Unless I could climb back into the saddle, and soon, I was finished with the top, finished with Empire City.

All residency was luxury on the Island. The Old Man decreed brutal rents which gave new meaning to what market would bear. My studio with kitchen digs commanded eighty-five percent of what I made at Merchant, more rent in a month than for similar digs elsewhere for a year. For some newcomers to the

City envisioning a seat at this table worth any sacrifice, ninety-five percent was a common rental peonage, and of course room-mates were forbidden in studios, I had to bear the rent alone. There was no margin for error.

Today there would be no plotting a course of action more future than my next breath, I knew well enough. I had no mind for it. The larger questions loomed with sad insistence, unspoken. I did not know what to do. I understood only that I was hurt and my wounds needed tending.

I don't know how the day passed. I was clouded, tired, dumb with feeling and bereft of mathematics. I was nearly broken, utterly. Evening came, darkness a balm to my injuries. I should be out shivering alone in the winter woods for the truth of my circumstances, I thought, not here sipping whiskey in rare comfort.

Tomorrow would be time enough for higher brain functions. There was no reprieve from the sullen glare of consciousness but sleep that would not come.

~

Day 21.

The facts seemed preferable to optimism. I had to price the car and dispose of it. I had to get a job, any job, no matter the atmosphere of doom within and without.

Once I named what I had to do, I directed myself through the motions, more like required calisthenics or an empty ceremony of will than anything I believed held real hope. I'd take a hit on the car for certain, given the time frame, not likely enough to cover me anyway. Then there was the chit card debt, for which I would still face bankruptcy. I would lose the license anyway. I should take the car money and leave the country, I thought.

There was someplace in the world I could ride for a few years on those dollars.

Instead, I called car dealers and responded to the margin notice. I readied letters filled with positive thinking I nowise possessed and tailored resumés for every hedge fund, investment bank, or financial institution at which I thought I might have a glimmer of plausibility. I registered with the agencies, picked through all advertised jobs, and set up automatic applications for future ones. Then, groomed and dressed for the camera, I called everyone I knew to test the steadiness of my voice and my frame of mind. I called one after the other with the news, no matter how slight the acquaintance, how sour the relationship, how nebulous the benefit: I was available.

I practiced my intonation to try to achieve some semblance of ego and self-assurance, but the speech analyzer showed rancor and distress. Worse, the analyzer yielded every political indicator on the chart but the upbeat free market Republican required. It seemed I was spoiled goods. One never knew if an analyzer was in play at an interview, so I persisted stubbornly until I could pass the black box, then launched the letter and resumé campaign.

I touched base with Robbie, hoping his despair would not add to my own. It turned out he was far more the realist than I, if no more optimistic. He was being auditioned at a limousine service, driving under the tutelage of an amiable elderly servant who assessed him meticulously through the lens of the rich and accustomed.

I called Neil too, who Rob said was picking brains out of the detritus of the crash, trying to bootstrap his own investment company amid still smoking ruins. For Neil, weiji was an opportunity, and how else to put his father's hoard to use? He said he would meet me for drinks in a week. I knew he caught the timbre of growing desperation in my voice as I countered with why not tomorrow, the weekend then, lunch Monday. No, he said, he was in operational overdrive and not a moment to spare. I knew he enjoyed dangling me, and why not? Were the tables turned, I'd rub it in.

Despite the ubiquitous ruin, or perhaps because of it, the sound of compassion was unheard, as if a strange breach of etiquette. I was a fat cat who got his tail burned when the market he had been getting rich on crashed. Sure we lived high jinx, but none of us juniors had been getting rich. I had to speculate to stay alive in the City. I had to save and scrounge to trade on my own account. I had to win just to stay in the game.

I might as well have 666 branded across my forehead for all the good my resumé would do me now. I had been flicked down within sight of the pinnacle. Keira, the job, the career, the apartment, the residency permit, the car: all gone or going and with them hope for the foreseeable future. There would be recessional layoffs for years, maybe depression for a decade. No one could tell. There were tens of thousands of us thrown out like used whores up and down the line and across the sector. We would all be trying to find a place to land that would let us keep our lives in the City. The consequences for the likes of me were no mystery. It had all happened before.

I was feeling damned sorry for myself, that was a fact, and I was peeved that no one, not even my foster parents, would really understand the magnitude of my personal disaster. To them, I was made of rubber. Until now, I had almost believed it myself. But I was made of glass, cracking with nervous fissures that might fall to pieces any moment, as the rest of my life already had. I had no particular talent for adversity.

It was late in the evening when I got around to calling Sean, my adoptive brother, at the monastery.

"I was wondering when I'd hear from you," he whispered in wide view, standing full length in the monitor in some sparse call room allowed to initiates. "Did you take a beating?" He was taller than me by two inches, all the more towering for being thin of limb, and older by three years. His long face and drooping bird-like posture on the screen made him seem penitent.

"No longer among the chosen would be another way of putting it," I said, marveling at his directness. "Not wasting words, are we?"

"I am alone with my thoughts and have lost the knack of conversation," was his quiet reply. "How are you?"

We were brothers together in the same home for most of our early years, but divorce in my adoptive family split us in our teens. He lived with his father and had progressed from a morose and suspiciously quiet kid to chanting vociferously in political marches as a young man. He joined radical groups, experimented with mind-altering drugs, and finally succumbed to alcoholism and heroine addiction. He was arrested for snatching a purse, not for a fix, but in a bid for the cost of treatment to rejoin the society he scorned. Then he found God.

"I may need a place to stay," I broached, only half in jest.

He entwined his fingers as if in prayer and looked down. He wore his cassock, but the collar was missing, the top buttons undone. He seemed like I'd awakened him from dozing or interrupted his reading.

"Then it's worse than I imagined. Of course, there's a room for you here. It won't be comfortable for you."

He was sentenced to rehabilitation by a lenient judge and later entered a Benedictine monastery with a view toward teaching.

"I'll likely get a place in the boroughs if nothing works out. Did I wake you?"

"About to turn in. Think of all the other people, now and in the future, who will go through the same thing again and again that you are going through. You aren't alone."

"That's small comfort, believe me," I offered. I was in no mood for commiseration.

I was in fact still winding down from the soldierly efforts of the day, and I realized with embarrassment that I was feeling sorry for him, pathetic as I was, even while he was feeling sorry for me. I didn't share his addictive demons. I drank, had taken drugs, and smoked, could not socialize without these, but no vice took hold. To him, my career was a vice from the start and an addiction thereafter. The tenor of his words had changed since he shocked us all and put on the cloth. He really did seem to have some Holy Spirit going.

"I've been talking to people all day. Everyone's bloodied, high and low," I volunteered wearily.

"Hubris Street," he said, shaking his head.

"Keira, too," I went on, ignoring his usual taunt. "I don't even know what happened. Nasty business at the Old Man's."

"The Old Man's?"

"Wellingham, her grandfather. Everyone calls him that. I went up to meet her at his estate. In all things, it seems I've been dumped. She's gone and the job's gone. Serious creditors are lining up to do me harm. If there's no break in a few weeks, I have to give up the City."

"Come here if there's nowhere else. Don't try to get through this alone."

"I want to be alone, to be honest, and that's the damned truth." Misery loathes company, I thought.

"The way you make a living makes you that way. Your pride isolates you, estranges you. Yet you do nothing but create different size numbers," he added with an exasperated gesture. "You should thank God for deflecting you from the path you're on. That is the silver lining for you."

"There's a whole lot of life in those numbers," I asserted.

"I know better than that and so do you."

"Do I? Well, I must have unlearned it. Anyway, I may as well have leprosy down on my resumé."

"You know how to hustle."

"Ha. Yeah, I guess so, if I can get in the door, but there's not a damn door left. And every minute here has a price tag. You don't hear the toll of the clock you hear the ka-ching of the register," I said, feeling the anger coming on. "I'm facing bankruptcy, by the way, and so it's not quite like I have the old Midas appeal. More like an infectious disease."

"Ken," he said, but I could hear consolation in his tone and so waved him off.

"The exodus they're calling it," I went on. "I imagine they could fill a few barges hauling all our sorry asses off to the boroughs. I saw a jumper make his grand exit from my terrace the other day. I was too far away to read his face but close enough to hear him smack the concrete."

"Christ have mercy," he mumbled, eyes closed, hands in fists at his side. When he looked at me again, he was resolute. "Ken, get out of there. The grounds here are beautiful. You don't have to be anything other than my brother. Don't wait until you have to leave. Give yourself a new perspective. Walk out on your own."

"I'm not big on the symbolism," I said. "Walking out on my own, as you say, it would not be. Getting booted is more accurate, whether I leave now or later. What I regret is being out of the game, mostly. I'd rack up a fortune now if I could get my hands on the stake."

He sighed with exasperation. "Admit it. You're addicted to gambling."

"Highly educated risk-reward management."

"Look at this rich guy club you want to join. They've declared themselves the chosen and built themselves an ark. You haven't lost your place. You've found your place. It's with the rest of us."

"I don't want to be with the rest. Sorry. Can't really seem to care much what's right or wrong. I want to retire young and live. If I'm addicted, it's to that, getting free of it all, making a bundle and getting out with it. Maybe then I can afford to care."

"Ken, if you come to your senses, you'll find yourself in the job not in the money. It will just get harder for you the longer you play at their table. You'll lose your conscience, and worse, you won't even know it. How long was I an alcoholic?"

"Don't start."

"I stank from suffering but so loved its causes; the way I went about getting happy was to feed the cause of suffering. That's what you're doing. You keep pushing now off for a later satisfaction that you should understand now more than ever won't happen. Even with millions, you'll want more. Your suffering, how you relate to your pain, isn't unavoidable. I'm telling you, walk out. Take your growing pains with you and leave the suffering behind with the damned you once worked for."

Sean's eyes were liquid on the screen, and for once I was at a loss for words. Nothing he ever said I couldn't parry half awake, but he was changed, and he seemed to know it.

"Not much choice in the matter, after all, is there?" I hedged. "'The damned I once worked for,'" I repeated, savoring the sound of his summation, and I nodded with a self-deprecating laugh. "And here I thought I was reaching for the American Dream."

"A carrot is what you're following, like the one dangled in front of a donkey to keep him moving forward. Hell, they have you dangling it in front of yourself. Those who are actually living that dream, who can claim this dream as their life, are a tiny few. Fewer still are those whose soul has not been warped in the getting, whose conscience is clear before God."

"The few, the proud…"

He sized me up with tired eyes. "Get some sleep."

"Yeah, good idea. Rest is a weapon, as they say." I said, as if there were a target left standing at which I could aim myself.

"Call me tomorrow, earlier in the evening, after Vespers. It'll be easier to get to the monitor, and this is late for me. Days start before the sun."

I bade him good night.

Religion didn't seem like the Church's unholy racket with Sean. He seemed apart from the institutional scam. Each time we spoke since he entered the monastery, his thinking grew less and less the cant of the church and more truly understanding. I was glad for him, I thought as the screen went blank. I have, at least, my brother Sean, I told myself and poured a whiskey, eyeing the level in the bottle before taking a sip.

~

Day 20.

Up late. Hung over. No messages. I debated horizontally just what I should get up to do for what seemed like hours. Then I did the same when vertical, deciding what to do next.

By evening I had not spoken a word. I ceased to exist but for myself. I idled on the Net, stared into space, got mad at myself and went limp before every possible course of action. I repeated this futile cycle until the day's hours were gone and dark had come again.

I gave myself up for useless. I did not call Sean after vespers. The best for me, I decided, was sleep without dreams. The problem was getting there.

~

Day 19.

The Market news wall double spoke:

"While expiration week trading will likely add some volatility, this week's slew of economic reports should have a bigger impact. Consider the market outlook as cautiously optimistic, as the major indices remain at short-term technical support. However, a move below the trend line will come at a cost, as the market will likely incur more prolonged selling due to weakening price activity while the market builds a bottom at current levels."

Something for everyone, I thought, remembering the Old Man's newsletter, Illuminati, which was a masterpiece of equivocation and so couldn't be wrong, including technical measures to support every stance. A one paragraph column, "The Gift Trade," was written in the Old Man's own tortured prose. Each issue featured his single recommendation, which I had followed with consistent profits. It was the only thing that kept the tiresome rag with its prohibitive subscription rate alive, and the Old Man knew it. All the hedge funds subscribed, and everyone wondered who was providing the insight. No one believed it was the Old Man himself or his regulars, and his words seemed to be little more than contorted attempts to interpret the recommendations.

But the tip was missing in the month leading up to the crash.

Would it not have had to contain a warning if the Old Man's source saw it coming? Had the bastard withheld it for himself?

Did it matter now?

~

Day 18.

I awoke in the dark before dawn. I had dreamed I was living in the Porsche as I traveled from town to town. In the dream, I had defaulted on the call, forfeited the license, and run away from the inevitable. I was a bankrupt-at-large, a carpetbagger running swindles on the impoverished in the fall towns. I laughed at my sleazy triumph and wept for myself at the same time. At this I had awakened, the emotions still flush in my face.

"Walk away from it all..." Sean's words came back to mind, seductive in their simplicity. Take a room in my brother's monastery or a studio in the lowest rent pit in the boroughs to mark time. How life would begin again would present itself or it wouldn't. That was tomorrow's problem.

This was not the first time in my 28 years I found myself flat on my butt, I reminded myself without mercy. I had been on a grand ride with my newly-minted MBA, flying high as I had been this time. I certainly went broke, but there was no stigma attached to it back then, it was just a bad bump. This time was radically different. Empire City was different. This was the big cut. You were in or out. There was no middle ground.

My market value was slashed 70% overnight. I was another suit on the rack, wearing a work history label. The shoppers would rummage through the lot in this fire sale, perhaps try one on, observe themselves in the mirror, then decide the cut was not right, made them look fat, the color perhaps a shade too dark.

What a relief to be passed over by these vainglorious shoppers I told myself, so punishing in their superiority. A bounding child-like hope would arrive when a good shopper came along, and then would follow the soul-jangling clink of my hanger politely returned to the rack, reason unknown, unknowable.

What way was this to run a world?

~

Day 17.

I was nearly paralyzed. I had no desire to move, and I could barely force myself. When I made it to a chair, I became one with it. At the balcony, I stood as mindlessly still as the dwarf spruce waiting for a breeze. I found that suffering was aggravated by movement of any kind, including the movement of consciousness itself. The slightest transition awakened possibility and brought its doom. Each pang of consciousness opened my wounds. The firing, the splat on the sidewalk, the humiliations at the Old Man's Estate, the humiliations of the job hunt...

Heavy of limb and emptied of spirit, I practiced stillness. Darkness came as a palpable relief. I stirred and began medicating the aggravation of stirring. Sleep would come sooner.

~

Day 16.

I awoke in the dark. I refused to think. I washed down a painkiller with the whiskey heedless of the level I'd marked on the bottle.

I awoke just before noon and declared myself a spoiled wretch unfit to live. It had been a day since I'd eaten. I made to rise and the lights streaked yellow and grey in rushing brush strokes as my eyes flittered closed and I fell back in a faint. An hour later, I slowly negotiated rising and drank the dregs of juice and ate two hard-boiled eggs. I drank coffee with whiskey and waited for a word from the City machine outside my fleeting sanctuary, its mechanism a calm, insouciant hum beyond the glass.

I slept again late in the afternoon and awoke at midnight. Consciousness, I realized, benefits from sleep when needed and suffers in the forced wakefulness of a work-a-day routine.

~

Day 15.

The wee hours were a solace for the hum was heard no more. My uselessness was free of its reminder. The dark congealed around me, held my body down on the bed. In my mind's eye, a kaleidoscope of half-awake dreams: faces, conversations, fantasies colliding and veering randomly. Imagination took me over. Dramas unlike any experience I'd known played out in my head, all of them ending in a fearful conundrum, strange and unwelcome.

I dreamed myself awake, opened my eyes, and raised my head to regard the familiar tower of four shelves that stood against the wall alongside the bed. The rising cubes of black walnut wore a battlement crown to resemble a chess piece rook. A Netbook monitor and its touch board lay on the shelf nearly level with the bed. The monitor was idle, its silent, oceanic scene of swimming fish played out endlessly. The lightest touch would awaken the sleeping dashboard to replace the undersea scene. The whiskey and tumbler were there on the shelf beside the monitor, glinting in the colors of its light, along with a silvery tin of small cigars and a sculptured glass ashtray with a swan's neck, all catching the flicker of sharks and rays and schools of colored fish.

Suddenly the scene vanished as the dashboard was tricked alight. I had touched nothing.

~

Day 14.

I awoke midmorning and eyed the sea aquarium in the faulty monitor, wondering if I had really been awake. And how could one know for certain?

Each day delivered an unbearable burden of time. I forced myself to dress and go out walking the streets to feel some modicum of being alive, to seek affirmation or revelation somewhere in the wider world beyond my apartment. In a matter of days I had become a ghost reflected in display windows, a hollow semblance meandering the antique neighborhoods and glittering commercial districts. The allure in shop windows conspired to remind me I dared not enter anywhere for my empty pockets. Life had become a museum for which I lacked admittance. I sought out streets that I'd never traversed. I felt at a crooked angle to time and space, not real, a ghost regarding the place of his passing.

The walk back to the apartment held no promise of discovery. The notion of home had disintegrated. I'd do what had to be done when the time came. Another day with no difference had passed.

Tomorrow would be follow-up day for all the futile resumés sent, so many paper boats set to sail in a make-believe sea. I would collect messages and inquire of outcomes. I would feel like I'd done due diligence.

Neil was still a chance, perhaps the only one, as dismal as the prospect seemed. Our friendship was ambivalent and careful, a truce of vipers. We had more than one duel of wit over matters as unlikely as the best symbolic color of neoconservatism or what his idea of freedom meant to a guy earning subsistence wages. I teased at the edges of his inhuman logic with illogic, as if that held a greater logic. He in turn made me squirm with feelings of dependency.

Neil, like the Old Man, wrapped himself in economic faiths and political values, the same ones that had coughed me up and spat me out. I was in the end just a suit he knew, an amiable challenger he could bring in to his startup because he would otherwise, sitting on his father's wealth, be surrounded by stooges.

Night became a sacred refuge. The fever outside the windows abated, and entertainment seekers filled the streets. I poured what I knew would be the first of several whiskies. At some point the pain would begin to numb and weariness would at last overcome the mouse chase in my head. I knew the value of getting drunk, and time needed wasting.

I measured three fingers down and decided that would be enough for the job. I sipped away, seeking release from whirling dead ends.

I wondered about such things as the possibilities that exist in every moment—were they finite or infinite? Were the possibilities, from time to time, one and then the other? I could never buy in to the folderol that you psyched your destiny, that desired realities are there for the picking if only you frame your mind just so. Psych jockeys had a hundred variations on the theme and even more names for them, but the message was always the same in the end. Shit's all your fault, and here's what I'm selling...

If I had a mind to, I could ascribe every shiny facet of my predicament to circumstance and exterior condition, and yet I also knew it was my own damned doing too. How could I have psyched myself to stake and leverage out like that? I was another greedy monkey who fell out of the tree for trying to grab all the bananas. In the glare of hindsight I damned myself aloud for pride and presumption.

When whiskey and weariness wore down to exhaustion, the possibilities were finite and infinite at once.

* * *

CHAPTER 4

Forever Sunday Island

Day 13.

I awoke before the alarm and prepared as if for work. I showered, had a touch of breakfast and coffee, then dressed and groomed for the monitor. I had my data book at the ready and recited what tongue teasers I knew to warm my voice and get mouth muscles and tongue working, as my daily measure of jawboning had dropped precipitously and put me out of practice.

Thus armed, I embarked upon the to-do list, beginning with follow-up for dormant applications and any openings newly advertised, attempting to get through the labyrinth of agencies and middle men to a company's HR for a first contact.

At some point I almost began to enjoy myself that morning, as if playing a game. A game is the only sense to make of an insensible activity, isn't it? I knew I could spend all day with the headhunter middlemen without coming an inch closer to a company's hiring manager. I well knew the uselessness of the time I expended. I was Sisyphus, grinning through the grimace of futile labor.

To my credit, I thought, I actually did manage to speak with a hiring manager, though it was plain this success against all odds was important to no one but me. I nearly fumbled the interview from the outset, as the guy resembled a childhood classmate in my adoptive town. Dennis, I remembered, gave me my first childhood taste of inequity. He was poster child for the kid who had everything—wealthy parents, a mansion home, toys of every craving—and he was handsome, popular, and intelligent too. He made me, a pimpled egghead in my early teens who was lucky to have foster parents, perfectly sick. In no time the interview soured, torpedoed by a memory. The chemistry quotient in every interaction seemed fickle and cruel.

Whoever gave me harbor in this financial storm would have my loyalty, but being fake was plainly sufficient for these people. Fake was perhaps preferred, in fact, since one is then ever on trial to make good on the fakery. Was I then not fake enough? Should I make my fakery more transparent? Was there a nuance to this art of the interview I was yet missing?

"You're a bastard bred to disloyalty..." The Old Man's words resounded in memory. If these employers believed I was the sharpshooter they sought, what could they expect for loyalty?

I played back call after call to try to hear myself through their ear. I winced, grit my teeth, turned away and groaned in the watching and listening, my voice indicator flashing political alarm all over the spectrum time and again. Inconclusive was better than a steady reading in the pink, but as the LieCo slogan said: "True blue shows through."

By the time I finagled another interview on the Net, I had arrived at the happy construct, and perhaps I even convinced myself as well, that they needed me as much I needed them; and eventually I settled into this self-assured tone, trumpeting my personal stock, my professional brand, like a shrewd and agile grifter.

The nuns at the orphanage had counseled me for being hypersensitive and prone to over thinking, and thanks to them I made myself learn countermeasures. I learned how to act, to perform and project the personality expected in a selective manner. I learned, in effect, to lie, and found I had a knack for it. So much silence now filled my days that I fairly enjoyed sounding off in the ego of the confident applicant. In this self-sell state, the semantic voice guard indicator on the Netbox did not once display a Democrat or pinko reading.

But the facade was exhausting and I wore down. In a long interview, what had begun so well turned tense, and in the end my words rang false to my own ear. Listening to myself fail at deception in replay, I was shamed both coming and going.

The end of business hours and the comfort of darkness arrived none too soon. I unwound myself from the forced pace of the day, and eventually managed to calm down altogether. Even sitting quietly still, every one, every thing, the very glue of customs and consciousness continued to constrain me, as if my very being were impermissible. I had no right to a living, but a nagging obligation to live.

There remained Neil, I reminded myself. A carefree affability was the operational mode required to deal with Neil. I felt like a dayshift whore playing these roles, but he was really the only game left to me. Neil was Dennis the-rich-kid all over again. Not that he had everything. With his long beak and big ears, icy personality, and lack of imagination, he surely didn't. But he had a mega-rich and powerful daddy and a decent trading average; he knew tech, and was a credible entrepreneur in this time of desperation. He should have no problem raising money. Daddy would make good if he fell on his face.

Out of expediency, if nothing else, he might yet make a job for me, a power I could scarcely forgive him for having over me. "He's smart enough to know he needs me," I said, pumping myself aloud. I warmed myself with a taste of whiskey as the idea of attempting a casual invitation to Neil began to gel. Soon my life seemed to hinge on pulling the escapade off. I ordered happy background music and hazarded a call.

"Yeah, not a party really," I pitched to him after preliminaries. "Not much to celebrate these days. Just you, maybe Robbie, whoever's still in town," I said. "Bring a date if you want. We'll knock back a few glasses and watch reruns of the crash, surf the Middle East for cheering," I joked. In certain unfriendly Muslim capitols, it was reported that people had gathered to roar their approval at news of the stock market crash, the prelude to the downfall of American imperialism, they hoped. Neil was not amused.

Something came over me with Neil; I couldn't help toying with him. He was a true believer. He called himself a Brandian objectivist, meaning you have to be one to know what that means. So, instead of encouraging him I'd tell him he looked like a Brandian objectivist, which annoyed him to no end.

He used the word "free" quite a lot, mostly in combination with markets, and he displayed a ruthless evangelism if provoked. I'd tell him that his righteous brand of capitalism didn't particularly need his help. This tease, that he and his ideological ilk might be entirely dispensable, invariably produced some weird pronouncement, in his detached, chilling way, some variation of being born to lead the charge for world domination. It was painful to endure, but we all live out delusions, don't we?

I knew if I fumbled this I'd be dropped to square one in Neil's game. He would disappear and I'd get the cold shoulder until happenstance again brought me into his orbit, which might easily be never.

"I have meetings all week," he explained dourly. "That Persian woman I mentioned, Hetty Sana, is coming around."

"Perfect. Bring her. I'll order Eastern hors d'oeuvres," I hazarded, wondering which credit chit was not over the limit.

"I don't want to crowd her with the fallout," he hedged.

"No crowding. Tell her I know Wellingham," I lied brazenly while speaking the truth, implying, in an inspiration, that the Old Man was accessible to me. Neil didn't know about the slap down from Wellingham. For all Neil knew, he and I were pals. It occurred to me, in his cleverness, that might be the reason he mentioned this contact of his in the fist place and why he sidled up to the idea with little resistance. With Neil one never knew who was zooming who.

"There's no need to talk business. We'll just have a good time and leave it alone for a while," I added before he drilled me on the Old Man.

"I'm working nonstop."

I could hear the uncertainty in his voice, and the excuse was lame. "Tomorrow night, then?"

"I don't know. I'm showing her the town."

I noted with optimism that he had backed down from an absolute no.

"She runs Adaptive," he explained, "that huge logistics firm in the Middle East. She has some business with my father."

The Texon daddy himself. I had just stepped into the deep.

"So where are you taking her?" I invited, as he sized me up quizzically.

"Sotheby's, then to see Visa, and dinner." "Visa Hee-Haw" was a musical comedy about competition for residency permits among the wealthier "burros," a spelling used by City snobs to disparage residents of the outlying municipal boroughs. I squelched the thought lest it trigger a disruptive emotion, then spied a likely interval in his plans I could exploit.

"Stop by for drinks after Sotheby's."

"I suppose there might be some time before the show," he acknowledged reluctantly.

I had him. "Would you rather I come along to Sotheby's or the theatre?" The teasing had slipped in and I feared the worst.

Instead he laughed, "We're getting along really well. She may want to invest in my startup. We'll most likely be working together at some point."

Ah, she scared him, I thought. It was scary all around, and perhaps I did not want to go along. Half an hour here would do the trick.

"Sixish? Drinks and appetizers?"

"Okay. Yes. If not, I'll give you a call."

"Hail, fundamentals."

"Power to the charts."

The screen went blank. I exhaled a breath of relief. Another five minutes and I'd surely have stuck my foot in my mouth or revealed my desperation. I sat staring at the black square until the screen resumed its undersea world of strange and menacing creatures. In my mind's eye, faces, voices, phrases from the day's drama resurfaced in mocking revue.

It was another hour before the churn in my brain wore down and I quieted. Finally, the music I had neglected to turn off grated. The light in the room glared. I ordered them off. The clothes I was wearing, the day's costume, I exchanged for a robe and sat alone in the dark.

I wondered what Sean's vespers were like. What time did they end? Should I call while buoyed by this sliver of hope while I still believed something might come of it? I reminded myself that

Sean had no inkling of the vicissitudes that ruled my life. He saw lies and games and hypocrisy. "Venal shenanigans," says he.

The transition was not easy from a Boston investment bank to a coveted position in an Empire City hedge fund. I had schooled in Philly, thence to trial by fire at a bank in Cambridge, then Boston proper, all a far cry from my adoptive home in the small town of Wickham, Vermont, not far from the orphanage.

"You can take a man from the country, but you can't take the country from the man," diddled idly through my head. But it wasn't so. I felt certifiably citified, a "flatlander" as Father Melakey of Wickham Parish would say.

Optimism would not take wing no matter what hope I entertained. I figured I would fiddle my way to the end, balls out, just for the record. What else could I really do?

Nothing could happen quickly enough. A start-up, now, of all times. There would be no telling if or when or how anyone got paid.

No, I disallowed, correcting myself to be positive. He'll set us up. We'll catch the rebound and I'll avoid bankruptcy, eviction. "Who's going to stop me?!" I challenged the darkness. But the psych pump did not work. My positive thinking reflexes were worn through. I drifted back to the threshold of depression.

Who would stop me seemed to have narrowed down to a foreigner I did not know named Hetty, and of course Neil, who could turn cold and acidic for reasons known only to him. I could end up on his shunned list in a blink and never understand why. He was afraid of this boss woman though. It was in his voice. "How can this work?" I asked the darkness.

I'd find an ethnic deli that delivered. Stake the last of my credit on this meeting. "Tomorrow," I said. I had to admit that the day-long gyrations had done me in and I was in no condition to fathom the absurdity of hope.

I poured another whiskey, grateful to exchange anxiety for a little numbness, unconsciousness my certain goal. I found the bed and propped myself in my customary position beside the tiered table with its battlement crown, making a pillow cushion for my back at the headboard, the glass and bottle stationed on the bedside shelf.

"Not 'til the fat lady sings," I told myself, making a mantra of the cliché as I sipped and watched the twinkling lights outside the transparent doors, among and beyond the hulking spires.

In time I no longer saw out of my eyes. Movies spun themselves in my head. Perhaps I was asleep, or drowsing, maybe only half-awake or maybe wide-awake daydreaming in the dark, illumined by the City glow.

~

Day 12.

I dreamed I lay on my side facing away from the strangers, weird in their low laughter, making taunts that I dared not turn to face. Fear rendered me immobile, pithed like a biology class frog with a jab to the spine. I kept my eyes closed as if asleep, defenseless as I was anyway. They were many—coarse, hillbilly, backwoods types making vengeful catcalls, enjoying my city-boy fear more than doing me harm. I pretended to sleep as they jeered at my pretending. Again and again, I knew cold, morbid fear, helplessness, and shame.

Another dream took its place. I was in my childhood bedroom in which the side wall sloped down from the ceiling, my adoptive brother asleep in the bed beside me. The window lattice cast its moonlit shadow on the slanted ceiling. I awoke within the dream to find that I was tiny, only inches tall. The darkness was enormous, cosmic but for the glow of the window and the latticed light. Then the bed vanished and I was falling backward in the dark, stomach churning as gravity pulled me down, an object of pure fear. The certainty of death eclipsed the fear of falling in the dark, and then, at the last moment, a huge hand reached as if from an unknown dimension to gently catch me. The hand, which I somehow knew was my unknown father's hand, upturned and dropped me again into a net which stretched safely away under my weight as I called out, "Father, father."

Then I came upon a woman, lovely in the huge moonlight of a summer clime. The light caught her small, jutting shoulder, a perfect knob, and illumined her thin angled arm. Her neck, long and exposed in the cut of her hair, was outlined in silver. Her hands were strong but petite, gathering in the stillness, awaiting my next touch to stir. "I love you, Keira."

"Do you love her?" came a low, musical voice, an unfamiliar woman's voice, from nearby in the room. It seemed to come from the netbook monitor on the shelf before me, as if the device had a mind of its own.

"I love her," I replied eyes closed in the dream, and out of it.

"She loves herself to surfeit, so little room for yours."

The voice had certainty, as if she knew Keira.

"She will always be some man's mark," she added.

"How do you know? How do you know?" I muttered.

The voice did not answer. I rolled over and faced away, and once settled there a childhood dream emerged. The kids I played with stood in the street, the world bathed in a reddish bronze dusk, the air charged with electricity and dread. I jumped the low hedges of my front yard to see what they saw up at the top of the dead end street where we lived. The intersection was blocked by a great wooden crib-like structure on giant rockers. The huge container seemed to be filled with all our households, our chairs, tables, sofas, and lamps; and it was slowly rocking, rocking. At that moment an ancient, propeller-driven airliner flew toward us low and slow, a gnarled tree with dead limbs snagged on its wing, old bark peeling off in the current of wind. The plane tipped its wing and shed the strange encumbrance to the ground, the limbs crashing significantly, silently in my yard, and I knew it was the final sign for the holocaust to follow. The air turned into woven fire, beams of orange crisscrossing in all dimensions without end in a checkered inferno, the end of the world.

I rolled over facing the shelf again and opened my eyes without stirring. A woman sat leaning on the edge of the whiskey tumbler on the rook shelf, resting one bare foot against the bottle beside it. She was dressed in black tights neck to ankle, a Goth version of Tinkerbelle, wearing a belt diagonally across her bosom which bound a long sword sheath to her back, the tail of which protruded behind her. She regarded me a with strange intelligence plainly written in her solemn face. I gasped.

In her hand was the haft of a long sword, fashioned heavily in the Samurai tradition but slightly longer and with a straight blade. The impressive weapon was belied by an impossibly wise, emotive, sensual, sharply cut face, her lower lip extending ever so slightly beyond the upper, these parting slowly in a confident smile that transformed her visage to that of a woman who calmly knows her power. Her raven hair was mounted high behind her head with a leather band and wooden peg. This was not a vision of Keira at all. I dreamt this, of course, or rather, I dreamt that I was not dreaming this. The surreal pervaded the dark in the silent wee hour.

"Greetings, Ken. I am Sahar," she said in a slow, nuanced, musical voice. "Fate has brought us together, most fortuitously I believe. I have a proposition for you."

I was smitten, open-mouthed, breathless. Among the impossible proportions before me, her penetrating black eyes, earnest and mature in their depth, riveted my attention.

"Quite the dreamer, aren't you?" she asked rhetorically of my stunned silence.

I gasped and shut my gaping mouth.

"I've been looking over your accounts," she said, indicating the monitor beside her which I recognized as the balance page to my bank account.

At that she stepped onto the keyboard and leapt key to key with trained balletic foot-chasing-foot steps, opening a window to show a transfer to my account awaiting execution. The amount was, to the dollar, the numbers I had run for what I needed to pay my debts and float for three months. The tip of her blade rested on the execution key. A touch and it was done.

I dreamt that I sat up with anxious focus, reaching impulsively for the aid of the whiskey on the shelf. Her blade swung with a glint toward my hand and stopped me. It showed a razor edge in the light, and I found her eyes as she probed mine. I pointed to the glass, and she nodded. I picked it up, sipped, then gulped it down, scarcely moving my eyes from her lithe, slender form, her taut, muscular articulation pushing every button of female allure.

"What," I tried for breath, "is the proposition?"

"We change the world, you and I." She smiled easily with those words, leaning lightly on the blade she'd stuck between the keys. "Starting with America."

My unconscious seemed to be making some kind of cosmic joke, I guessed. Here was this impossibly tiny woman I distinctly heard say change the world, you and I, starting with America. Limp with relief at such silliness, I closed my eyes and fell back into the warm pillow behind me, replacing the tumbler without looking, confident of her unreality, the words "starting with America" reeling in my head. A tingling bubble rose from the depth of my unconscious, buoyed by the mirth that filled it, until it popped the surface in hilarity at that change-the-world notion. I laughed, then laughed a little more, and then laughter overtook me. I lay there and shook, belly laughing until it hurt, tears running down my face. By the time I could properly see, I was flushed and sweating. The apparition was gone. The ocean creatures had resumed their aimless display. I was silent a long time, the lonely quiet gathering around me. I didn't know what to make of myself. Was I losing my mind?

I slept again; or rather, I slept on but dreamed no more that night and awoke to the alarm sounding. I did not remember having set it as I groped for the mechanism, then dozed back into the warmth of the pillow until the chime returned at its relentless interval. "Off," I growled, and it ceased. It was nearly noon when I awoke with a start, searching my empty head for what it was I had missed by oversleeping.

Of course, I had missed nothing and was not missed. As I rubbed my eyes and massaged my temple, I realized I did in fact today have a raison d'être. It was Neil and Hetty day.

I jumped up and ordered hors d'oeuvres, a bottle of Bekaa Valley red and a vintage California white, heedless of expense, for 5:30, jousting with a nagging fear he'd cancel out too late to nix the order, and leave me the idiot. "Call Bob Sandler, full view." There was no answer. "Try his alternate." A moment later, Robbie's broad heavy face appeared cropped tight.

"Hey, man. What's up?" he asked.

"Same bear trap. Where are you?" He switched to full view and I saw him in livery cap and suit. He was sitting in the driver's seat of a limousine, part of the partition visible behind him. Out his window in clear focus was the bustle of the street and far sidewalk.

"Madison and 77th," he answered matter-of-factly.

"What's doing there?"

"Ha. Not a thing. I have to wait here for a dispatch, not a thing in three hours already. At least this outfit pays waiting time. Most don't."

"Schlep anybody worth talking to?"

"Nah, only the tourists talk."

"Is that keeping you together?"

"I moved to Brooklyn last week, Coney Island. Three fares a day keeps me alive, just about, but it can take twelve, fourteen hours for the damn dispatcher to hand them out to me."

"Seniority?"

"That and how well you kiss his ass." He puckered his thick lips and smooched obscenely at the lens.

"No telling if it's gonna be a one-fare day or a five-fare day," he continued. "Had a 20 hour, five-fare day my first weekend, which was decent money. Most days are waiting around, that's the job, waiting, five hours on end yesterday. Only so much you can do on the Net. Brutal waste of time. I'll take a snooze in the back if I don't get a call soon."

"Why not freelance on your downtime?"

"They have this thing rigged with every sensor known to man. My position is blinking on a map right now."

"Any way to hack the GPS?" I wondered.

"Yeah there is, but everything is monitored, every watt in the battery and every thimble of booze in the icebox, even how many times each door opens and closes. There may be a damn camera hidden somewhere too."

"Sell the car to a fence," I joked.

"Yeah, the exchange rate in Venezuela is still good, and no extradition. They probably got me on a list at the airport. I had to get re-bonded for this crap. Can you believe that?"

"You're schlepping crème de nabobs?" I inquired, surprised at the security requirement.

"Nah, anal execs mostly, middle tier, and well-off tourists."

"How's Coney?"

"Found what they call a studio in a 200 year-old building. It's the Stone Age, man. The bathtub is in the kitchen and I yank a chain to flush the toilet. I kid you not. Tank's up against the ceiling. I'm having a ball trapping the mice, though. Got four this week." He paused and added philosophically, "Life has its simple pleasures."

"Listen. Neil said he'd come over for a drink sixish, along with a bigwig backer. Can you get here?"

"For real? Hot shit, man. Jeez, I'd hate to miss that. Hmn." He pondered, absently biting a thumbnail. "Okay, if I don't have a fare right then, I'll make something up for the detour. The problem is the uniform."

"Hey, we're all friends. Neil knows what's going on."

"Yeah," he huffed, nodding. "But bad for his game, a beggar boy in livery."

"Lose the cap and jacket."

"Bad for your game too, bucko."

He was right, of course. "Look, spring for a new shirt."

"Cheapest thing in town is half a day's pay," he said, shaking his head as he thought it over.

"Pick one up. It's on me. Nothing Hawaiian," I warned, and he laughed.

"You're getting by?" he asked of me incredulously.

"I'm going down fiddling."

"If I can, I'll show." He was obviously discomfited and wanted to go.

"Show, Bob. This could turn into something for both of us."

"Yeah, it could. Alright, see you then. Thanks." His downfall gig was painful to witness, and I'd soon be there, somewhere, another notch down on my way to trickle town.

"*De nada*," I said. He'd do the same for me, I figured as the screen went blank from his end.

Keep the ball rolling, I admonished myself, and set about weeding through messages and spam. Then I dutifully checked the daily ads to which my auto responder had proffered applications and followed up where I conceivably could. I did not bother myself with the voice box. I was doing all I could to sound right wing, neo-con, Republican. Of necessity I was getting better at it.

I shifted gears yet again and tried Keira's numbers, certain of the futility. Her doting granddaddy was a grand master at keeping people out of his protective circle. If she had wanted to reach me, she would have by now. One way or the other, I was history.

"What shall I do with my sorry sack until party time?" I wondered aloud nervously, afraid to lose the positive momentum I could already feel slipping away.

Should I stick to the job hunt, so as not to jinx my prospects with Neil? Continue with cold calls? Revisit the want ads? Catch up on the latest networking strategies? Practice technique with power interviewing software? The whole wretched culture of job seeking was just a click away. Every kind of gung-ho psych jockey was out there selling their wares, from positive thinking to laws of attraction, bidding me improve my chances in a more perfect union with the great white lie.

The afternoon stretched before me like a featureless sea. For all my gamesmanship, I was just another shrivel wrapped soul. Unemployment defined me.

There was one business owner who had baldly asked me in an interview, "Can you devote yourself to my furthest enrichment?" His very words, and in fact the very real essence of my job. Yet, that was my problem: Like him, I lacked true enthusiasm for any enrichment but my own.

"What else?" I asked aloud, in mock incrimination of my self-marketing failures, of which there seemed to be no end.

For the liberal guy in his Birkers and T-shirt, I would need to dress down and re-brand. For the conservative in his buttoned-up suit, I would need a new tailor and a haircut. I should shave my head for wigs, with a supply for every occasion. Overall, I concluded, my chameleon skills needed buffing.

For the woman who'd rather hire a man, I would need a sex change. For the old man, I needed grey hairs. For the geeky child wonders, glasses and an owlish glare. For the Black man, soul dye. For the WASP, a better family. The religious required a sorely lacking piety; for the sage that certain acolyte something. For the socialite, names to drop; for the fat, girth; for the short, fewer inches. For the plain dumb, a better practiced patience and humility for the privilege to serve them. And for all the unguessed office politics behind their bright shiny smiles, I would need to somehow be a feather in their camp's cap.

Whims and hiring peccadilloes ruled my life. Was indignation and rage ever quite appropriate in an eat-shit-and-smile-brown world? It seemed to me that euthanasia made more sense than this grinding degradation, or else disconnect survival from the god-damn job, why don't you? What kind of world didn't get this? Ah, yes, the free world.

I had to get out or I'd explode. I still had claim to the sidewalks and parks. Or some of them, I corrected myself, recalling the many gated parks and reserved walkways of Empire City.

"When the going gets tough, the tough go shopping" floated up from somewhere. There seemed a perverse wisdom to the prescription. I'd go buy something, something useless and fanciful—and cheap. Stir yourself, I silently ordered.

I went to the closet and finished dressing. When is having a drink with friends not? In a few short hours. I stuffed my feet into shoes and laced. I debated outerwear for the mild February, and decided I'd walk fast to keep warm and go with just the suit jacket.

The apartment door opened and closed behind me. That's what I'd buy, I decided, a book by An Brand, the misshapen Natalie Woods of neoconservatives, and use it as a prop for the evening affair. The situation with Neil had not really changed for the better. I could at least stop teasing him about his attachment to this shivery gal's cant. A showcase Brand book was just the ticket, a hard copy bible for the extremes so dear to him. I'd stage the thing where he couldn't miss seeing it lying around. I'd get it used and well-worn if I could. That would tweak his head some.

I ordered my environment for the ride down. The Wagner began low, growing in volume until the thrilling refrain boomed from all sides, the car walls illumined in real time with a breathtaking panorama of my 27 floor descent from lenses outside the building. The joy ride elevator was a staple of high rise residences in Empire City. I left the car energized.

For Hetty the enigma, who do you need to be? Global. With stocks in the toilet, maybe currencies? The US crash had crippled stocks around the world, and interest rates would be eased to stave off recession. Would the resulting currency sump be slower in Japan, London, or Shanghai?

Crossing the lobby I cast my customary wink to the sexy, older concierge with great legs. She nodded noncommittally, as trained, but I got the smile others didn't.

The smaller currencies were more vulnerable, and Shanghai would likely ease ahead of the other central banks. I'd shine if I could make a case for the right currency pairs...

I headed downtown from my East Village apartment out of habit, wandering through the NYU housing with Picasso's "Sylvette." I never missed a chance to visit her. She reminded me of Keira with her two faces. It was not Sylvette's constraint or Keira's apparent duplicity, but a simple facial resemblance from either side. Or did every man find his lover's face in her faces? I turned to savor the wide precipice of jaw and cheek, the nexus with her neck as I continued past, turning my head until I would have to walk backward to keep her in view. Then I stepped up the archway over Houston Street, the private gardens of the new archway towers on either side.

Soho was a residential park closed to vehicles. Many of the streets were cobblestone, some were no longer paved from building edge to building edge. Trees stood about in designer array, evergreens the only color left among them in the season.

Down here amid the ancient low buildings, the ivy grew in thick beards across the stone faces, windows lost in the wintry auburn of Virginia creepers. I was already warm from hike as I spied the used bookstore I had passed many times but never entered. Apart from the digital catalog, it was every bit the quaint Vintage Book Store it claimed to be, all but the most popular volumes in a storeroom out of sight.

The An Brand query produced a voluminous list of organizations and articles as well as the author's books. I shrugged and ordered her hallmark tome "Atlas Chugged," surprised how fast it slipped up the vacuum chute to the register. I'd chosen the most beat up of three paperbacks, for which I paid the price of dinner with wine at a modest restaurant, and grimaced as I tapped my chit that the old cow must be mooing from her grave.

Before I knew it I had reached the Canal Street archway, where Chinese architecture rose incongruously into the city skyline basking in the afternoon sun.

Many blocks later the Memorial Park with its massive Freedom Tower, the new One World Trade Center, came into view. I'd never acknowledged the thought, but I knew I had been heading there all along. I had on the same suit I wore the fateful day of the crash, I realized as I approached the plaza. Instead of the data case, I held a prop for the coming show with my erstwhile colleague and, God only knew, prospective boss.

I retraced that day's steps until I stood at the Memorial pool. "So what are you doing here?" I asked myself. I was not here to pay tribute or sentimentalize. I had no feeling for the dead of yesteryear. The attacks that followed, all the draconian vigilance to prevent them notwithstanding, had diffused the uniqueness of 9/11.

Only one of the major attacks occurred in my lifetime, long before I'd ever visited Empire City or its surrounding boroughs, then still quaintly considered New York City with Manhattan but one of five public municipalities. Every attack since 2001 had its own amazing news clips, its own bloviating, its own rage and misbegotten military action. The attack in my time line eclipsed 9/11 in carnage, and played well into the plans of those set on taking Manhattan private, even though it did not occur in Manhattan but across the 59th Street Bridge in Queens. The #7 subway line ran atop an elevated platform, old and dilapidated, before descending into the tunnel under the East River into Manhattan. Underneath the elevated trestle were, of all things, parking lots, while to each side ran Queens Boulevard, one of a handful of bottleneck bridge and tunnel roads to and from the City Isle where rush hour traffic massed in the workday morning for the river crossing.

Early one Tuesday morning in September, six drivers parked their trailer trucks under the length of the Queensboro Plaza Station and walked away. At the peak of the morning commute, when trains in both directions were stopped and people thronged the station, traffic honking in the jammed roadway below, they detonated their truckloads of home made explosives. The elevated rail structure, of fragile ancient construction, heaved up and then rained down in pieces huge and small, as did railcars crammed with thousands on their way to and from their daily shifts.

It was later learned that the spectacular newsreels of the explosion and the horrendous footage of the aftermath was taken from nearby rooftops with ordinary camcorders. It was allegedly provided to Box News by a member of the terrorist group for an exorbitant sum. And of course, the perps had made fortunes on the headlong dive the market took that day and for months thereafter. They blithely closed out their shorts and vanished with enough loot to finance such carnage for generations to come.

The same crisis rhetoric was dragged out for reuse, filling media walls relentlessly, as personal freedom and privacy were raided in new rounds of laws, closing the proverbial barn doors after the horses had fled while shoring up our passion for war in some far reach of the planet.

I subscribed to nothing, least of all the Democrat or Republican cant. They scarcely differed to me and both had the odor of the unclean. I was taxed without representation, indeed. My ism was me-ism, but it was obvious to me that Neil's darling of me-ism, An Brand, was just some dame making hay for herself as an emigre from communist Russia. For a mite of moral seeming, the illusion of clothes on the naked emperor, her grateful barons made her high priestess. Bully for her.

It seemed that was all an ex-commie had to do was come here and fawn over capitalism. What trick could I turn? What gimmick did I have to please the powers that be? Certainly, the market for flattering robes was a sellers' market, with keen high end demand for such, and few in supply that weren't a hash job, but that wasn't my calling. I had trained for math, not moral diddling. I shuddered involuntarily, remembering the curious sound of the jumper as he smacked the pavement, jellied. That was the answer to Brand.

I fancied I was a chameleon, motionless in the carefully crafted public space, blending in, an actor by absence, a master of urban camouflage. Perhaps I was not even really there. I looked at the prop in my hand, eulogies for unbridled Schweinerei marching across its back cover, and I hated myself, hated the Tower looming beside me. What could I say to true believers? I care nothing for your laws! I am an animal, a two-legged appetite, a beast like you are but I don't rationalize or pretend!

I knew what beasts we were.

"The predatory stage of humanity" came to mind, and this thought squared off with boxing mitts against "you don't know how lucky you are to be born in America," as my adoptive mother never failed to remind me. I was sick of the voices in my head.

I regarded the vile volume in my hand and looked out to the pool memorializing the September 11 dead. I imagined myself hurling the thick paper brick into the tranquility of the reflecting pool, imagined the splash as Brand's tome found its true place in the universe, but I checked my arm in time. The symbolism would end in handcuffs, which would not do, not today, not on Neil and Hetty day. I peered around at the eyes, the guards, the cameras, that were ubiquitous. Terror Central. What had I come here for?

Get out before you do something stupid, I admonished myself. I could feel my body shifting into high gear as adrenalin began its ascent, and I fled the place as quickly as I dared. To remain invisible, a blur-body in an ever changing scene, seemed the best strategy when I had anger like this, especially when I could not quite sort out the source of it. By the time I reached the street, I was nearly livid, rage tears welled and I slapped at my face for calm—to no avail. I felt caged in time for all time. What did freedom in space matter? Walking with determination to nowhere was pointless, and standing still, time galloped on all around. I was unable to stay or go, a perfect hell in being there.

"Go ahead then," I growled to myself. "Lash out, throttle someone to death, smash them about the head with a rock, extinguish yourself in accordance with civilized principles." That's what I wanted to do.

How well I understood fanatics, all of them, every kind: Muslim fundamentalists, white supremacists, eco-terrorists, fascists, skinheads, Black revolutionaries, communist guerillas, anti-abortionists, right-wing assassins. With sufficient betrayal, oppression, or impotent rage, there was no kind of killer I could not become. The same was true for most anyone, I knew, whatever their pretense of pieties.

I headed back uptown out of sullen habit, as senseless as the idea of home had become. The sidewalk crowd were to me no more than ambulating obstacles with whom I had nothing in common. What was death? A little thing, a part of life, like birth, that comes to all. The world doesn't owe you a living, as my adoptive father would harp. Live and let die then, of course.

The world doesn't owe me; then I owe nothing in return, do I? I owed no restraint, no morality, not even sanity. I could just as soon kill you as look at you, the truth of this owe-nothing ethos be told.

"I could kill you," I snarled menacingly, glaring down a startled old man in a suit. Peel away the house training and we would be left with mad dogs homegrown by the millions from the naked truth of live-and-let-die.

The jokers who made the headlines, the ones with billion dollar scams, merely bilked too vigorously, ignoring the rules of etiquette otherwise known as the laws of the land. They were criminals largely by dint of getting caught. Cheating was not "fair" in live-and-let-die land, of course, but we were all one dose of enthusiasm away from being criminals in Empire City.

I could not sustain the intensity of indignation that had swept me up. It dissipated with every step until I was, after a ferocious fit of barking, once again the well-conditioned middle-class puppy, replete with collar, tag, and leash.

I angled east, wondering how I'd shake this malevolent turn and un-scowl my face for pleasantries with Neil and this big shot woman he was bringing with him. I passed over Canal and then Houston without answer, in a reckless free-fall of emotions.

What's this all about now? "Scamper on home," I aimed at myself in derision. "Amuse your masters and maybe they'll let you back in the kennel."

As I neared home, I again questioned the exchange of the public street for the private place that was the apartment, an exchange of true cold for false comfort. I was homeless inside and out. I did not bestow a flirting smile on the concierge as I crossed the lobby. I did not request a surround sound elevator ride. I put my thumb to the door lock and stood looking around the studio apartment as if seeing it for the first and last time.

The Netbox on my desk was lit. It had been off when I left, hadn't it? My email was displayed, a message open. The subject: "What now?"

The first line read, "The US crash dragged down global markets, and interest rates are now key. Declines in rates will be quickest progressing to slowest in the following order:" Then came the currency list followed by the option pairs to play.

The question with which I'd left the apartment lay answered before me in detail. The note was signed Sahar, and there was an address and surrounding verbiage identifying the sender as a member of a forum belonging to a high school investment club, Henderson High, in Courtney, Alabama. I reread the lines leaning over the desk monitor. The post was not half an hour old. "Reply," I ordered. "Write. How do you know? Send."

Oddly enough, the trades seemed to make sense, though presuming to know the precise order of currency ripples over the time frame was preposterous. I observed some of the trading pairs read out as syllogisms, as if it were a game. And yet, to judge from the trade overall, this was no high school kid slinging lingo.

The question remained: what was my Netbox monitor doing with this email open? Did I imagine that it had been off? I took in the apartment, looking for some hint of intrusion. There was none. Unless someone were here, or some unheard of malware had wormed its way to the power hub, I must have forgotten to shut the thing off.

"A sign from God," I mocked aloud. The leading trades, at least, seemed likely bets to me, what I would myself predict, as for the rest, even an amateur could come up with some kind of rationalization for the scenario. I searched the name Sahar, which I did not know: "Female, Arabic, meaning dawn."

Keep on track, I admonished myself, rising to doff my jacket and tie, choosing from among my best casual shirts with care and trying to remember ever visiting a teener forum.

A chime preceded the voice of the concierge. "Delivery 76760."

"Confirm," I said. "Send him right up."

It was already dark, and the lamps were on. The door chimed and I ordered "Preview" as I made toward the door. It was a young Arab in a white service uniform.

"Open," I said. "Come on in and set that down right there on the counter." He extended his transceiver card and I tapped my chit.

"Thank you, suh," he said in an indistinguishable accent. Knowing I'd feel better, and in an effort at bribing the gods, I handed him a generous tip in paper bills. His eyes lit up with a smile and he bowed backing toward the door, intoning variations on "Thank you, suh."

I unwrapped the delicacies and rummaged for plates on which to arrange them. I put out the last bottle of my favorite Irish, the two bottles of wine I'd ordered, and appropriate glasses, fussing with their arrangement. A bucket of ice and a carafe of water completed the picture.

A chime preceded the announcement "Robert Sanford." Robbie, a/k/a Bob.

"Send him up, please."

He arrived at the door flushed but presentable, wearing the new shirt, not anything I would choose but appropriately conforming. His shoes, however, were patent leather, a garish part of the uniform. He stood short and squarishly stout in the doorway, the unmended space in his front teeth showing between thick lips.

"Let me guess: Diana Ross, open air, fast," I said by way of greeting. He was an old, old, oldie fan.

"Not half right. Elvis, open air, slow. 'Love me tender, love me true,'" he intoned awfully. "Am I early?"

"Nah, right on time. No dodges from Neil so I assume he'll be here any minute with this Hetty."

"That the Iraqi?"

"Iraqi national. Iranian and Saudi by birth believe it or not."

"What's to believe?" he asked.

"Sunni-Shiite thing."

"Young?"

"Nah, old. A big CEO and all," I reminded him. "She has Neil on edge."

"Ha, Neil on edge. Does he know I'm coming?"

I shrugged without answering. Robbie poured a glass of the chilled white and helped himself to an hors d'oeuvre.

"Mmm. What is this stuff?" He picked up the package label and read its description.

"Iranian fig rolls. Yum."

"Still on your shift?"

He nodded. "The car's parked down the block. One fare all day, so I'll sit it out a few hours more. The overnights to Tokyo pop up sometimes in early evening. Lousy tippers, but an easy ride to the airport, and with any luck a pickup for the ride back."

"Take a look at this." I led him to the Net monitor and swiveled the chair for him to sit. He read in silence, munching.

"The timing of rates too, hah! Who is this shyster? He scrolled up to the masthead. Whoa. Henderson High in Alabamee." He turned to look at me quizzically. I shrugged again.

"Damned if I know. I came home and there it was." His brow furrowed as he looked it over again.

"That doesn't just happen," he said.

"And I'd swear the box was off when I left."

"Don't start cracking up on me, man. You're my last hope."

"Then you're in the muck deeper than you think," I replied. "If true, the play would be worth a fortune. That's no kid coming up with this prognostication, not even a wonder kid. Look at the back play in the Sucre. A lateral exchange with a non-market currency for shifting in and out of pairs. The lead trades make sense on fundamentals."

"If I had the minimums, I'd play the front end at least," he confirmed, nodding.

"So would I, I'm afraid, which is what got me in this mess to begin with."

"Weird."

"Think we should show it to them?" I asked with a bit of mischief.

"Sure. Just ditch the source." He grinned at me infectiously, searching my eyes.

"Okay," I said, "but let me do the talking."

"All yours. I'll throw in the sequence as a joke. Let me get it down." He turned to the screen and began memorizing. It was a mistake to underestimate Rob, but people did it all the time.

"The trouble is, this will be all over in a week," I said.

"Says who?"

"The author, look." I pointed out a line below the fold where she gave the time-frame.

"It would take me a year to save the minimum stake."

"In two weeks I'll be trapping mice with you in Coney."

"Speaking of which…" He fished in a pocket and dug up a receipt and placed it on the desk. "Thanks again," he said. "I'll pay you back when I get it." He returned to the monitor, ostensibly to test his memory.

With a chime, the concierge announced, "Neil Busch. Hetty Sana."

"Send them right up. Oh, and Maggie, ask them to try 'Valkyries,' open air, slow." The off light flickered.

"You wanna charge them up?" Rob asked.

"Get them smiling anyway. I need a conspicuous place to put this." I held up the Brand book. "To give Neil a hard on."

"There, on those," Robbie suggested pointing to the economic classics of the decade by the celebrated economist Milton Creedman, Dame Brand's own living Lenin.

"Not enough contrast," I said, pulling down a few other worn paperbacks from a bookshelf and arranging them on the edge of the desk with only one spine showing. As an afterthought I turned "Moll Flanders" to face front along with "Atlas Chugged" on top.

"There's a happy couple," I joked aloud.

We were laughing when the door sounded, freezing the ruddy smiles that lingered on our faces, and were still collecting our good spirits when Hetty entered followed by Neil.

A stricken silence came with them. She wore a magnificently embroidered Nehru jacket of pearl and gold with black highlights, her black silk slacks tucked mid-calf in low heeled mock-riding boots. Her hair, jet black with wisps of grey, was cropped short. She was in her late forties, petite with a tenacious hold on her ground, her feet planted apart mannishly as she peered at us with the most remarkable face.

The recognition was immediate, and I checked with Neil to confirm what I saw. Her face was the slightly feminized and well-groomed face of Mohammed Atta, the 9/11 terrorist whose intense, glaring photo was infamous the world over. A simulacrum for dark intensity and deadly intent, Atta seemed to stand in splendid drag right before my eyes. I had a chill.

"Welcome. You must be Hetty. Thanks so much for stopping up." I took her hand and turned it palm down with a press filled more with compassion than greeting. "Neil." I shook his hand squarely. "You've aged since I saw you last."

"Keeping late hours. You look the worse for wear yourself," he said.

"It's been a rough go around," I answered.

"Hi, I'm Bob," Robbie announced, rising from the desk chair to take Hetty's hand in an all-American shake. "Bob Sanford." She was surprised by his gesture but took his hand in good humor. Thank God for her smile, I thought, as the stern visage of terror dissolved in facial crinkles of amusement, small even white teeth, and a wry, pleasant smile. The sudden and complete transformation came as a shock of relief. Neil was amusing himself with my reactions, which he obviously well understood.

"Let's have a drink to friends, old and new, here and now," I ventured. "I have wine and whiskey. Choose your poison. Tell me what you think of this baklava."

"Thank you," she said. "Is that thirty-year Irish? Yes, that will do. Straight up, please."

"A woman after my own heart. Neil?"

"Ah, the white. Look at that," he added, hefting up the bottle for Hetty to glance at the label.

"Very thoughtful of you, but to tell you the truth, I know little of Western wine." Her English was British-learned the way she hollowed her vowels, but she had virtually none of the accent otherwise. That bare remnant of British mixed with her own faint Arabic accent in a clear, friendly voice that, with her potent smile, diminished the stern intensity from her eyes.

"I've left the labels on the hor d'oeuvres for those of us unfamiliar with the cuisine. How do you pronounce this one?"

I indicated one of the description placards with its English lettered Persian name. Hetty pronounced the name, which I repeated carefully, earning a compliment.

"He has an ear for language," Neil said in a tentative monotone.

"Best strumpet player in town," added Bob.

"Strumpet?"

"Phone artist," Bob explained.

"It's what we used to call the Netbox video, our instrument," Neil explained.

"Back in the sell side days," added Bob.

"That's how we all started out," I said. "Cold calling at an investment bank."

"A kind of initiation by torture," Bob added.

"The larva stage," said Neil.

"Selling your services, a very good way to start. We do the same at our investment banks. It is a difficult time to be selling such services," she said, her face consolidating once again into Atta. She looked at each of us in turn and said, "Gentlemen, I understand the times. I am looking to take advantage of them." It was the cocking of the gun we'd been waiting to hear.

"Robert is a bond analyst primarily, and I'm more of a maverick: equities, currencies, whatever is hot. Speaking of larva stages though, right now I'm developing some ideas on option spreads in currencies for the short term." I pitched this to Hetty but was careful to stay in Neil's orbit. He knew I could poach in his preserve and he couldn't stop me, but he would never forgive me either.

"Currencies? Yes, stocks will be consolidating for some time yet." She sipped from the tumbler.

"How did you meet Neil?" I asked.

"We met by chance in a computer store in Geneva some months ago," she informed matter-of-factly.

We cracked up. Even nerdy Neil, turning red, had to laugh at himself, and he shrugged, opening his arms from the elbows, palms up, in a baleful gesture. Only Hetty did not get the joke.

"Neil is known to spend more time at the monitor than anyone alive," I explained. "He only leaves the trading station to pick up a new one, and he can rig it up blindfolded."

"They think I am a geek because I enjoy research and technology. Actually, Hetty had advice for me on a six monitor set up."

"Would you trade the currencies he mentioned?" she asked of Robbie, surprising everyone.

"Yes. I'm with Ken on the spreads," he contributed solemnly.

"The idea is to paint the divergence in rate lowering in rolling currency pairs over the next few days," I explained quietly.

"Is a pattern emerging?" Hetty asked, intrigued.

"There are many ways to educate a viewpoint, I favor interest rate fundamentals and historical behavior in parallel conditions." Hetty nodded at this, and Neil raised an eyebrow. "It remains speculative," I added.

Robbie backed me up by reciting the list of currency pairs, ending with, "In that order." He was grinning widely.

Neil snorted. "You get that from a crystal ball?"

"That was confidential information, Bob," I chided. "Of course, the ordering is malleable and needs tending intra-day."

"This works on national economy fundamentals," Robbie offered, overextending the pitch I thought, and I shot him a look.

"Care to bet on it?" Neil taunted him.

"You're on," Robbie said, playing the part, though I could see his relief when Neil did not pursue terms. Hetty's eye wandered to the bookcase, taking in the titles. Neil's eye followed, and I smiled inside as both observed the side cover of the planted title. Neil looked back at me in some surprise. She was thoughtful for a moment, as if we were not there.

"There are opportunities, I am sure," she finally said. "How else would you trade the post-crash situation?" she asked.

It was like a rifle shot. With that, we were off, passing through the threshold from stranger and uneasy friends to prospective partners, fellow analysts, and traders. We talked markets and national economies, rates and currencies, and I put in an occasional stock or fund that one might not have guessed stood to benefit from the general rout.

I showed them the balcony, and since it was still mild, left the doors open when we returned. Hetty had insight into the oil markets and the Middle East bourses. We each had a second drink, dug into the food without embarrassment, and talked freely. The get-together was a success, and I was nearly stumbling with vertigo by the time they gathered themselves to leave.

I saw them to the door, followed by Robbie. "I really must thank you for a charming and informative time," Hetty said. "And I forgot to mention the elevator ride—quite exhilarating. We shall do it again on the way down?" Neil nodded.

"The pleasure is mine," I said genuinely. "Let's talk again soon."

I nodded and she seemed receptive, or at least not forbidding. "Neil, take good care of her," I called after them in the hall, and I ventured a wink. She smiled, her terror mask melting away.

They stepped into the elevator and were gone. Bob and I were silent. Sounds from the street far below wafted in from the open balcony door. I was exhausted and relieved. He poured himself another glass of wine and popped a delicacy into his mouth, waiting for my appraisal.

"Do you think she knows?" he asked, unable to keep it in any longer and starting to laugh while chewing, nearly spilling his wine.

"Oh, she knows," I said, remembering her face in the hall.

"Man, what a tough break for a chick. I'd wear the hair long at least."

"She knows and knows we know."

"Sure would take some brass to mention it to her."

"Monitor. Open wall one. Photo of terrorist Mohammed Atta." The search result was instantaneous.

We stared back at the stark sinister face covering the wall.

"His face speaks volumes," I said. "Off, please."

"Still so polite," Robbie noted, poking at my lingering schmooze mode. Then he added seriously, "Ken, I can't thank you enough for letting me in on this."

"Don't thank me and don't get your hopes up."

"Apart from the face, she was great. Hard to believe that was the CEO of Adaptive."

"Damn sharp," I agreed. "They have the Middle East sewn up, more partners and affiliates than anyone knows and the list is changing all the time. She was laughing right along with us, like there was no age or class difference," I said, more wondering aloud than outright assertion.

"She has clients here, and Neil thinks she's going to back him?" I nodded.

"At a minimum, he's a back door to his daddy and Texon." I shrugged. "All I know is I've got to get some kind of commitment out of Neil. I've got zero credit left, Rob. No sublet rights and less than two weeks before eviction. I can't pay the rent with a pie in the sky."

"I'll line up a two bedroom for us in Brooklyn, if it makes you feel any better. We can work just as well out of the boroughs."

I nodded, then shook my head. I well knew it mattered a lot where you worked from, and that being on Empire Island was far more than appearances: we were equals with Hetty's lot, more or less, had access here that we would not have anywhere else on earth. The island was a club, and getting booted had grave career consequences. "Just a crimp in the grand scheme," I recited vacantly.

"You'll sell them, alright. I have a good feeling about this. If she'll work with us pipsqueaks, we can sure work with her, no matter her..."

"Liability?" came out of my mouth.

We laughed cruelly, emboldened by alcohol and hope. Then it was Bob's turn to go and I found myself alone again.

The meeting had gone well, a stunning end to a dark, angry day, but nothing had actually changed. There was the financial toll in food, booze, and Robbie's shirt, but worst of all, hope had been exacerbated. I propped myself on the bed and sipped, adjusting my back into the pillow. I did not subscribe to the cult of wishful thinkers. "Believe, and it will happen." Or its counterpoint: "If you don't believe, it won't."

I poured another drink and sipped for half an hour, focused on nothing, vanquishing each malingering doubt the moment I felt its chemistry. As the hour wore on, however, powerful misgivings insinuated their way through the many chinks in fortress hope.

This very day, I had returned from ground zero to greet the face of the terror leader who brought it about, and she might now be my ticket out of the market's imploded ruins. I was partly in awe of the cosmic irony, and wondered in part what larger significance I might yet be missing.

I had lived and breathed financial news for a decade and knew the history well enough. America and friends had made the Middle East safe for capitalism through a series of grueling wars beginning in Iraq and Afghanistan, then Syria and Iran. Baghdad was now the center of a regional stock and commodity exchange, the Grand Bourse, with Israel the richest participant after the Saudis. Intermingling investments dissuaded the US installed oligarchies from making further war among themselves.

There was little bother with pretensions at home or abroad about waging war on terror, liberating people from tyranny, or spreading democratic freedom. The United Nations' fig leaf could be dispensed with too. The US was openly the honcho everyone always knew us to be, and we made no apologies. Russia and China chafed, Muslim fascists bloodied America's nose, South American communists taunted us and our allies. The fringes right and left were aided by the discovery of new explosives, the ubiquitous ingredients of which, for the time being, remained beyond government control.

It was an open debate in mainstream media whether the CIA was behind a few choice attacks abroad, those among the dead so convenient from a certain political perspective and the rupture of terror so well suited to nearby elections. Rogue agency actions were as common as bad weather, many believed. A few scandals made the news, and business went on as usual.

War was the happiest of conditions for spooks and the Mil-Con Index. The spooks provided full spectrum briefings to the President, who would then implement a plan to keep the military contractors happy. And with national security legislation and Supreme Court dictates regime after regime, which party was in power was a scarcely distinguishable nuance. What distinguished the two parties was lost on all but the thirty percent who still bothered to vote. While divergent rhetoric roused the same addicts to participate in the same ceremony of democracy, political power had shifted ever rightward in the cosmic void.

The American fabric grew less and less porous, the economic divide concrete, and the news cast a daily aura of government crackdown on one threat or another, at home and abroad, all glibly promulgated on news walls with the assurance of universal assent and approbation, as if to think otherwise made a public enemy of you. The free Net and blogosphere labored under routine ISP tapping, and anonymous connections were criminalized. The electronic backbones were owned by global media and telephony conglomerates, all monitored by the National Security Agency.

Two decades ago America had once again been "made safe for the lives of the unborn" as the media commonly phrased the Supreme Court reversal, and pro-choice protests had become ever since a strident staple of the news. An industry of orphanages arose overnight, funded by tax and church dollars. It was at St. Mary's side door that I had been abandoned, an unwanted burden, not a year after my birth.

All this blood and turmoil in the far reaches of the world, it seemed to my egocentric mind, so that Ms. Saudi-Iran-aqi can peck among the detritus of a US crash. All this so she can present herself as my employer of last resort, or not, as a matter of cocktail chatter. My life, so righteously preserved from prenatal suction, was now at the whim of Atta the angel.

"And for that," I told myself aloud, "I should be grateful." But I wasn't grateful. I resented the whole schmoozing world even if I won at the game. Why should I be grateful?

Cry, baby, cry.

The winter moon made shadows in the room as I undressed, overripe for bed, the morrow a blank slate. I was drunk and for that I was indeed thankful. I crawled into the warm promise of oblivion, where the unconscious unwound its nocturnal life in the making of dreams.

~

Wee Hours, Day 11.

I lean my hatted head out the window of the control booth and look back to find her standing on the train platform waiting to board. Why had we left our bed of love? We had peeled our skins apart scarcely more than an hour ago, severed our one beating heart to put on clothes and go to work. In a flurry of habit, we trotted ourselves off to the wail of the rush-hour siren, clopetty clop to jobbidy-job, to action without heart, complicit in the murder of time. Again today a lovers' strike left undeclared, that soul entwined in mine so short a time ago now food for great machines. The doors bit her aboard. I lurched the beast forward on its tracks.

A voice is speaking into my ear, clear, low in tone, womanly and musical. I lay with my eyes closed facing toward the bed table. "If you were not confused, Ken, you would not be in grasp of what is happening to you. Life in your culture is indeed as sudden and perverse as you experience it, and as illogical as you find it to be. You don't need a head full of religion or politics to know you are twisting in an evil wind. It will take time for you to know in your bones the truths of which I will speak. I will give you time and the means to heal yourself. I ask only that you bear with me."

I opened my eyes and looked across to the shelf moving my head a little from the pillow. There she stood again, leaning against the netbook monitor, dressed in black tights, sword in hand, concern on her face, her beauty a melting blow to my focused eyes. We searched each other's face until she blurred and the booze swayed my lids closed again.

"It looks like I'll need to be your drunken dream for a while yet," came the voice again.

My eyes were heavy and I didn't want to wake up from the deep comfort of the whiskey.

"Soon I will meet you in the light of day. I have to trust you, and I am unused to such a need. More than I can say depends on you."

She said nothing for a while and it seemed the dream had ended.

"If you will not, then I will talk. Hide behind your eyelids if you must. I know you can hear me from their movement. I will be perhaps a little better known to you when you face me."

Again it seemed the drunken dream had passed, and I nearly slept before she spoke once more.

"I am as I seem, living in the Big world, your world, a person diminutive in scale and a human being. I live among you, and I study you and the world you have made."

Time stretched on before she spoke again.

"To regard a great city, one must ask: Are we humans not a species of master path-makers and habitat-shapers? We are. And yet we dare not take our craft to the social estate, nor to the state of our lives beyond the physical. In this our higher realm, we remain like deer, making a trail through the woods as we find them, no vision of a human garden, but paths made in forage of instinct alone. Generation after generation follows these single-minded trails of scent and happenstance through the tangled woods, until we have worn a whole civilization of paths.

"Why not? One might ask, if the experience of conscious creatures depends on the laws of nature, why not follow the vitality of instinct for our paths? Why allow higher faculties, like Science or the Arts, to show us the way to move through the social domain?"

She paused, gathering silence, then answered her question.

"Because we are not deer. Our faculties can be applied to the most fateful decisions in the navigation of human life. Science transcends bias and self-deception to observe with reason, why then does a Science of moral paths have no standing in the order and economy of human life? Why do the Big require that a Science of Ethos be what no other science is required to be: the Word of God?"

Quiet enveloped her words again before she spoke.

"The moral landscape of your world is wretched in its trade-offs and sanctioned evils. Morals, human values, these can be understood when viewed through the lens of Science and of Art, but your political twisting has made true Science and true Art all but impossible."

I exhaled out of rhythm at the novel complexity of the thought. I dared not stir.

"The world we share stumbles from technology to technology, the marketplace your god and guide for want of moral knowledge of the kind only Science and Art can offer to you. We cannot learn habitat-shaping of the human estate from the sniffing beast in us. Our instincts take the short view of all matters, grave and slight. Living, laissez-faire deer in the wild are in a game of brinkmanship with extinction, and yet the Big imitate deer in their political economy at much the same brink. Dressed in your law and ingenuity are centuries of sylvan accidents, tree falls and paths around them, a myopia of culture and legal ways.

"Even animals do not share in the worst of your behavior. In extremis animals are known to eat their young and each other, but you have made an economy of cannibalism. As a matter of course, you eat your young and old alike. There is human blood and tears in all you produce and consume. Those who live for tomorrow's world are eaten by those who live heedless for today. You celebrate this appetite with names like freedom. You even sacrifice yourselves for the sacred cause of other-eating."

Her voice had grown impassioned, which made the ensuing silence all the emptier.

"I am not a creature of sacrifice nor do I bring visions of utopia," she began again calmly. "I have with my wealth the means to redress some small symptoms in your current ills, but I am no altruist. I will neither partake of the human meal, consuming others for my gain, nor the hypocrisy of giving alms thus earned. Alleviate the suffering ordained by a system, and leave the system free to ordain and perpetuate the self-same suffering? The altruist has no moral standing. Such benevolence is itself guilty of the wrongs it would address. I would obviate this shameful need of charity, and do so in accord with man's rational nature and the cultivation of genius, far higher ideals than alms for the poor, the sorry stuff of laissez-faire."

I heard the faint sound of her movements on the shelf in the silence that ensued. Her strange words had a drug-like effect, muting my fears, which seized me again in the long quiet. This was not happening, I told myself in an attempt to calm the panic rising in me, but when had I ever dreamed this way? A chill ran down my spine.

"There was a time," she continued, and my ears seemed to reach out, hungry for the bare assurance of her voice. "I lay forlorn and vulnerable on a moonless night alone in the forest. I knew there were snakes about feeding because I'd injured myself killing one. A fortress around me would not have been enough to calm my fears. I had then your selfish, stubborn sense of self-reliance and preservation. Yet there was a selfless side to my selfish fear, and the reverse, selfishness to my common vulnerability. I learned that fearful night, self-ness is not a true pivot of argument but rather an instance of language confounding thought. So much of Big thinking seems wasted at battling straw constructs of language, words made the servant of thoughts made the servant of words in cycles of misgiving."

The silence was brief.

"The earth is finite, like our lives. Such facts bind us, if nothing else. Common cause and commonweal are for your own selfish sake and for the planet of such alike as well. To see beyond property is hard when you are at the teat of it, but the root of all scarcity is there to be found for the looking. I refuse the ethos of owners, alms and trickle downs. Thus, I am a revolutionary."

She quieted.

"In time, you will understand me so. There are consequences to knowing me. A point shall come there will be no turning back for either of us. I do not appeal to your concern for others. When I say to you, 'join me in revolution,' it is because you are yourself afflicted. You have a bad case of affluenza, the disease of a culture of scarcity. You do not want to be tramping down Hetty and Neil's path, following their scent, widening the way for the next assenting generation, quite selfishly, because it aggrieves you, and quite as selfishly, because it infects and afflicts everyone.

"Genius lives best for itself living the truth of its commonality with all. This is not obvious to the Big. To restore clarity to the individual and all fair meaning of distinction, our human needs must be met unconditionally. There is no other valid purpose, or moral justification, for governing structures."

She paused. I strained my ears, but the quiet was absolute. My stomach churned. I swallowed, tasting booze. At last she launched her voice again into the void.

"The job will be yours for your life if you can keep it," she explained. "You saw last night I can set you free from your money problems. Free for conscience, I'd rather say. That you are capable, I have no doubt, but I must know you are trustworthy. With me, you will in time grow into a more powerful man than your furthest dream. I offer you the best lifetime you could ever live."

The silence was broken by little sounds, as if she were stretching and yawning.

"Day is dawning, and now we will sleep. Do not fear to wake, Ken."

I spun, round and round, lying horizontally. The bed and room spun, dizzying, until I knew I would be sick. I awoke sitting upright in a sweat, nauseous and gasping for air, struggling to fix my eyes on something. I swung my feet to the floor and, attempting to stand, stumbled to the carpet in the whirl. I stood up and walked as the way to the bathroom revolved out of sight. I stumbled again. I crawled to the toilet bowl, where I heaved up my sickness until it seemed my own guts were demanding to vacate my body.

~

Day 11, Daylight.

The alarm made its appeal to consciousness, but I was in protest.

I listened to the chime, motionless, until I dozed again. I woke hours later, the sun high, pouring into my studio.

I seldom had dreams before the crash, or remembered them, but now it seemed they were kicking in the womb of my unconscious and birthing themselves willy-nilly. Yet if I tried to conjure them into conscious memory, the words, the sequence, the details would fade as I chased them until I could reassemble only fragments of what had so moved me in my sleep. Days later, with its own apparent volition, the dream would drop full born into memory, and I could replay it from beginning to end.

I'd had the last dream before, that much I knew. And the dream seemed sequential, like a new episode of the same dream. A miniature woman, some eight or nine inches, speaking at length in dire portents I did not understand.

I felt relieved, a comfortable lightness to my being, and yet perplexed by this little Robin Hood-ess so earnestly posing some big question of life, the meaning of which tantalized but eluded me. But, small wonder, I did understand the fantasy to contain a job offer.

Until I remembered more, I decided, my dreams would have to wait. I dared not estimate how likely a call from Neil would be, let alone whether he or Hetty would make a job for me. If I didn't hear from him today, I should try to pin him down on a timeframe. The day was otherwise free, without to-do.

Coffee, I thought, and a cigarillo. I'd make this day my private Sunday. "Dreams," I said with a laugh, shaking my head. I rose to go to the kitchen but stopped at the bathroom door. I'd been sick, I remembered, but felt so much better for it that I could hardly believe the trauma had been real.

I felt unusually settled, returned to myself, as if looking upon my troubles from a plateau of immunity, as if they were the dream. I felt here-and-now alive, with a day to spend anyhow I pleased, and for all anyone ever knew, my last such day. This one was another cloudless blue sky day, unusually mild for the season, though the wind had picked up and blustered the balcony spruce.

"Coffee for the cobwebs," I said, padding off again. They had been so real, these sleep time visions, and there seemed to be no controlling them, as if they had a mind of their own. Now there was a thought.

I sat at my desk in my robe, the coffee steaming in the demitasse, a small cigar idling in the ashtray. More than a sunny morning of rest, this was my island of time for reflection. Something tectonic had shifted to bring me to this Sunday-like serenity, some semblance of equilibrium was at last restored to me. I felt a delicious frame of mind coming on, bitter and flavorful like the espresso mixed with the smoke of the cigar, or like the windy reminder of nature's serene indifference outside the glass wall.

It was with the indifference of the wind and of mathematics that I considered my life's travail. I wondered, how many Sunday mornings does a man need to call a life? When does life become a habit of living? Did I really need more days, or decades, or want more? The world would keep without my tiny claim on consciousness. My brother would mourn and pray. Keira would think I'd gone off pining for her. Robbie would suffer because I failed to chase the lead with Neil, but I do not live for them, do I?

If I could be no more with the snap of my fingers, in this serene moment I would snap my fingers, I thought. What better time should I expect there to be?

Saying good-bye, making mental farewells, this was the happy sadness of a man choosing to die, robbing death as well as life of their claim. If I was manic and depressive, so was life; but this morning I was neither, nor was life. The party seemed less dear than leaving early. That was all. There was no drama to it.

I would need no farewell to my so-called self. We'd be parting company gladly I figured. If only I had the strength for seppuku, I mulled. That was awesome power. There would be no second to lop off my head once I'd slit open my gut though. And I did not have the courage to inflict on my body such conscious brutality and pain. I was no samurai, though I wished I were.

Pills and whiskey would be the way to go. I'd change my mind on the way down if I took wing out the balcony, and then I'd leave a big mess on the floor of the public crock, and this was private. Wrist slitting in a long hot bath was a suitably bloody and time honored way to go, but not foolproof. And there were detectors in the drains.

"No, the coward's way out suits me fine," I thought aloud, sipping the rich black mixture and savoring a draw on the cigar.

For all the wrath gone by, I should take someone with me, I imagined, strike a blow, go down in a hail of civic gunfire: Unemployed Wall Street analyst kills tycoon, subdued by authorities. But I had no rancor this morning.

Was this really not, indeed, my time to go? I had no problem with being dead. I feared no afterlife. I had no use for any god that would not forgive me for bowing out early. Who can say I was ever meant to die otherwise? And absent all in death, one misses nothing left behind. I'll be a handsome corpse, my young life a tear in the ocean.

Is now the time? I could not change the world's wantonness, but should I continue to live with it? If thinking, even of suicide, were a waste of time, for whom should it matter more than me? This morning I had no heart for enterprise and it did not matter to me. How much of my lifetime must I rent to others' wasting?

Were every day a Sunday, I thought calmly, mildly elated, with all the freedom and delight that money could buy, how soon would I tire of it? What, in all the world, that I or anyone could do to feel alive would not, in time, become a loveless clinging, more habit than delight?

The less one has to worry about, it occurred to me, the larger what's left looms. There was no shortage of affluent suicides. A healthy heiress in her fifties, with no broken heart or personal tragedy to excuse her, took her life after surviving a car wreck unscathed because, she said in a note, the car, a perfectly restored first edition Thunderbird convertible, was irreplaceable. I assumed even as I read the news that she was just tired and bored, perhaps thinking, "Death? I'll try anything once."

No shortage of affluent loony tunes either. Which kind of rich nut would I become if things went differently? A kindly old Mr. Softy of Altruism, Inc.?

In truth, I loved the beauty and clarity of math more than making money. In the peculiar chemistries of greed and fear, my specialty was supposed to be their valence. Was I even any good at it, considering my plight? Was this what I had to live for? A game of probabilities that was sometimes rigged, sometimes random? Where succeeding had no virtue? What did I want of a term in the world if the whole game was meaningless?

That was the killer. I stood and dropped my robe, slipped off my underwear and wristwatch, and knelt naked on the plush buffalo skin rug, sitting on my heels as if the pills and alcohol were before me, awaiting the ceremony of consumption. Such a simple matter, a holy communion of sorts, in reverse: eat of no more body, drink of no more blood.

I emptied my mind to meditate on no-more. Sun and shadow changed in their angles as time passed in this reverie, until a single word, "cannibalism," opened the sluices and the living dream shunted into consciousness. I ran through the drunken visions I'd been having, replaying word for word. These were dreams of mine? This was the stuff of some kind of... What?

The dark dream elf with the sword and the promises was asking me to pass on the Neil and Hetty nexus. This hot little swashbuckler in tights was all set to give me a pile of money if... If what?

My memory returned to the real world, depriving me of an answer what the quid pro quo had been, if indeed she'd told me. I had found, I thought, a different answer though. Maybe that was the message of the dream. This was not my time to die.

"There's always time for suicide," I whispered quietly without irony, and got to my feet. Call Neil instead, I thought, mildly amused, slowly warming to the idea.

I felt carefree, almost reckless, beyond the consequence of whatever I might do. "Call Neil, cam close-up," I said, comfortably naked. I watched the camera find my voice and focus as my cropped face appeared in a smaller window within the transmission. I reached him on his Puck. He was also in close-up.

"Neil."

"Ken."

"How'd it go last night?"

"I'm on the way back from the airport." He widened the view to show the luxurious cabin of his limousine.

"The Rolls?"

"She'd expect it."

"So where do we stand?"

"She likes you, and she tried your trade out on some of her people, Persians mostly. They took it seriously. Is it?"

I grinned and winked.

"They'll be joining her in London. She's scouting everywhere she goes, Ken. There are people in London she wants to meet, then oil business takes her to Finland."

"What's the time-frame?"

He shook his head. "Whenever she decides. She's not interested in Bob. That's all I know."

"How's that?"

"She thinks you're a sap for bringing him into this."

"Go on."

"We think alike. Robbie is smarter than he talks, but he has no philosophy."

"What is that supposed to mean?"

"She only wants you if she understands you to be someone who doesn't need her, who would make it no matter how you started in life."

"Like you, Neil?"

"Yes, like me. We can't all start where you did. Don't start talking like a looter."

"Did you say loser?"

"Looter. As in gate crasher." Ah, his An Brand lingo, I vaguely recalled, indicating the way he divided the world into moochers, looters and the self-anointed elite who got things done.

"I want more than a company," he continued. "I don't just plan to make money. I want to restore freedom to markets and capital flows, a pristine laissez-faire."

"You want to blow profits on politics?!"

"You see the news, don't you?" He searched my face for further reaction, but whatever he was getting at, I drew a blank. "We'll pay ourselves first. That's hardly the question," he assured. "We'll make more money making policy than from marketing is what I mean."

Thinking big was well and good, but this was delusional for a start-up, even with his father's backstop. "Bob's a good man," I argued.

"He can't be reasoned out of who he is. You don't have to be. And you are connected with virtuous people."

"Virtuous people" was his peculiar synonym for the wealthy. He meant the Old Man. So that was it.

"It's either me or some Persian guy in London?" I asked to displace a roiling emotion.

"I can't say, but we want to start small."

"When?"

He made a face.

"Neil, please. Try to pin the time frame down for me. I have decisions to make."

"Things might go the wrong way for you in London if I do."

"Let me talk to her," I gambled.

He was impassive, ignoring the request. "Line up Wellingham if you want to clinch it," he countered, cutting to the naked chase.

"It is not a good time to approach Wellingham," I lied without lying and shook my head gravely for effect. "When will you be in touch with her again?"

"In a few days I expect. She has no reason to hurry, but we ought to get in on the market flat line."

"Ask her to call me. I'll take the consequences. You can tell her the best roast lamb in Europe is hidden away in London and I know where." This I ventured having no such knowledge, but it would make it all the easier for him to mention me to her, and I figured I could come up with something.

Neil looked away as if peeved at the insistence behind the breezy suggestion, but I could see that it registered. Then he looked me squarely in the eye again, odd, cold bird Neil, without affirming or denying.

"Hang tight," he said, plainly putting the conversation to an end.

"Stay loose," I obliged in ritual reply, hating him.

He leaned out of frame and touched off. The monitor went blank as the end transmission screen faded in, glowing green in the dark of the apartment before the screensaver kicked in. I would have no answer for days on end, at the earliest.

Poison comfort for me and plain poison for Robbie. I didn't want to have to break it to him. "Sorry, buddy, Neil thinks you're a looter, so does Hetty. They figure you aren't quite…rich material," I sounded off, reveling in the sarcasm. "If only you fixed your teeth and worked on your vocabulary. Nothing personal."

Let him find out from Neil, I thought. Let Neil do his own dirty work. Maybe he will learn something from the experience. I should think a skinny egghead like him would not take such a shine to "Social Darwinism." Bob, at least, will forgive me. He'd understand, say he is glad for me… hate my guts.

I opened my email out of habit without hope. My auto-responder had completed thirteen applications, each with a personalized cover letter, in response to jobs located anywhere in the country. I scanned the prior day's submissions for nibbles or bites, then took in the new ads. There was a nice opening for an analyst in San Francisco, but "applicants must speak Chinese." There were several junior analyst openings in the mid-west, all looking for kids just out of school. A few hedge funds here required seven years management background, and I had only one year with some fudging. Two more were senior jobs with investment banks in the City, positions offering three times more than I had ever made, a luxury compartment on the gravy train. Unobtainium.

I toyed with the idea of graying my hair and presenting a forged identity. They might even keep me when they found out. Likely as not, they were frauds themselves.

There was nothing. I expected nothing. "Financial Times news," I ordered mechanically, conscious of my habit of reading the news after email.

A bomb had gone off near the Grand Bourse in Baghdad, which dwarfed the Damascus, Teheran, and Bombay bourses. Along with its status as a regional financial hub, amidst its myriad fountains, splendid desert architecture, bustling oil and currency exchanges, and its affluent population, Baghdad had become a kind of gaveling table for settling regional disputes. The bombing preempted market news because the exchange was hit while the Iraqi finance minister was giving a state of the economy address.

Of the mélange of groups from all over the globe who used the place for terror statements, the local Marxist Baathist group had claimed responsibility. They had been outlawed by American decree since before I was even born. The carnage was extensive but the minister was not among the dismembered attendees.

The oil sector would rally on the news, and the dollar would find a new bottom. Otherwise the market lay flat lined. No one believed rigor mortis would set in, and Shanghai and Brasilia were already showing signs of life. A bargain-hunter bounce would not be long in coming and everyone knew it.

"I could kill for a stake," I said aloud. It had become a mantra lately.

Not being able to trade an easy win was a nagging affliction. I could accept any financial calamity if I could yet consummate my way out of it, but no one was in a lending mood, least of all to casualties like me. I should find a mark to peddle a trade to, maybe something in commodities, but I had no heart for hustling, and fool's money was in short supply.

The only question was how long until the bounce? I could strad-dle the flat line for the time value of options, I observed out of dutiful habit, though I knew it was small pickings without a huge stake and that it took too long.

Broke, one's options are all contingent on other people, I ob-served as if it were an immutable truth, and I had only Neil and Hetty left. I could not fathom why my distaste for them had grown so strong. It seemed to have something to do with that dream, but the tag-along, dangling dependency now chafed my ego raw. In the end it seemed little more than a life of humilia-tion would survive these circumstances, the desirability of which remained at question.

I should administer self-therapy, I told myself, dress, go out, and let others have a whack at my demons. The prospect of prowling after female companionship arose vacantly, as if I could smile let alone laugh. The very idea of a stranger seemed strange, never mind launching my personality in some lame strategy, chatting up what feminine prey proximity and cunning might provide.

In my current state, I was bereft of cunning or charm. To venture out would only confirm the demons, this I knew. Such a paradox was the City. There was so little potential in strangers, the more attractive the less accessible. The greater the number of them, the ubiquitous proximity, the less opportunity to crack the shell of any one.

My stomach growled and I debated whether to humor it, then headed for the kitchen to forage. I ordered the fridge door to the camera illusion of transparency and surveyed, then opened it and distractedly assembled a sandwich, placing it on a plate along with a few of the remaining hors d'oeuvres. I set the plate on the counter to regard it. It had been days since I'd had a prop-er meal. I picked at the hors d'oeuvres and learned the sad taste of leftovers. Mine was no longer an appetite, I realized, but the habit of one.

I returned the dish to the fridge, placed a cup and ordered an espresso from the coffee maker, returning with it to the studio where I relit the half smoked cigar, pouring a short whiskey to the glass.

Each little act was deeply satisfying, as if performed at once for the first and last time.

~

I passed the day in calm reflection, posing questions of life and death, and the sun had at last come down on my forever Sunday island. The twilight was clear, the early moon's luminance on the balcony lovely to the eye. Soon the moon would swing away and the city lights would dwindle, allowing the glimmer of stars.

I reached for the cold coffee, drank, and replaced the cup, reached for the whiskey and mixed the delicious flavors, chasing the taste of the smoke. How many more pleasures do you want, I asked myself? My luxuries, at least, I would spend to the last.

I was finished then, no more flip-flopping. The future was too late. All this looking in, looking out, was my consciousness, awaiting the inevitable and permanent power outage. That was the long and short of it.

I had saved my prescriptions. Before finals one year in college I was diagnosed with acute insomnia, which quickly passed, leaving me with extra pills. Later, for a few years, I was prone to cluster migraines. These, one blessed day, stopped. I so feared their return, and still did, that I hoarded whatever opiates I could from dentists and doctors. I had a collection of prescriptions stretching back to my pimpled teens. I had a stash.

I felt as light as air, emptied of compulsions. I was wide awake. I stood and stretched and made myself feel the life in my body.

Then I poured and drank the liquid warmth and drew on the small cigar.

"Open," I commanded the window doors. The room filled with chill. Out on the balcony, the coolness clung to my bare skin. "No melodrama, no tears, no self-pity," I said to the night. "Out of strength, not weakness." The whole stone City seemed jealous of the warmth of life in me. Let the option expire worthless, I thought.

Trivial pendulums of the heart, little arcs of joy and sorrow, then a money changer's corpse. End of story. With a slough of the skin, like a snake in its season, I'd wriggle out of the whole she-bang. As mother might have preferred but for the law, I'd scrape myself from the womb of the world.

I no longer cared to know the meaning of my humiliations. That was for those who would live. The all of nothing, never to know again—there seemed to me no bravado to dying beyond the body's fear. The only choice was when, not whether. Why let the habit of living ingrain me further? Will I be capable, old and disintegrating, seduced in the ways of resignation? For whom should I put in the time when I myself decline its uses?

I breathed in the chill air and returned to the room, drank from the tumbler, sat in the chair by the desk, and ordered the wind shut out.

I looked back to the fridge with its stash of pills and a chill ran down my spine, subsiding into a queasy relief that grew by stages until it was longing. Then I set myself in solemn motion. I retrieved my stash from the refrigerator and laid it on the floor beside the bottle of whiskey and its tumbler in the window's glow. The prescriptions were long expired, some more than a decade, but the meds didn't have to be fresh to be potent, and I had enough for two.

I eyed the satchel. Wake up dead or put it back. To open was to use. That was the rule. There was no time limit.

Always time for suicide.

I relit the cigar and studied the sports satchel that was not much different from a doctor's bag. "All of these drugs, or none," I said. I maundered over how drunk I should get for what seemed a long time. It would make no difference at all, I concluded. I never had a reason to blame booze for anything. I was a good drunk and would be one to the end.

Passing out conclusively was the option on the table: a cushy, painless, Americanized seppuku. Euthanasia done right. Bad dreams on the way out would be the worst of it. Such a weightless thing is life to the mind.

How do I trick the stubborn body to cooperate? Let drinking wind down to the threshold of sleep, then have the gorge of pills.

"Money is the measure of a man's worth." The Old Man said it. Neil. The lot of them. Therefore, I was worthless. The idea of dying by the Old Man's creed stung my pride, but not for long. His world was mine, after all—there was no other world. There was no compelling reason not to extinguish my ego and desire in selfish harmony with culture and custom. I had no place here. I no longer wanted one.

The room vanished but for the satchel. I felt my nakedness from head to toe in the dim as two luminous snakes extended into my vision and moved toward it, took the satchel on either side, and brought it up against my knees. I looked at my hands, turning them palm up and moving the fingers.

What I do is my responsibility. No one else's. I renounce ever wanting to be at the top of the game. I renounce all pleasure, all love, all future tense to be spared the present and the past, free at once from the human condition and from myself.

My brother had God. I had Will. "Be done with it!" I unzipped the satchel and turned it upside down, spilling the assortment of containers to the rug before me. My hands clasped one after the other, unscrewing, unfolding, or unwrapping and chucking the contents into my mouth, one after the other to the very last pill.

I rose up from my haunches without knowing why, eyed the entrance to the bathroom, and set off to witness my face in the looking glass. I could feel the saliva accumulating in my mouth around the pills. Swallowing would be easy.

The only light penetrating the bathroom came from the far wall where a small window of frosted glass cut a rectangle of light in the wall across the room, reflecting just enough to see myself looking back in the dim of the mirror, cheeks farcically puffed with the enormity of death.

A sound came from the living room, as if something knocked over with a thunk followed by the sound of the plastic Rx containers colliding and a furious female shout.

"Damn it, Ken! Where are you?!"

In the bathroom saying good-bye, I answered absently in my mind at the improbable alarm of a human voice demanding my attention. The absurdity of my state became at that moment fully apparent, and I felt myself beginning to laugh with an odd sound, my stuffed mouth in charge of life and death.

A running pace of footsteps, faint, as if far away at the edge of hearing, suddenly grew louder at the hardwood floor outside the doorframe dark as ink.

"Spit it out!" came the voice, and the next instant a searing pain in the tender space between the bigger toes on my right foot ricocheted to my brain. A gooey white glob dropped with a splat into the sink basin as I let out a short sharp "aaaah," followed by "shit!" as I crashed my head on the glass in reaching down to take hold of my agonized foot. The mirror shattered and bloodied my crown as I fell backward to the nearby wall, my vision reeling in the dark, my left eye hindered by blood.

Leaning back I managed to clutch the offending foot in my hands and raise it up to where light would catch it. I saw, without understanding what I saw, a slender sword in miniature extending from between my toes, its heft and razor edge cutting me further with each swinging movement occasioned by my shaky hold.

I reached for the hilt with two fingers, which disobediently missed it, as the weight of my leg overcame my one-handed grasp and I dropped the foot to the floor, the impact shaking the blade loose. The sword skittered an impossibly long time across the hard tile with a diminutive metallic clatter.

The silent dark took on oppressive mass. I gave up trying to use my eyes and slid down under the weight of my eyelids, my back pressed against the wall, arms squared across my belly.

* * *

CHAPTER 5

Perchance to dream

Days 10–9.

Consciousness arose from a deep compression of darkness and animal silence. I floated up from being there to a knowledge of being there. From its long incubation in silence, I remembered being aware before, but no other memory yet emerged, nor language or reasoning. That momentary sentience exhausted me, and then darkness closed around. When a glimmer re-emerged, a first thought and context: I was no longer alone in my being, a lone light in a vast lightless universe. A clear, musical voice spoke from the ponderous dark beyond my illumined sphere.

"Your eyelids tell me that you can hear me. Hear me, Ken. There were risks for both of us before. Now the risks have grown."

I was apprehensive in the dark, unable to locate the voice, unable to fathom the meaning of its song.

"I'm afraid this is as new to me as to you. I must risk putting you over the edge. I have to trust your resilience."

Voice music. Not for me. "I" was a speck of light.

"It's been two days that you haven't stirred, but according to MedCam, you're not in danger of dying. Your vitals are good. You will wake up soon."

"I" would wake up? The idea infused me with warmth, safety, and my speck of light swelled.

"I spoke to you in your drowsing to make my voice known. I will live apart from your dreams now. Forgive me for the shock, Ken, but I have to take a chance with you in spite of your weakness."

"I" was a thing lost in a mind, or perhaps dreamed in one.

"I don't blame you for wanting out. The great wonder to me is not that people take their lives but that many more do not, worse indeed that many more do not take the lives of others. Stripped of its disguises, survival in your culture breeds despair and ruthlessness, and should by rights make suicidal lemmings of great swaths of people, and killers as well in answer to first and last resort. In statistical fact, more die from suicide in your culture than from car crashes, if you didn't know, and taking others with you is a staple of the news.

"Yet weeks have passed that I am confined in your apartment. There is some urgency that we reach an understanding."

Dreams are real, as dreams: this bloomed as knowledge. I knew that. But who was the "I" who knew?

"I need you strong. That you are the one, or will be, I am certain. Your trials are a necessary part of so becoming. This time is critical for us."

Her music resounded in the void like a solemn hymn in a cathedral hall.

"Ken, I need to get back to the manor."

I was Ken. I was real. I would awaken to "us." Rapturous warmth infused me and my luminous speck expanded in the void, itself a luxurious repose of silence.

I dreamed I was a radiant fleck within an immense hulking body. I dreamed that I remembered a world of hulking forms and bodies, dreamed that I ambulated among multifarious streams of bodies, an endlessly long march of hulks undulating through a rectangular city, their light hidden within their inner dark, as mine was invisible to them. I passed faces, clothed bodies, shapes, sexes, ages, a world of human hulk-flecks, a world of contexts, familiar, strange, a tapestry of cultures complex beyond knowing. I was in awe of a world that could never be real, could only be a dream, a fearful dream and exhausting. Luckily it twinkled out of consciousness, along with my tiny white fleck.

~

Day 9.

"Third day you've been asleep or half awake, but the worst is over. More and more REM, more often and for longer periods, but I have to get more water into you, Ken. I know you hear my voice. Open your eyes, please."

Her words permeated my consciousness before the fleck in the hulk knew its twinkling. I hung suspended in the music of the great dark voice. The I-fleck radiated joy at the sound of her.

"For a few hundred in cash your building people were more than happy to get you into bed for me. CamDoc says you need more water than I can get into you without your cooperation, and this will be a problem if you are unwilling to wake up."

A "you" said "I." These I's, I's...

"Ken, don't let me lose you to the hospital. So much is at stake. Wake up."

"What I's?"

"You said something. You said 'eyes.' Yes, Ken, I'm drizzling your eyelids with water now. Can you feel your eyes opening?"

"Who...?" The dark cracked and a blinding nova exploded pitilessly in silence, silhouetting shapes. From directly above, a black shifting wedge seemed to be observing me from within a cosmic radiance.

"A croak is a start. Here. Let me get down from your face. Can you see me, Ken?

The molten lights and shadows turned to red and then darkened into dreamlessness.

~

Day 8.

The light awoke inside the hulk-dream, the hulk contained the dark. And beyond the dark, outside the hulk, somehow I knew there was a hulk street rising and falling over hill and dale, with ambulating hulks moving one way or the other along its length, maneuvering around each other, their fleck selves unseen within them.

I am one of them lying on my side, remembering them. But my hulk does not move. I can only join them in a dream. Why doesn't my hulk move? Am I a moving hulk's dream?

"You're close to waking. I can tell."

I absorbed the sound of the voice, then the silence.

"You've slept very deeply, a month of nights by my reckoning, though it has only been days. Come. Don't leave me here talking to myself. I have gifts for you, new bearings for your course. You will not awaken to what brought you down to this."

Her voice filtered away as it had filtered into the dark, replacing the dream. She spoke from an unknown dimension. "Grueling work, Ken, nursing you. You must wake up and help me."

Her voice returned at my ear. "Ken, dear. You've been more or less asleep nearly sixty hours. The mass you spat out dried, and I managed to weigh it against the containers' contents. If every one were full, which I doubt, sedation should be diminishing rapidly. You couldn't possibly have swallowed that much. I am afraid your own reluctance to awaken is to blame. Come awake, and join me, for I do have wonderful news."

I felt a sensation along the side of my hulk shape, as the voice moved, until her speaking song was coming from one place, there before my... "Eyes," I said.

"Yes, open your eyes, Ken. There is a new world at hand."

I was I, and she was in front of the eyes of the me-hulk.

"That's it. Open them up."

Sweet music.

The light smashed into the darkness but didn't overwhelm the "I." Shape colors seemed to absorb the light and materialize. Then, something moved.

"Thank you, Ken."

A woman shape was on top of the me-hulk, a wiry, athletic young woman with a mass of black hair around a chiseled face. She was dressed neck to ankle in tights, a leather strap across her chest. My gaze followed her as she propelled herself from my chest to the bed and onto the shelf, her white ankles and hands flashing in turn.

"Welcome back."

"Oh," came out of me like a breath.

My hulk shell shifted. The I spoke, "I."

"Aye. We haven't properly met, Ken, but it is early morning. You're in bed, and you've been out for three days, two of them on the bathroom floor."

My hulk shell shifted. Hulk hand touched the hulk head. "Awwwww, shhhhii..." The hulk turned inside out in rocking spasms of pain and color. The fleck-I dissolved in the me-hulk.

Throbbing, I saw a body stretched before me, mine I gathered, and beyond, a transparency framed the light that was day's dawning. I knew this. I tried to move a leg but couldn't. I moved my head and eyes slowly up and to the left where a rectangle of shade marked the bathroom doorway, and I saw beyond it a pillow and blanket on the floor. I moved my head ever more slowly back across to the right, unfolding a world of baffling intensity in the panorama. The wall, the counter, the radiant glass door and spires beyond, the desk with its hulking monitor... It all seemed unreal in its stillness.

I turned my head further to the right until I could see the light emanating from the rectangle of fish. She stood on the shelf in front of the Netbook, etched against the light behind her and illumined from the daylight on one side. She had a wide-eyed and touching expression of concern and apprehension on her half-shaded face.

I moved my head back to face the great radiance in front of me and then closed my eyes, exhausted. There was something eluding me, something truly momentous. This is my bed, and I live in this room. I am awake with my eyes closed, lying on my back, naked under a sheet and seemingly unable to move. There is a woman standing on my shelf, watching me. Something was gravely wrong with this. It was the woman.

"Ken. Look at me."

I did not. Her voice was familiar, like a lover's voice. That was not the anomaly. A woman could not stand on the shelf. That was it. Had she walked out of the screen behind her? Strange things were possible. That was not one of them.

"Ken, darling. I know perfectly well that you hear me."

I knew she did not fit there. Impossible, yes, but that was not all of it. Some nebulous thing was still eluding me.

"I have water here, ice cold. You'll recover rapidly once you're hydrated and fed. Can you take the bite-tube from me?"

My consciousness, such as it was, flowed wholeheartedly into the idea of ice cold water. I calculated I would have to move my hand, take the drinking tube, and retrieve it to my mouth. Was this possible? No. There were missing steps. I needed to turn my head, open my eyes, move my hand toward the woman on my shelf, and take the tube from her hands. I kept my eyes shut.

"Here, let me help."

She was manipulating the tube into my right hand as it lay at my side. Her hands were cold, but pressed against my thigh, her body was hot.

"Are you smiling? I think you are trying to. Okay, I'm going to give your hand a shove, and you lift it up to your chest, no further. You've already given yourself one black eye. One, two, three, up!"

I moved my hand and it flopped like a frog onto my chest.

"Good. Now, can you inch it straight up to your chin?"

The frog leapt again, jabbing the mouthpiece at my nose.

"Close enough." I felt the tube in my hand being tugged downward and did not resist. I felt the bite-top at my lower lip and awaited further instructions.

"Can you put it into your mouth?"

I struggled to unglue the top and bottom of my mouth. Finally they came apart. I could smell the water under my nose.

"Let's try mouth to water then. Can you lift your head just a little? The mouthpiece will go right in."

I struggled with my neck but my head weighed too much. I rested, tried again, reflexively nudging my hand upward while unsticking the stuck halves of my mouth. The complexity of the maneuver I had accomplished flitted across my mind, but the thought was replaced by an ecstasy of cold water gliding down my throat.

"Easy does it. Slowly, Ken."

I could feel her climbing my upper arm to my shoulder, then her bare footsteps across my bare chest as light as a kitten. There was a gentle tug on the mouthpiece, and I paused, sipped. Each swallow was an orgasm of delight. I was breathless.

"Too much at one time is no good. I'm going to pull it down now but keep it in your hand."

Tears flowed from the joyous relief of drinking cold water, and I sucked a last gulp before letting the mouthpiece go. I felt the heels of her bare feet dig in, and then her toes as she hauled tube and hand away from my mouth.

"Let me dry your eyes."

I could feel her step along my solar plexus until I felt her knees against my chin, and then a chilly hand occupied an oval space on my cheekbone as she daubed at my tears with a tissue.

"Care to open them?"

I opened my eyes and struggled to attain focus in front of my nose. Her knees planted in the nook of my chin, she surveyed my eyes, one then the other. The glow from the side stand illuminated a small, smiling, dark-eyed face, though I was cross-eyed to make her out.

"To judge from your pupils, you are nearly back," she said, climbing down to my chest and standing full length before me on my solar plexus, the tissue still in her hand flowing white at her side.

My eyes roved over her body, lingering on the light between her legs, back up to her white neck gleaming from the black stretch sheathing she wore, then settled on her face before beginning all over again. She seemed amused to watch me take her in part by part. Her breast curves were mesmerizing. Her ribs and breast-bone showed through the tights, and a curve sloped inward over her belly. The space between her thighs was riveting. There was not a part of her which did not bear aesthetic contemplation.

"You are smiling. That's a good sign," she said, reclaiming my attention. "Well, this is as big as I get, my love." She took a few steps back so I could see her better, then turned her palms and arms out in a slow, elegant bow.

"I am Sahar," she said, standing on the flat of my solar plexus as if born to it and looking into my eyes, a tiny smile playing across her mouth.

"Sarrr," I growled.

"Sa–har."

"Sahr," I croaked.

"You can call me Sa, for short. Fate has brought us together most remarkably."

"Sah," I whispered with a sigh.

"Sa, Sa-Sa, Sasita. Any of those will get my attention." She was smiling. "We'll have plenty of time to get acquainted. A little more rest and you'll have motor control. We'll feed you, then all will come back."

She searched my eyes. "You'll be well enough to talk when next you wake. I've left the water tube in your hand. You can rest now."

My eyelids lowered obediently taking her image with me into slumber.

~

Day 7.

There is a sidling motion of the head that a lover makes, face pressed here and there as if it were a caressing hand. The face discovers in the curve of the beloved's neck, or the slope of her bosom, or cheek or hair, a surrender of pride and a profound repose.

Eyes closed, unseeing, dark within dark, a woman applied her brow to my shoulder in this moving submission, and then her cheek opened my heart to her listening ear.

Eternity had been violated and a set of questions invaded my consciousness: Who is this? What face? Who is in my arms, bestowing love? Who am I? Who...

"Angh." A white light eclipsed my vision and I shut my eyelids. I raised them again narrowly, squinted unseeing at a room and window framing a cityscape in the bright of day.

I was lying on a bed in a room. My body weighed several gravities, and I could scarcely budge a limb. My forehead was throbbing. My left eye hurt. I was starved and I needed to pee. Peeing took precedence, I reckoned. In order to accomplish this, I had to get myself upright and ambulate to the bathroom, a Herculean undertaking.

I tried to move onto my side. Eventually, it worked.

I contemplated each momentous, exhausting stage in the process, then executed the maneuver until I sat on the bed, feet on the floor, elbows on knees, head in hands. I remembered the dream, wondering what she was.

I was Ken, alright, which was not a good thing to be. That was all I knew.

I rose from seated to standing, a red roar of light blinding my eyes, and dropped like a stone to seated again, then sailed backward to the bed in a faint.

When I came to, I remained still, eyes staring open, unseeing. I remembered kneeling in the moonlit dark, emptying bottles of pills into my mouth, going into the bathroom. I tried to kill myself. I was now awake and sick from the pills. I did not die. This was no damned afterlife. I had botched my suicide and this was a mortal hangover. I wept until I wept my eyes dry.

Cry, baby, cry.

I rose on an elbow and regrouped for the bathroom attempt. Soon I was sitting up again. I opted not to risk trying to stand. I slid to my knees on the rug and caught my fall with forearms and elbows, resting my head on the rug. I raised myself up, pushing with my hands, and sat back to eye the distance. I would leave the protective rug in a few steps on my knees, then it would be hardwood and then ceramic before I reached the bedding on the bathroom floor. From there I could hoist myself to the toilet seat.

I pawed my way to the bathroom doorway. The bedding reeked. I was humiliated. I had to stand or crawl through it.

Clutching either side of the entrance, I inched my way up from my knees by shouldering myself against the doorjamb as the blood drained from my head. I held each gain until the urge to faint passed, until finally I was standing.

My bladder insisted I pay attention, but my eyes turned to the empty sink. The unswallowed gob of pills I expected to find there was gone, though streaks of dried saliva led down the drain. My precious stash was wasted and gone. I was the more perfectly damned for no longer having an easy way out. The mirror bore a shatter star from the impact of my head, and I noted that my head bore the scab of a wound surrounded by a purple bruise. Did I start the faucet on my way down, washing it away?

A desolate hilarity began to overtake me. I was giddy at still being alive. I had a good laugh out loud. If anyone found me naked, cackling, the bedding on the floor already pissed, ready to piss the floor, they'd think... The notion that I'd lost my mind was instantly sobering. I was okay. I was not dead and not insane, able to laugh in spite of myself. Right?

Sobriety brought me to the moment of truth. I had to take this leak or it too would be on the floor. I gauged the distance to the toilet across the bedding. Too difficult, I thought. In an inspiration I lurched forward, grasping the rim of the sink, and pulled my crotch against it. My humiliations were overtaken by sweet relief as I urinated extravagantly into the sink bowl, groaning aloud with the unwounded side of my head pressed against the cool glass of the cabinet mirror, wondering if I could possibly be half as sane as I thought.

Whether minutes or hours later, I cannot say. I awoke face down, half sprawled on the bed, half off. I had no memory of getting there, but I vaguely knew I'd accomplished something magnificent and was deeply entitled to rest.

~

Day 6.

"Awaken to your new life, Ken."

Her voice buoyed me up from the slumbering ocean of dark and I surfaced with a smile I could feel on my face. My loins awakened too.

"I am here, beside you."

She was alive in my room on the bed level shelf at my back.

"I can tell when you're conscious without even seeing your face. Your breathing gives you away. My, you are stubborn about facing up. I should apologize for hurting your foot. I am sorry. It was necessary."

The music settled into words, making sense. I felt my brow furrow. More was missing, the gap nagged at me.

"I have nutra-tea for you here on the shelf, and it was quite a lot of work getting it there. Come, everything your body needs, as they say. You haven't eaten in days. There's a tube, if you'd rather not sit up."

I grunted.

"Don't let it get cold. It won't be as nice."

I grunted again and rolled onto my back.

"Neil left a message. Robbie left one too. Neither seems happy with you. Your brother left two messages and he's expecting you to call him. The world awaits you, Ken. The world awaits us both."

I opened my eyes, rolled in slow motion onto my side, adjusting my head to face her. There was a long still silence as a chill descended my spine. I could feel my scalp prickling.

She stood on the black chestnut shelf beside a tube cup, steam rising from a sipping aperture. A fruit aroma filled the air, a wonderful distraction. Manta rays roamed the monitor behind her. She wore a form-fitting tank top now, exposing her arms and shoulders, the leather strap angled between her breasts, the sword on her back showing its hilt above her shoulder. The end of the sheath was like a straight tail behind her black clad legs and reached nearly to her pale bare feet. Her eyes were as black as her attire, and her mop of hair was tied back and almost blue in its blackness. In contrast her skin, a fluid of curvatures and concavities, gleamed white where it showed. Laughing oval eyes, slanting slightly, searched my own. Her features showed a poised, bird-like alertness. Her lower lip jutted ever so slightly beyond the upper, giving an air of dignity to her smile. She was, in all, as lovely as she was impossible.

Conflict assailed my brain. Thinking seized up. The impossible woman seemed anything but a dream.

"I've been at your side looking after you. I am in fact what you see, a diminutive woman standing on your bedside shelf. I am possible, real, not a dream, and I can explain most of everything."

I shut my eyes, reasonably certain I was now wide awake, if for no other reason than I felt alert and had no desire to keep my eyes closed. I opened them on her again, half expecting she would be gone.

"Can you put aside my size long enough to talk to me? I promise you'll have all the time you need to express disbelief, astonishment, curiosity, even fear. I ask you to accept for the time being that I am real, no more astonishing than human nature itself. I am a woman in every way, and I will not harm you unless you try to harm me or harm yourself again."

I pulled the sheet reflexively to my chest, shut my eyes again, crippled with the thought that I'd ruined my sanity with a pile of barbiturates.

"My goodness, Ken. Such a baby."

Her laughter was warm and light, unexpected. I opened my eyes and followed her smiling gaze to see I'd inadvertently exposed myself and an erection stood up to greet the day.

"Were you thinking of me?"

I stared at her, riveted, and the erection grew palpably, straining against the air.

"Nothing I haven't seen before, you know. If it's easier to believe you are dreaming, then believe that for now. Just don't be afraid. Yes, I must be a dream, too small to be real.

"But if I am real, you are encountering a natural phenomenon. That's rather exciting, isn't it? I suggest it is a privilege, if you are up to accepting this fact. And if I am a dream, you'll wake up soon enough and I'll be gone.

"Have some of this. Come. You're strong enough to reach for it. Go ahead, up with the right arm. Good. Now take the tube."

I obeyed without taking my eyes from her, bit the mouthpiece and sucked at the tube, the hot, berry taste exploding in my mouth. A glow of warmth radiated outward from my belly. I sucked the liquid down greedily.

"Can we talk?" she inquired. I shook my head and paused, panting for breath, eyes tearful at the effect of the nourishment on my body. I remembered the erection and covered it, returning my speechless gaze to her.

"Yes, cover up. We should get to know each other before we mess around," she teased.

I took her in again, her impish humor, the miniature jewel of fascination that was her body. She smiled and moved about the shelf self-consciously, knowingly feline and provocative in every fluid moment or pose she casually took. She was playing at sex kitten.

At last she sat down on the wrist rest of the keyboard, stretching her legs and letting them rest akimbo before her, leaning her elbows back on the shift and 'X' keys. Her shoulders bloomed into balls, the curvatures within her bare arms, chest and neck rearranged themselves in a new algorithm of beauty.

"You know," she said with a gesture of her head toward my cock, "I may never have a drunken sailor. A sleepy headed Ken may be the closest I shall ever come."

Her humor hit me like a blow. I was stupefied. She was purring. She sat up, stretching her back, her breasts jutting attentively on either side of the strap.

"Can you say 'yes?'"

"Yes," I said, the sound hoarse in my throat. I felt my volume and weight and the gnawing tension concentrated below.

She considered me, generously I thought. Then she changed. In an instant she seemed to implode and her face became solemn, angular and deliberative. She seemed to become someone else in her demeanor, to be somewhere else, deep inside herself.

In a slow transformation, her face and eyes softened to a smile, as if her serious self had left the world to decide something of great importance and the feline imp had come back satisfied. She looked across at me, and a flash quivered through me.

"I'd love to give you relief, Ken, and have relief with you. I shouldn't take advantage of you in your condition, though, should I?" she cooed seductively.

Yes, yes, take me, surged the thought. "I'm okay," I managed to gasp in a whisper.

"Are you now?"

"Yes," I managed distinctly, still whispering.

She dropped herself to the bed. "Ken, my love, keep your hands still. If you move them I will have to stop."

I exhaled in a gasp, and nodded. She put her hands on my hip bone and swung herself up to my thigh. She locked eyes with me and stepped slowly to the bulge beneath the white sheet.

"I'm a poor nurse, but looking after you has affected me, I would like you to know."

I struggled to find a self to express, stuttering, "I... I..."

"Speak later. The sleep to come will be the last before you are fully recovered. No more excuses." She smiled knowingly. "Let's clear our heads before we dream in them."

Yes, I thought in nodding silence. She was intensely desirable, but I understood she meant to please herself too. She meant to make love with me.

She stood beside the bulge and ran her bare foot across its length, then straddled it, her crotch at the base. I could feel her heat through her tights and the sheet. She leaned forward, guiding her warm hands slowly up my length. I saw the breath along her ribs quicken, and she repeated the caress, reaching from lower still to higher still, her thighs contracting against me, her coccyx moving against me in slow rhythm. I'd been too long without and knew I had no restraint. I groaned at her stroke and climaxed under the sheet at the pinnacle of her reach, the bulge rocking convulsively as she tightened the grip of her thighs and leaned forward, eyes closed. In a soft, spasmodic moan, she surrendered herself in my surrender.

I exhaled her name in the last glimmer of consciousness, carrying the sight of her down with me into a long exquisite swoon.

~

Day 5.

"Wake!"

I awoke with a start to the sound of her voice and looked at her. She was seated on the edge of the shelf, smiling expectantly.

I gazed at her my mind a blank, then a groundswell of memory rolled under me. I sat up. The pills, the dreams, her sword, the water, the tea, the sex, the whole wretched mess of my life came back in a torrent.

"Sahar," I said, like any other name. "Sa for short."

"Yes, you remember." She beamed at me. "You look yourself again, almost. How do you feel?"

"Weak."

"You managed to swallow some drugs."

I nodded and rummaged for memory, then turned to the bathroom doorway, and remembered the clattering sword. I turned back to her and saw it now strapped to her back. "You stabbed me with that thing," I said, indicating the weapon on her back.

"I had to act. As it is, you've been in-and-out of consciousness going on four days now."

"What's the date?"

"Sunday, March 1st. Do you feel clear?"

"I think so," I said aloud in a clear voice. A wave of memory washed over me. "The rent is due today. Friday, the Marshal comes knocking. You can't be real," I added matter-of-factly.

She frowned with a shrug and shook her head, plainly disappointed.

"You can't be, can you?"

"As you wish. I am not real. I can't be. There is no such thing as a miniature woman like me, of course. You must be hallucinating if you're awake, dreaming if you're not. Are you awake?"

I looked around the apartment as I assessed my condition. My head throbbed where I'd banged it, and the empty feeling in my loins corroborated the cum stain on the sheet. The tea bottle stood on the shelf as before, the drinking tube resting on the bed. My stomach growled audibly.

"I think so."

"Then it must be you're hallucinating. Don't be hard on yourself, Ken. You're barely awake and half-starved, with a nasty bang to your head. If you must appease your rational mind, imagine your subconscious has conjured me to help you."

"That can't be either."

"No?"

"You seem—as real as I do."

"There you have it, then. Truth be told, I am as real as you."

"You just said…"

"I'm trying to help you along, Ken. Call me a freak of nature, if you will. Not at all an impossible one, biologically speaking."

"I have to be dreaming this."

"Actually, you don't. Can you get up?"

"I've lost my mind."

"Technically, you are preserving yourself, mind and body, by saying that."

"You are not real."

"I am or I'm not, as you wish."

"Four days…"

"The world is still flat on its arse."

"Neil. The job." The message light on the monitor blinked the numeral 3. Sharks swam lazily on the screen.

"I told you about the messages. Your life is waiting for you."

I fell back to the bed with a groan.

"I can help you."

"You? A fantasy, a wet dream? Uh, uh—succubus?"

"Succubus," she said with some surprise. "Do you really believe in such things?"

"No."

"Nor do I."

"Okay, wake up. Wake up." I slapped myself, fingertips touching my temple. "Oww." I explored the bump and scab above the eye and gingerly surveyed the larger area of sensitivity with my fingertips.

"You feel real now? You have a mild concussion, and I am stuck here because the Old Man shot down my plane and my chute took me to your car. With the guards watching, dogs at hand, I had no choice but to steer my descent into your backseat. I would rather we met under other circumstances, but perhaps this way is for the best. I have nursed you back from oblivion. Will you hear me out?"

"Christ, do I have a choice?"

"No. You must be famished."

"Yes."

"A light breakfast, then. Too much food too soon will make you ill. Concierge," she called toward the automated dumbwaiter chute. "Please send up two scrambled eggs, bran muffin toasted, a large glass of orange juice, and an espresso. Suite 47, guest account."

The order appeared in a corner of the screen along with the exorbitant fee and an x'd out account number that ended in four unfamiliar digits.

"Three minutes, please," came the synthesized voice.

"So you do room service too."

"Why not? If you persist in believing I'm not really here, nothing will be sent up, right?" She smiled. "Not pain, not pleasure, no sound or sight or touch—what is left to be real? Life itself may be a dream then, which I appreciate is a defensible proposition, but even so, you are stuck with it."

"If I'm not mad, I'm going mad." I was scared.

"Just leave it alone. If the order arrives, will you give your sanity a rest?"

I considered. "I could be dreaming food or be insane and hallucinating it."

"Such lucidity from one so mad. I'm nearly convinced myself. You will eat though, won't you?"

"I'll dream I'm eating if I dream it gets here." I was in a fog, groping.

"Tenacious!" She laughed. "Now, don't be peeved."

"I'm not peeved," I said, peeved. "Let's pretend you are real. Alright? Now just leave me alone. I'm in enough of a shit hole." This seemed eminently true.

"Well, Ken, I can't leave you alone. I am a forced guest here. I could have Papa finagle his way into town, but that is not as easy for us as it sounds. So I'm stuck here, as I have been for weeks now."

"Weeks?" I sat up straight.

"Since you left the Old Man's Estate in your Porsche."

"You've been here?" I swung my legs from the bed and faced her, my head going light for a moment with the sudden movement.

"Yes."

"Where?"

"There are a few nooks where a clever girl can hide."

"What are you doing here?"

"Making the most of serendipity."

"What do you mean?"

"There is a fatefulness that can hardly be denied to falling from the sky into the backseat of your convertible just as the roof is going up. Do you remember? When you stopped before the gate, I thought I caught your eye in the rearview for a second. Thankfully, you were preoccupied with the guards, as was I. No telling what would ensue were I caught in the open with their dogs loose."

I did remember. "I saw a leaf."

"The chute was leaf camouflage. It's under the seat of your car. As I said, the old man shot at me by the skeet range. The plane was hit. I nearly made it all the way back when a cable came loose. I had to bail out. There was much loving work in that plane. With luck, there'll be something to salvage."

"You're saying you were there."

"You haven't given a thought to my predicament, what I have been through, and nursing you to boot. Put yourself in my place, why don't you?"

"In your place?" Of course, from her vantage point I was being insensitive and selfish, but then again, she'd stuck me rather hard in the foot, caused me to bang my head, and her very being there seemed an assault on my consciousness. The service chute chimed.

"You'll have to get it, but don't move too quickly or you'll pass out."

Grasping a corner column of the rook shelves with one hand and clasping the sheet around me with the other, I raised myself onto my feet. I waited for the light-headedness to pass and then took my first tentative steps toward the dumbwaiter.

She greeted the spectacle of my progress with laughter and taunts of "Atta-boy" and "Go on, you can do it," which made me laugh in spite of myself. Ambulating did indeed seem a dazzling achievement. I felt like the first ape on two legs, the smell of breakfast and a growl in my stomach leading me on. I made it to the chute and leaned on its counter. An array of string and miniature pulleys, some kind of hoisting mechanism adorned its façade, stretching down to my feet.

"That's some of the gear I had Papa send in. I hope you don't mind. It's been quite a workout even with lifts."

I turned to face her standing on the second level shelf and noticed similar strings running down a corner column. The rook-like bed table was crowded with the containers from which she had been nursing me.

"Ungh," I grunted in response. What was growing more feasibly real gave me a chill. I shut my eyes tight and tried to shake my confusion. Everything remained when I reopened them, including the doll-sized woman standing on my shelf and the fragrant breakfast sitting in the dumbwaiter. I gave up searching for the flaw in my perception.

Even the mad must eat, I reasoned, opening the thermal door and sliding the covered tray out. Testing its weight in both hands, I gauged the effort I had to expend in order to regain the safety of the bed versus standing shakily at the counter. I tried a step.

"Easy does it, Ken. One foot at a time. Almost there. Let me make room."

She shoved the tea bottle to a corner with outstretched arms, then used her foot to push the keyboard back under the vid and then the ashtray into another corner. With one arm she pushed the whiskey tumbler out of harm's way.

Just in time I let the plate onto the space on the shelf and fell seated onto the bed. When my head cleared again I moved back until seated up against the wall, blood draining away before shut eyes. I was exhausted with near starvation.

Again I expected the fantastical to be purged when I opened my eyes, hoping against hope the food at least would remain. It was all there, however, the food, and the woman searching my eyes, her impossible little face full of shrewd concern.

"Are you okay?" came the beguiling music of her voice with a smile. I felt tenderness toward my miniature savior. I noticed a red bruise on her bare ankle. Was this from climbing to attend me?

"How can you...be so small?" was the question I finally asked.

The sound of my voice rebounded at me, checking the reality of the speaker.

"The short answer is that I don't know, but there's a longer answer. Here, strengthen yourself. You will need sustenance to hear my story." She lifted the wrapper, crumpled it up noisily in a ball half as big as she, and tossed it playfully in the remaining free corner.

She forked some egg with the plastic implement and proffered the handle to me, which I carefully took from her hands. The taste was eye-watering ecstasy.

"You have never met one so small, and this is a shock to you, naturally. Consider for a moment that individuality itself is a freakish thing, and so are we all a little mutant. Who is to say my size is not evolutionary? A change the species needs. If the Big were smaller, a great many problems would cease. A lack of space, food, and all the dwindling resources would not be a problem for millennia, if ever, providing time for the species to mature before it extinguishes itself. But if I am merely a defect, not an adaptation for survival but a random biological event, then so be it. Despite family myths that say I have antecedents, I live with the assumption I am unique in stature in the known universe. Perhaps in other ways as well. I find many differences with the Big."

"The Big?" I prompted, despite the nagging wonder whether I should participate willingly in whatever dementia engulfed me.

"Yes, normal-size creatures like yourself. In deference to my father, I call you 'the Big.'"

"Father?" I ventured, hoisting the plate to my face, shoveling, savoring, feeling stronger by the second.

"In deference to him because I have a litany of other names for the Big. My father and mother were both Big. I am of the Big born, you could say. That's where some knowledge yet unknown comes in, how I came to be, but it is from my mother's side, my father swears. She died giving birth to me, in what was considered a miscarriage. Due to lack of facilities in the village in

Mexico, she bled to death, but Papa saved me. He slipped me into his pocket, he says. It were better to have drowned in her blood than be born in a hospital. If they had found me alive..." She shivered, shaking her head.

I had polished off all the egg and half the muffin and taken several gulps of juice. I could almost hear my cells trumpeting in gratitude.

"Papa took me away with him. But you know my father. He is Pedro Clavel at the Old Man's Estate."

I stopped mid-chew as the obvious connection overtook me.

"You are still a little fuzzy in the head. It will wear off."

"You read minds too?"

"Your expression betrays you. I have taken every measure to come easily into your life," she continued, "but you have forced my hand. Now there is nothing for our differences but to face them."

"Pedro is your father," I stated, unbelieving.

"Yes, wise, skillful, dependable Pedro is my ingenious father."

"You live with Pedro at the manor..." I recited absently, more intent on the food than my own incredulity.

"I don't know how I'd have survived without the talent in his hands or his wisdom. He built most of my gear: the plane, my bow and arrows, my skis and snowmobile, those lifts on the counter. He forged this sword that never leaves me." I was not about to interrupt her.

"My mother was not Mexican, as you might guess," the little woman added. "She was part Hungarian with some tribal Gypsy blood, and part Lebanese. She wanted to name me Sahar, Arabic for the dawn. So that's what Papa named me. He says I have her

Tartar eyes and his mouth and nose. Can you see the resemblance?"

I shook my head and swallowed.

"My father is a great man, who has endured many struggles
keeping me safe."

"You are the only one, like this, in the world," I said in honest, if
not yet believing awe.

"Just as you are the only one like you in the world. But yes, as
far as I know, I am the only diminutive on earth. My mother
believed there were antecedents in her Gypsy bloodline, that this
is a recurring genetic event. The story was retold to her by her
mother and her mother's mother that there had been strange
births, other diminutives like me, at different times in history."

I did not pause in my feast, and she went on.

"Like my father, I don't put much store in these family rumors.
It is preferable to believe I am unique in history, and I imagine if
others like me ever existed, they would see themselves that way
as well."

I continued to strip the plate of all but a pair of black olives, feeling the chemistry of my brain changing as renewal made its way
through the bloodstream. I motioned with the plate in advance
of returning it to the space on the shelf.

"Give me an olive," she said. I took one and handed it into her
extended palm with my two fingers. The olive looked the size of
an eggplant in her hands as she took a bite of its blackness.

"There are family stories of others like you?" I asked, wondering
dismally what else this charming phantasm might have in store.

"The family legend has it these diminutives were actors behind
the scenes in events of history."

"Like?"

"The Reformation, the Magna Carta, the American Revolution… The list is long and goes back to Moses. Papa tells me my mother's stories as best he can bear to remember them."

She took a bite and laughed at her appetite. "I love olives. I can eat a whole one." Her white face bit off chunks of the soft black flesh, a marvel to behold.

"There is no separating wheat from chaff in a family fantasy mill," she said as she searched out the napkin. "But how Grandma bent Papa's ear about it. She'd claim the invention of fire, the wheel, nuclear fission, and the microchip were all little whispers in some Big's ear.

"Grandma used peyote in her declining years, however, so make of such claims what you will. I've researched my genealogy as well as possible, paid investigators to dig, and even my father does not even know this about her. I'd rather believe she was delusional and I am unique in all time. Are you feeling better?"

My brain at last had nourished blood. I could feel my body transforming itself with fuel. I was astonished how much better I felt, and I nodded saying, "Yes, thanks," attempting a smile that did not quite succeed. Nothing she said mattered quite so much as the fact she was still quite there, impossibly little and talking a storm.

"One may well conjecture all individuality has an evolutionary mission. Stories and myths of diminutives aside, I intend to transform the broken civilization in which I find myself. As I understand myself and your world, I believe I am able to do this in my lifetime. That is the long and short of the offer I have for you." She munched the diminishing olive.

I looked at the pillows and blanket in the bathroom doorway, wondering if I'd yet wake up there to find all this had gelled in a doped-up doze.

"This encounter is as radical for me as for you. Again I ask you: try to put yourself in my place. You are my first Big, in person, apart from my father, as I am your first diminutive. Not to mystify the happenstance, but this encounter shows every sign of being meant to be."

I was her first real guy? Where did she get her ease in the world?

"I live online over the Netbox vid. I am largely self-educated, so pardon my manner of speech. I am 34 and quite worldly in the ways of Big culture."

Was she reading my mind? I took her in critically.

"I am intuitive and so it may seem I read minds sometimes, but I cannot." She returned the half-eaten olive to the plate.

Should I humor my symptoms, talk with them, eat with them, make love with them? Indeed, was I being seduced into insanity? If I gave in, might I never get out? If I ignored her, would she go away? I'd perhaps tire of imagining her, I reasoned, but then I'd be completely alone. Unbearably alone. I knew in my bones I would not fail to end myself a second time. I contemplated the balcony.

"I cannot stop you from jumping if you're quick. I see you are still willing to reject the evidence of your senses. You are waiting for me to vanish into thin air. Well, I am neither Houdini nor Tinkerbelle. There is nothing I can do about my human condition, but neither am I your private Mother Teresa. I am about a mission, and I am choosing you."

I stared at her as if at a wayward part of my own body.

"Be at ease with me for the time being, Ken."

"A wonder of nature," I said to myself. Or the balcony, I thought. Surely there was a better choice. I should not trust my brain, no matter how well I felt. I forbade myself any meaningful decisions in this frame of mind, but this decision did not provide the relief I hoped for.

"Look at me," she ordered, and I obeyed.

"I am only human, a pituitary expression, a trick of DNA if you will. Did nature intend to tweak the genome? I cannot say, who can? As far as I know, there is no other in this world of my dimension, but I am like you, a human being, a fact I regret sometimes, much as you do. Think of me as the miniature version. I am faster too, I think. I worry my experience of time is not quite the same as yours, though I age no differently and expect to live as long as anyone may."

"Christ, I don't know." Emotion was crowding out what sense I thought I had a moment ago.

"Maybe I should leave you alone for a while. You can try your legs and satisfy yourself you're still alive and well. She stretched herself casually, as if readying for bed, and continued, "I've been up most of the night. I could use some rest. I won't be any farther than the shoebox in your closet. When you're ready to talk, just give me a shout."

"Wait. If someone else saw you too…"

"Who?"

"Anyone."

"You could dream or hallucinate it, just like breakfast," she teased.

"No. Yes." The cat chased its tail in a conundrum of consciousness.

"I have several sets of false records, Ken, and no official identity. Apart from fake electronic IDs, I'm an undocumented alien from Mexico, technically speaking, though I keep this to myself for my father's sake. He is here under papers I forged for him long ago. The Old Man hired my father because he is among the best landscapers in the world, and the Old Man's estate has been a sanctuary and godsend for both of us.

"There was a time in my childhood I longed to be a human phenomenon, accepted among the Big. I craved to be known to the world. I expected to be cherished for the uniqueness of my being. My father and I fought over this well into my teens. I wanted to be a star among you. He warned me of discovery. Well, I know now my secret life has been his greatest gift among a treasure of them.

"With technology and this sword I have all the identity I need. I am alone and glad of it. None of my life options can be managed safely. I have chosen my risks and revel in my calling, as you shall too in yours."

She stood quietly, smiling a little. She was waiting for me to speak, I thought, but listening to her had emptied my head. Her voice and body defeated my critical faculties.

"Many freakish and tragic creatures are born," she went on, filling the void. "We see and hear nothing of them because they are hid away from the world. Am I freakish or tragic?" She extended her hand upturned in question. "My gene print shows anomalies. I have subsidized millions in research, diverting crumbs from the Old Man's accounts. The foundation had no idea where my eggs came from or who was behind the grant. They were just scientists facing an impossible reality, as you are now. But they ran with it. In the end, they tried to fertilize my eggs with stem cell DNA but could not. I had to know with certainty whether I could somehow bear a child, absurd as the notion may seem. Their efforts confirmed that I cannot get pregnant, fertile as I am."

"The research is documented?"

"Sorry, Sherlock. It's not mine and would be difficult to get, and you'd say you dreamed it anyway. When there is greater hope from Science, I'll see that work renewed."

If anyone ever sounded like they spoke their personal truth, she did.

"Ken, you're not far gone. The old idea, the one that nearly killed you, is behind you. You have a new life, my secret notwithstanding. Do you remember I appeared to you when you'd been drinking?"

"I wasn't sleeping." I remembered. "You set up a transfer to my account but didn't execute it," I said without hiding my displeasure.

"Your money emotions rule all others. Do you remember my offer? I'd have completed the transfer if you were up to conversation at the time."

"Some save America, save the world stuff." Like neocon Neil, I thought.

"What Neil and Hetty want from you is much the same though the politics and scope of imagination differ. Like them, I want you to help me with capital investments. Is that not your profession?"

"You want me…to do my job?"

"More or less. Yes."

"For you?"

"Yes."

"Now I am surely dreaming or hallucinating. Or both," I declaimed aloud. "I can't just have a guilty little win-the-lottery fantasy. No, I have to conjure up a sword slinging revolutionary…doll, Papa Pedro's kid no less, who parachutes into my car with a job offer."

"Bravo," she laughed out loud. "A life adventure, not a job, is what I have to offer. It is indeed as remarkable as you say," she added, quieting me.

Time for some clothes, I thought. Enough of this. I gathered the sheet and swung my feet to the floor on her side of the bed. My face was quite close to hers for a second as I rose and finally stood, the sheet over my shoulder. If I didn't do a single other thing, I had to do some kind of damage assessment. Maybe that's all it would take to get square with this... whatever she was. No decisions, I admonished myself shakily without speaking.

"Go ahead. Dress and go out. I will not follow you. On your return we shall be as we are now. If you want someone else to see me, you can meet my father in town when you take me back to the estate. But not if you're going to tell me you're dreaming when we get there."

I faced away, held by the magnetism of her voice.

"You can't help hear the sense I make because you are sane, awake, and relatively well for someone who has been playing dice with his vital signs. You're sufficiently intact for recruitment. Consider, you are now on the threshold of your own personal renaissance."

I replaced myself to the desk chair and leaned forward on the desktop, facing away from her and massaging the unhurt side of my brow with the palm of my hand.

"Are you so clever to dream me up in all these particulars?" she asked. "You must have a singular talent. No, Ken. I was shot out of the sky and ended up here, to watch over a suicide's drooling."

"I don't drool."

"Of course you don't, except on special occasions."

"It was special enough until you butted in," I protested, confronting her.

"Yes, I spoiled the moment for you. Now you have to live and bear witness, poor thing. We shouldn't spar. We should get to know each other for a lot of nice reasons. Just leave judgments of possibility aside. If you can do that, Ken," she said in honey tones, "I will let you in on more than you could ever dream you were hallucinating."

She wasn't making this easy. There was a devilish spell in her voice and demeanor I could hardly resist. And the notion I was neither mad nor hallucinating had begun to take hold.

"Would you like to know how a three inch child grows up in the Old Man's wilderness? Or are you ready to talk about money? I can't have you flying off on wings of fancy."

"I'm not making any guarantees," I muttered, feeling cornered. "I have no idea what I can or can't make up. Why shouldn't I make any of this up? It's just the sort of thing I'd make up," I rattled off nervously, doubting it was true.

"Why would you make up something you refuse to believe?"

"If I refuse to believe what I make up, I know it isn't real."

"God and universe, you are a well-reasoned nut."

"I banged my head on the mirror, maybe the sink too," I stated, standing and facing the bathroom. "I fell asleep on the floor. I ended up in bed. You said you paid maintenance to put me there?"

"I told them there was a party, a lot of drinking. I left cash on the table and sang with the shower running while they hauled your ass over to the bed. I can name them if you care to corroborate."

I was fairly sure what I saw and heard was credibly real. Still I was reluctant to give up the game. "They took a bleeding man from the floor, a man more dead than alive, and put him, put me, to bed?"

"I'd cleaned you up some, and they hauled your dead weight to bed, bruised, piss-wet, and all."

I understood this was convincing, or should be, and considered she would likely go on being utterly convincing.

"You've been watching me, spying on me," I stated matter-of-factly.

"Not closely enough, I'm afraid. I live empathetically, being alone, vicariously if you will. I make no apologies for being an eavesdropper, voyeur, spy, imposter, or thief. Those pills you had on hand suggest you have been dancing with this devil for some time. This is true?"

The question took me by surprise, and I was flustered to come up with a reply. "No, not really. It's an option one shouldn't lose sight of, that's all."

"Perhaps one should not. I have myself been near to self-killing—but I cannot permit you."

"It's none of your business," I said with petulance.

She stood defiantly for a moment then gave up the thought. With a pantomime's shrug, she refused to argue.

"How could I have swallowed so much," I asked myself, ignoring her, still feeling the weight of my limbs.

"Roughly one tenth of the dry mass was missing. I am afraid you were experiencing a nervous breakdown concurrently and did not want to wake up."

"No one else knows about this?" I asked.

"Rest assured I have been discreet. I used MedCam services under a false ID. No one knows but you and me what has happened here."

"Thanks," I said. "I think." I was not sure which was worse, the hospital and attempted suicide on my record or this surreal wrench in my mental machinery.

"Your physical prognosis is excellent. The dissonance in cognition should reconcile favorably soon. I expect you will be ready for work in a day or two."

"You stabbed me in the foot." I leaned over to examine the still smarting wound between my toes."

"To stop you."

"You had no right to stop me."

"You so love the games of capitalism, when the calculus fails to break even, you finish off with self-loathing what self-blame has begun. Your murder is indeed my right to stop even if you are the tool of your murder. But I did not save you for my right, I saved you for my purpose."

"I dropped the stuff out in the sink when I yelled," I said, ignoring her, drawing myself up, and making my way around the bed to the bathroom doorway. "I banged my head on the mirror, bent over from the pain. But I… I was laughing."

"You made sobbing sounds."

"I was laughing with my mouth full," I said, stepping inside to regard myself in the splintered mirror. "I saw the comedy, the absurdity. My face…was a cosmic joke." I puffed my cheeks in the mirror. I would have laughed it out, I thought. "I was going to laugh it out," I said to her. "You hear? That is the last thing I remember before you stuck me."

She considered what I had said for a moment. "You encountered absurdity and lost the will to die. I like your version better," she finally said. "I could have killed you myself for putting yourself down like a Wellingham dog."

"Dog nothing. I was master. And you didn't save my life," I continued. "You damn well nearly killed me. Sure, when I yelled I dropped the stuff out, but then I swallowed whatever was left. Had to, its a reflex."

"For you this was an edge of life ceremony," she said, mulling over my revelation.

"You think I'm fudging?"

"No, I think I am hearing the truth, and I am profoundly glad of it, for your sake and ours together. You wish to blame me for believing your suicide theater, or for the swallowing reflex?"

"It wasn't theater, damn it. You had no right to butt in."

She considered this, then took a new tack. "That you are alive is what matters to me, Ken. Do you have any idea how much the Old Man made on the recent crash?"

"Yes," I said, drawn in. "A lot."

"He could buy a small country with it."

"How would you know?"

"There is little I do not know about the great Avery Wellingham. I grew up on his grounds and educated myself in his manor. I was trading with his money, on his account, with his own computers before I had two digits in years."

"Bull."

"I spend days at a time hidden in his lair, his libraries, his collections, his data. I swim in his granite pool summer nights, and I raid his pantry. I know more than he does about his holdings and the property he lives on."

"Then you know Keira."

"Since she arrived as an infant. We grew up there together in a way. I spent time with her, close to her, whenever she was there. I lived through her. The Old Man has been protective to extremes since she was born. At night the guesthouse is wrapped in a perimeter field. I've set off many an alarm probing his security. Do you still love her?"

"Yes. I don't know. Maybe."

"She is not a complete airhead, and the least noxious of the lot."

"You can't be so close to a woman like that without imagining a life with a woman like that," I said, "in a family like that. Wait a minute. You said you were flying the plane while we were shooting skeet. Did you see her leave the guesthouse?"

"A limo rolled around after you left with the Old Man."

"And?"

"And nothing. A suit got out and went to the door. They left together."

"She didn't struggle? She walked?"

"Yes, she walked. He carried her suitcase. Does that matter?"

"I don't know. I just don't know. Maybe it means she dumped me after all. Maybe she was under his thumb the whole time."

"You are unnecessarily hard on yourself."

"Or he played her too, somehow, supplied a driver with a story to tell her. He is capable of anything. He gloated that I'd never know."

"Much in the world is under his thumb. You have been beaten up pretty badly, I know. But you can put that behind you now. Will you hear me?"

I made no protest.

"I know there is no love between you and the Old Man. I know him as a man, and I know him as an enemy of mankind. I could ruin him with what I already have on him, ruin him overnight and at any time, but my father lives and works there. We both do, and that estate has been my lifelong sanctuary. It would break Papa's heart to see the grounds auctioned off, and the truth is I don't want to see that either. My father has made that land beautiful to man and a most productive habitat for wildlife. There is no better hunting in the Catskills, and the grounds are toured by many students and ecologists.

"Papa was still young when we first came there, soon after my birth. He lives on his salary and will take no money from me. *El dinero del diablo.* Yet he knows he would not have the work he loves but for *el bastardo rico.*"

"I've heard him pull the Old Man's whiskers pretty hard."

"Yes, the two of them are in a game. Papa goes too far, but the Old Man goads him to it and then bullies him. They are each, in their way, addicted to your class war. Papa is a devout communist, just as the Old Man accuses him. That is the irony. He avoids the buzzwords and slogans. He could never work in America if he did not learn the ways of pretending, but Papa speaks his mind well nonetheless, as a Democrat, and the Old Man is none the wiser of his true heart."

"Isn't it hypocritical to work for such a..." I searched for the word.

"Dangerous capitalist? Don't be absurd. Wellingham is a man as well as a monster, and there are few jobs in America where you are not working for a dangerous capitalist. We are all in service to extraction, until we are not. No one is pure. In order to make a moral point, one must be able to survive. That is the long and short of it. I have worked for a living remotely on the Net and well know what the job market is. Before we came to the manor, my father had many hard choices in picking which thief to work for. He has made a good life for us working for the King of Thieves."

Pedro was, I always thought, a good if harmless guy. He was a communist, for real? And had this creature born to him? I tried but couldn't get my bearings.

"No one is born an ideologue, you know. The capitalist world begets its opposing ism. Nature abhors a vacuum. To Papa, the failed experiments in history are national happenstance. The best ideas remain, he says. The communist dream is under his skin. Perhaps that is why he has such a miracle in his hands. He has never practiced capitalism, *el trabajo del diablo.*"

"But you have."

"I have no ideological barriers to my learning. I have three going enterprises, businesses if you will. I've come a long way with a modest stake."

"Trading?"

"As you might imagine, given that I'm a creature of the Net. When I first poked into the Old Man's trading station, it was a revelation for me. I was obsessive for the longest time, studying all I could. At first I paper traded, then used the Old Man's cash overnight in Japan, Hong Kong, and Singapore. As a child this was my serious play.

"In the beginning, Papa was frantic with my disappearances until at last he found out what I did at night, and then he wouldn't talk to me for a long time. Sometimes I know he is afraid for me, and I know sometimes he is afraid of me because I know so much of the devil's work. I cannot help that. When he finally did speak to me, we argued for months. We still argue over the course I have chosen."

"The Old Man didn't find out you broke into his account?"

"Not for the longest time. Then he was in denial for years despite suspicions. He has his bank set up for playing at God in the world, and his personal portfolio is on autopilot or tended by others. The core of his wealth is in bonds. At home, he has a state of the art setup he uses for little more than master accounts. All his attention is on the tithe of money he has allocated to his bank and its subsidiaries.

"His cash allocation was unusually high one time, and I doubled billions overnight. That was the first serious extraction. There have been many since. I have zero liabilities. I see now you are alert," she teased as I realized my face had brightened and mouth hung opened in a small "o." She continued.

"Wellingham went through a stretch of time much as you do now with me, doubting his sanity and doubling security. I no longer need his accounts. If I use them, it is to torment him.

"I had fed him anonymous tips before I placed my own trades. Eventually, he could no longer ignore them and started trading on them. He ended up publishing them."

"You're the Golden Goose?!" I exclaimed.

"Yes. I send him a bare bones trade, which he publishes in the Illuminati with his own absurd embellishments."

"Why?!"

"Why give it to him? Because when I influence what he and his stupendously wealthy subscribers are doing, the trade becomes a self-fulfilling prophecy. Even where it fails on fundamentals, it succeeds technically in volume, and where it succeeds, it does so extremely well. I think of them as my lemmings rushing en masse to make my trades outperform."

"You're making insiders rich."

"I've seen your trading account, you did alright with Golden Goose trades when you could access your employer's subscription. Well, he did not publish my tip about this correction. Mind you, I did not anticipate such severity. Still, he kept the insight for himself and omitted the column last month."

"Why should I believe a thing you have said?"

"Let me show you some lucre, that should convince you," she said, turning to the Netbox on the shelf. "It's 11:25 AM Eastern." She tapped out a series of keystrokes, hand and foot, summoning a Level IX account. She swung the monitor to face me. "This is a small speculative account where I'm entirely in cash. Let me assess and analyze, okay?" After a few moments she exclaimed with a smile, "Here. Italy's banking news is worrying the Euro trend line, but the Turkish Finance Minister is scheduled to speak in a few minutes. I'll drop all this into euro options, near month, long. Set a few stops. This trade shouldn't take long from the looks of it."

I watched her take a position, betting the euro would rise on the news. She was staking millions for a fraction of a percent in gains.

"Alright, the old news of Italian central bank problems is digested and the tick is moving my way. That was probable. Let's go live to the speech. There, you see. He is announcing a successful vote on the IMF austerity measures. Now, we get out before the counter-reaction reasserts the trend. I'm going to exit now and go short. Done. Okay, missed the top by a little, and there it goes back down again, twice as fast. I'll close it out now at the trend line. The profit is six months of your rent here in less than a minute."

I had just witnessed a simple news trade that happened to work beautifully, catching a bounce even I might have guessed in a better moment. Still watching it made me sweat, and it wasn't even my money. Her sureness, her ease, the calm in her eyes spoke more about her than stumbling on a piece of news.

"You didn't know what he'd say."

"That particular Turk would not have scheduled a meeting if he didn't have good news. Let's run something like that again. Breaking news, currency repercussions... Here is some inside news. The prime minister of Nigeria has just now introduced legislation aborting the gold standard, pegging the naira to the euro. The story has not yet broken in the mainstream news. There's a Middle-Eastern three way I like for this. I say we're going south. Let's compute a custom chart for this."

This one went past me even on my best day. She was staking even more this time, using three currency trades, none of them the naira, each with triggers set to move into alternate positions, hedging her risk on the downside at each branch. Plainly she knew something I didn't about these currencies right now and what Nigeria's gold standard mattered to them. I stood up to watch more closely as she placed her trades with the graph rising against her, then the story broke and the graph keeled over and dived, deep and fast.

"Out we go. Another seven months of rent. I'm staking a lot in deeply leveraged risk, but news reactions are reasonably predictable. There goes the counter-reaction. Very short-lived and so would hardly have paid to flip."

"You know something about this news?"

"That gold and petro-dollar are related, and for oil rich Nigeria to abandon gold will affect nearby currencies. Here. I am transferring the profits to your account. You have more than a year's rent just for hearing me out."

I was speechless with warring emotions, joy and relief on the one hand and on the other a new surge of disbelief, this time at the reversal of misfortune. In the end came unease at the origins of my suffering. Gratitude came last. This was either a self-serving fantasy or I was mad, but either way my great financial fall had become a shameful triviality. I put my hands to my whirling head, inadvertently touching the sore spot and groaned as my legs buckled and I groped for the bed then let myself down onto the rug in many levels of pain.

"I have gone crazy," I sobbed to myself, kneeling on the floor bent over, certain the compounded evidence was conclusive.

"Go ahead and spend it. You're running late fees as it is," she countered without sympathy.

I attempted to recover myself from the floor but was too weak. "Look, if you can do this, what do you want with me?" I said. "You could make millions a day like that."

"I have no time for trading, and less love for it. One must keep up with all-consuming diligence, as you well know. For me it was a compulsion, a bad habit I have broken, but also a drain on my talents that I can no longer permit. And millions a day are not enough. I calculate I will need tens of billions net profit a year at minimum. Steady businesses suit the purpose better for having a purpose in themselves, and I prefer revenue streams that are reliable over a lifetime. I can teach you a few things I have learned from trading, but I am myself disgusted with market vagaries and the buying and selling of financial abstractions. I have real work to do."

A peal of thunder broke outside in the day's dark umbrage. On the balcony, the wind shook the spruce and drops began to paint the tiles in dark splotches.

"I love storms," she said and was quiet for a moment as sheets of windblown rain draped down the glass doors.

"You could be rich, famous, without a care in the world," was all I could come up with.

"Put on display and exploited, if not caged and dissected. I'd lose my life, as surely as if killed."

"With the right agent, you could wrangle…"

"I'd be wrangled in the end."

"You could get a lawyer, establish legal rights."

"I prefer natural rights. No, Ken. You make the money, with my help. I must free myself for what only I can do. I will need your investment banking and acquisition skills initially, not trading, though we will want to get a hedge fund working at some point. You will manage certain development projects, place investments, merge and acquire. Later on, you will run a number of companies and chair boards on others. I'll pay you incentively as long as you earn your keep. We will change the world and you will be rich. Think you're up to it, slugger?"

"Yeah. Look at me now," I said, struggling with gravity and noodle limbs to gain my feet.

"I'd have been caught in the crash too but for a hunch, an intuition I can no more explain than the universe."

"That's what they all say."

"Ha. Maybe so."

"Stake me my own account?"

"Sure, if you'll return the stake in a year. I am not making handouts to feed a gambling addiction. You'll have to eat your own losses."

"Go ahead."

"Before we part, I shall. I ask only that you return me to the estate when I require and that you speak no more of insanity or delusion. Agreed?"

I was effectively shut up.

"Well?" she prodded.

"I can still ask questions?"

"Yes," she said, laughing at me. "And you may think what you like. Don't imagine you can hide an hysterical relapse with or without words. I ask in return that you squelch your doubts entirely as long as we are together."

"You're some kind of wonder woman?"

"I sweat like you, and if I don't bathe, I stink—if that's your idea of a wonder woman. Speaking of a bath, I need relief from tending you night and day. I've been climbing the place like a spider." She stretched with luxurious expertise as she had before. "And you've exhausted me, no small feat. Can I trust you to run the kitchen sink at 92 degrees?"

Her smile made me smile in spite of myself.

"You shall soon see how banal your wonder woman is."

I looked to her on the shelf. At this distance she seemed to express herself more theatrically in pose and demeanor, intuitively compensating for her smallness a few yards away. She was bafflingly clever it seemed, and I set forth dutifully for the small kitchen area off the main room. "How high do you want it?" I tossed to her over my shoulder, then realized with a jolt that we were even now at the aforesaid banality.

"Three inches will do. Then I will retire for the afternoon," she went on, projecting her voice with surprising resonance. "I suggest you take a bath and rest as well. I will join you for dinner."

Her request fulfilled, I returned to the foot of the bed, watching as she maneuvered past the ashtray to a corner post, snatching a scarcely visible harness at the end of a string. She held out the harness for a moment.

"My rappelling gear," she said from her stage. "I am no less bound by natural law than anyone of size. Like you, I am a miracle to myself and a mystery in the universe. Like you, I learn myself as I live. I am not omniscient, and God does not speak to me.

"That," she said, indicating a toy like platform with wheels on the floor at the foot of the table piece. "...unfolds into a dolly. I have lever and fulcrum for lifting onto it. With the mechanical lifts you see on your counter tops, I can move most anything here. I designed this gear and Papa has built it. He sent it along to me here. He used to make everything before I could outsource."

I was amazed.

"I've been climbing all my life," she continued proudly. "It is the same as walking or running for me. You could say I can't live without it, and such conditioning is necessary for my survival, in a way I can't expect you to understand."

"Tell me."

"Ha. I wouldn't know where to begin. Peril is a way of life for me at the estate. I have become accomplished in many forms of self-defense. Consider that, at the age of five, a black ant stood as high as my knees, its pincers the size of knives, and several of them were the equivalent of a wolf pack for a Big.

"Nature is an unforgiving school to be sure. Almost everything alive is potentially deadly to me. I have shed a good deal of blood with the blade on my back. I have battle scars from a horned owl." She turned down the shoulder of her tights to show me a scar.

"A Doberman is a shocking, snapping monster such as never found in your pre-history, and a feral cat is an enemy I cannot defeat save by luck or poison."

It was terrifying to contemplate what the size and ferocity of a hungry dog or cat would mean to her.

"Poor Papa is 200 years old on my account," she continued, her face softening. "And I must return to him as soon as I can. I am just a house guest, Ken, no matter how strange or fortuitous. I had no idea I'd be dropping in on you any more than you did. A miraculous bit of luck for both of us, after all."

I nodded, dumbfounded.

"What shall we do for dinner?" she added, brightening.

"Whatever you like," I finally remembered to say as she waited, my mind still on a Doberman the size of a house. What kind of guts would it take to live in such a world?

"It's still storming, so I'll order in for us. I'd really love to see the City before I leave, though."

"How can you do that?"

"In a pouch on your backpack. If you like, I'll spook a stranger, just for you."

"That doesn't worry you?"

"I've been seen many times but never believed. The servants speak of the gremlin in the manor. It may help you believe if, outdoors in the wider world, someone were to take note of me."

I wondered if it would, but nodded and plodded my huge hulk to run the tub for my own badly needed ablutions. The mess on the bathroom floor was gone I finally realized, having taken it for granted. I regarded her standing on the far side of the bed, the monitor on the shelf flickering over her darkened form as she browsed restaurants and fares.

"I had maids up for the bedding and piss while you slept," she called to me absently across the room without looking back at me.

Again, she seemed to know my mind. How could she, if not a figment of it? I made the bargain, and I realized in so doing I had short-sold fear itself, but the edgy pertinence of everything she said or did remained unsettling.

I took in the face in the mirror. I was bearded and pale, a head of hair sprouting in all directions from which dull eyes peered. The welter on my temple was fairly purple, and the cuts had scabbed. It felt much worse than it looked.

In the quiet interlude, it appeared we were just some very odd couple negotiating a ho-hum afternoon. Banality aided and abetted the inconceivable. I filled the tub and fell soundly asleep in the hot water.

~

When I awoke later in the dim of twilight, the tepid water seemed black, as if with my filth. I dried and exited the bathroom in my robe, looking for her. The sky was nearly dark. I stopped to check my account, confirmed the amounts she had added, and paid the cursed rent.

I found her in the hall to the apartment door, all but head, hands, and bare feet covered in black tights as before, shadow fighting with her sword. The display was impressive. She finally acknowledged me as she whirled low to deliver an upward thrust.

"Hi," she said smiling, breathless. "Feeling better?"

"Like a new man," I said. Feeling huge and threatening standing there, I squatted down.

"I wanted to get my practice in before dinner. Do you fence?"

"I tried it once. Too hot and confining in the suit."

"I have to warn you. I can't allow anyone to handle me. You will suffer if your hand comes close," she warned. "I can be crushed, quite inadvertently."

"Your father must have handled you."

"He's told me it took him years to learn how. Erring on the side of caution, he would carry me on a tissue and bathe me with a soapy feather until he learned to trust his finger and hand. Make no mistake, a Big will fall from this blade," she said, holding it out. "There is a quicker means than its point or edge. A hollow, like a hypodermic, lies within the length, what the hilt contains I can release at will."

"Poison?"

"The merest nick and a man your size will not know he's hit the floor," she said, resuming her exercise. "Just don't move your hands toward me suddenly," she said in cadence with a series of offensive moves.

"You've killed?"

"Many times."

"I meant…"

"I know what you meant. If slaying an overly attentive mouse is unimpressive, you should try your own hand with a kangaroo in close quarters."

"Overly attentive?"

"I didn't wait to find out what it had in mind. I stood all of four inches the first time and carried a sailcloth needle. It wasn't pretty, but I was quick about it. Since I've been old enough to know fear, fighting has been a way of life. I have become proficient at killing, in self-defense and as huntress. I've learned the ways of many creatures as no Big knows them. How not to fear them. How to communicate with them. How to make them fear me."

"What's the biggest you've killed?"

"That would not be wise to say. I will tell you my father is fond of squirrel stew. I snare rabbits for him. I hunt with a bow and sling, defend myself with spear and shield, and do battle with dagger and sword. I have had life and death scraps with fishers and hawks.

"To surprise me asleep is a grave danger you must understand," she said, resuming her moves as she spoke. "I can trust you, can't I?"

"Liars ask you to trust them," I offered by way of reassurance.

"Good, but I shall require much more of you. Dinner should be here soon," she added, snapping sheath and weapon solidly together in a fluid instant. She slung the sheath across her back. "It is a joy not to have to wake you up again, sleepy-head."

It occurred to me that I could never go back to a world without her in it. I congratulated myself for my open mind. It was a talent not to judge, I thought, not a fissure in my sanity. It was for me to rise to an occasion for which I had no deserving.

That for which there is no deserving was a definition of love, I recalled someone had said. I tried on this new perspective as if a suit in a dressing room. It became me. The burden of her being there was a privilege either way, even if she were a phantasm, it seemed to me. Despite her sharp claw and tough talk, she was a friend, at once miraculous and approachable. For the moment, imperfectly unreal or not, she would do.

The dumbwaiter chimed. "Are you as famished as I am?" she said. "You like lamb, if I recall."

"How do you know... Never mind. I'm starved."

"It's Lebanese. *Kibbeh b'Sounieh*," she called after me as I made for the chute. "And Chateau Musar Bekaa Valley to wash it down."

"Are you coming?" I tossed back at her. "I could eat a horse."

"As the occasion requires," she called without humor from behind, then seated herself lotus style on the buffalo rug, her eyes closed as if in meditation.

"I am thanking the buffalo for the pleasure of his fur. I honor his life and ask forgiveness for its taking. This is my prayer to all life

I take. In your goods of manufacture, I make this prayer for the human lives consumed in their making. Let's eat here."

I remembered my last meal there and what I had sought to do. She saw me hesitate.

"One large plate for both of us. And the biggest candle you have. We'll banish all memory while our candle burns."

"I'll put the cutting board down for a table," I said, nodding at her suggestion, as if such banishing were a thing I could do.

The first date banter continued as the candle shone over our faces in the dark, working over the food, pouring and drinking the wine, flavors rampaging in my starved palate. I fairly hummed with involuntary "ummn"s.

I towered above her as we ate, sitting as she did cross-legged on the floor. I imagined my face a huge sign in the sky, an open book to her acumen.

I felt like a beast in her delicate presence, which did not deter me from stuffing myself until I could hold no more. At last I reclined against the foot of the bed with a full glass of wine as she continued stabbing at the plate with a toothpick, each piece of food seeming a meal itself in proportion to her mouth, and yet she ate prodigiously.

"Fast metabolism," she explained without my asking.

"You didn't just now read my mind?" I asked at last, quietly. "You answered the question I was thinking."

"I saw you watching me devour the food. Papa complains just so. *Pídola* he calls it, leapfrog. I intuit much and quickly, but there is a wealth that is plain to read in the Big body. With Papa it is more intuition, and there is more occasion for such consilience, but I will tell you what I tell him: the times I do not seem to read a thought are many and the times I seem to do so are few. I do not know I leapfrog your thoughts unless you tell me of it or I see it in your face. Your mighty mite does not come equipped with paranormal powers."

"Are you sure?"

"What powers I have," she shrugged shaking her head, "are human powers. What I can do, so can others do whether they know it or not. I am hyper-developed in some areas and lacking in others, as are we all."

With that she wiped her hands and stepped away from the food to face the thick candle burning on its holder of coarse-hewn oak. Her breath flickered the flame. She sat down and was still for a moment, then lay down on the rug, extending her arms and legs in a gesture of abandon. She went limp in the black cushion of winter fur and closed her eyes. Her sword and strap lay detached by her side. Quietude settled over us.

* * *

CHAPTER 6

The world according to Sa

I nodded off, dozing lightly in the comfort of the food and wine, and awoke to find her standing again before the flame of the candle, her stillness fervent and calm. Watching her there, elbow propped on folded arm, fingers lightly on her chin, I wondered what kind of genie it was standing there before me, what spell she might release into the night.

"I have been pondering what words to say to you, Ken. There are words you will understand, words that are truer than your understanding, and words of my own anger and revulsion. I cannot educate you much less convert you in any meaningful way. Volumes of words would scarcely scratch the surface.

"I closely follow research in the ways of learning, ways to make true understanding gel, and no shortcuts have been found among fine theories. Our narrow learning bandwidth and slow development are great banes of the human condition. It is arduous enough to learn a profession in thirty years. How can we squeeze a universe of understanding through human nature's pinhole?

"What words then? I ask you."

I was preoccupied with watching her during this speech, a creature of fascination in her physical grace, and as a woman, arousing—somehow all the more for being miniature and un-attainable. What had passed between us had been a gift to my helplessness. She could only come to me, I knew, and I had yet to earn her trust.

"While I'm busy with your business, what will you be doing?" I finally asked.

"The test of true democracy is the impossibility of being owned," she tossed off with a dismissive flick of the hand. "The first task must be to transform the electoral system, that great hoax of capitalism, hostage and whore to funding and bribes. For democracy to have meaning, it must be impossible for one reflex-ive ideology or ism to own parties and process outright as communism did and capitalism does. I would reclaim democracy from feudal ownership and unlock its wheel."

She spoke slowly. "Without democracy unowned and unown-able, our political discourse will remain framed as it is, the blundering of government or the plundering of markets, as if this either/or were ordained by God. We still have today a racist, patriarchal, elitist Electoral College designed by and for the slave holders of yesteryear. With both congress and president for sale, in two-party, winner-take-all voting, check and balance has become institutionalized gridlock, servant of a stasis most immoral and destructive. With democracy reclaimed, those powers over governance now in corporate hands will revert to the people."

I followed politics from a market perspective and knew only clichés and slogans beyond mainstream media. Alt News, the alternative, did not move markets. As for political opinions, I made every effort to avoid them, and took pains not to get my-self pinned down with labels, all of which seemed to me over-simple and confining.

Smiling and slow speaking, she seemed sure of her command

over my attention, her voice at ease in conviction. It was all I could do to keep up with her.

"We have a democracy based on consumer focus groups," she said, "sound bites tested as in the marketing of toiletries. Capitalism is beyond questioning and socialism is a dirty word that may not be spoken. The American democratic ideal is a vague memory, mistakenly assumed, falsely defined, and all but dead in our time," she recited evenly.

"Question free markets and the beaten dog of state communism is dragged out to remind us how lucky we are to be free to pose so reckless a question. This is the child of Noah's thinking: the external threat, be it wrath of God or foreign ism, should make us grateful for our privations, being so much worse elsewhere in the flood."

The room seemed to float, sealed from the world. It had been a long time since I had sat in the dark with a candle alight. There was a lightness to her voice at odds with the sweep of her words. This kind of talk seemed play to her. It occurred to me she did not often have a chance to sound off. She studied my face, and when I found her eyes, began anew.

"In the media we hear the voice of democracy made synonymous with the voice of capitalism, its extractive license made out to be the meaning of liberty. It takes mental fortitude to see through the fog of washed history, through a media dedicated to misleading us, the conspiracies of silence, and the vagaries of a suck-up culture. We have to school that fortitude."

She was silent, and it dawned on me. "Schooling, that's what you have in mind?" I asked in some surprise. I imagined her intentions were darker. I did not know whether I was relieved or disappointed.

"All manner of schooling, if you will. Education is a powerful means to make, as well as prevent, a structural revolution," she explained. "All economic culture is school of a conditioning kind. We will have to educate people to part them from the conditioning of your culture, then further for the tasks at hand."

"What tasks?"

"Political and economic culture follows organically from beneficial structures. I shall see to their building. Unless schooled in creating these new structures, revolutionary governments are prone to resort to cultural tyranny, purges, state terror, the guillotine or gulag found in yesteryear's cultural revolutions. The new regimes then outdo the extremophilia of capitalism with fresh brutality."

"You really think some kind of revolution is possible, here of all places?" I asked with a shrug. "No one really believes in revolution."

"I could as easily say everyone believes in revolution but does not know it yet." She seated herself on the candle holder, leaning back against the handle. Her shoulders and bosom stood out. I watched her rib cage move with her breathing.

"We have, for example, a wealth of conspiracy theories that range from the crackpot to the well-grounded, all of them born of the same intuition: that we as a people are well screwed. Taken together these theories so condemn our political economy as to make war against it a moral necessity, and yet who wages war? The conspiracists allege crimes too secret to expose and rely on general disbelief to excuse themselves from such service.

"The theories themselves, whether they involve a private or government cabal, propose a specific corruption within the system, one to be fixed, instead of systemic change. The least provable of these theories seem designed to obscure class consciousness and invite instead a paranoid consciousness outside the real politik. I would reclaim and redirect this and all wasted moral energy. There is only one conspiracy at the root of our ills, that is capitalism, and it trumpets barefaced in the noon of day."

This whack at the system had more resonance with me than I could explain, as if something clicked too far inside my head for me to know outright. I thought of Sean, and my own misgivings.

She regarded me, smiled to one side, and asked, "This is not true?"

"It does seem a conspiracy of sorts, banks running the country for profit and all that, wealth and power compounding at the top, but that's the real world," I said, "the only one that matters."

"The future must matter more, if it is to be longer than the past. Planet and species are at stake. I sense in these times a critical mass of understanding, a catalyzing evolution in consciousness, a level of willingness to break with the past. A Zeitgeist fertile for revolution, despite raw power to the contrary."

She made the impossible seem possible, being possible herself.

"America has a last gasp in her, I think," she added, getting up and pacing again. "The foundations of capital are decrepit and weak on their own merits, have been running on the fumes of war since Honest Abe. They are overripe to fall.

"What do we replace capitalism with?" She asked my unsaid question. "The Big have no thought leader to help them reinvent themselves when the chance arrives, no path to discover their better nature and provision for its happiness.

"The Big botch the implementation. When the fog of revolution clears, you are left with a reversal of understanding, not a higher one. We, the species, have not yet seen a revolution where the level of understanding was up to the task. With careful research in post-revolutionary periods and some applied science, there is a way to make this understanding. I should think we could produce blueprints any freshly elected citizen could implement. We will need a clear a path toward revolution and the re-invention of bottom-up governance in its aftermath."

"We don't really have capitalism anymore."

"Capitalism compounds into the neo-feudalism we have, much as socialism aggregates into centralized state capitalism under a rhetorical veneer. We cannot pretend away the tendencies of these isms. Yet so much has never been aired or tried."

The question remained, "You're talking about a democratic revolution?"

"Only a revolution in democracy will make that possible," she replied.

"You don't want to make everyone a poor proletariat in some commie regime," I half-stated half-asked, seeking assurance.

"For a while, I would see everything our culture contains, good and ill, continue. Let the ills be grandfathered out. The question 'Why?' should clamor loudly back at every question of new law forbidding old practice. We do not ask how to forbid capitalist culture. We ask instead how can every silly thing be made tolerable, even billionaires."

"Switching anything around in America would have to be a bloody mess. Wouldn't it?"

She turned pensively back to the candle. "That is also my fear," she affirmed quietly. "My cherished dream is that these transformations come to pass without violence. With imagination and will, I am certain there is a way; but it would be naïve to think fervor can always be controlled. I am afraid, as we are mortal beasts, bloodshed cannot be avoided more than sweat or tears.

"Violence here and now, however, would be a failure of imagination and of will," she continued, pacing and pausing as if seeking the words. "I do not agree with those who believe the wronged must become more like the thing despised to overcome it. Soldiers are best disqualified from holding power in the aftermath of revolution, as part furthermost of their great sacrifice. I will occupy and subvert the thing despised, use its excess to bring it down. Revolution," she added with finality, "has never been properly capitalized."

"You want to capitalize a revolution," I repeated, nodding as I marveled at the idea. Finance was rife with convolutions, inverse relationships, and contrarian thinking. Though her assertion made my head spin, I got the idea. Revolution could be funded much like any social enterprise. Why not?

"If someone is buying something," she explained, "why should the lucre not go toward progress? So long as extractive enterprise takes place, to what end could its surfeits be better applied? Let capitalism serve its undoing as long as we must live with it. We could keep to high-end product to soak the rich or those that serve business-to-business purposes, let corporations pay for the people's emancipation, as is most fitting."

Her simplicity boggled the mind.

"Adequate funding is key to a well-reasoned revolution. Capitalism, I think, could be voted out of existence for the price of one resource war, a few hundred billion at the going rate, a notion seemingly beyond the Bigs' collective imagination. With a well-researched plan, its basic structures could be dismantled and transformed within a generation."

Where did her sureness come from? How did she come by this tone of voice? She played with huge ideas like a cat with a mouse.

"There are ways of arousing awareness and desire in a people," she continued. "My change managers will discover and invent them. There are no trails in terra nova. Leave the path making to me. From you, I need revenue structures. That is the first milestone. Then growth strategies. Peaceful revolution is extremely expensive."

"So what, you're just making all these plans up as you go along?" I asked in some doubt.

"You could say that," she agreed. "But I have good help, and my make up is not yours," she added, angling her head to the side and jutting her chin. "I have perspective of scale and a calling."

She paused to let this sink in, then faced into the flame of the candle. "I burn in this flame of consciousness and I must act, but I cannot act alone." She faced me again. "I will school hungry ears to teach in turn, but I need you for business, not politics."

"Go ahead. I have to know what you're all about, right?"

"No, you don't, really."

"Tell me anyway." I was going to add "please" but left off. In truth, I was spellbound by her words, the intelligence in her eyes, the art in her movements. She was herself experiencing her own first-time encounter—with me, the only Big who was not her father. She was feeling her way forward. Unlike me, however, she was unfazed, an actress improvising on the stage in the magic of opening night.

Pieces of understanding struggled for a way to surface and form a whole I could comprehend. I was myself part and parcel of her indictment, that much was clear.

Even so, her commitment was infectious. I hung on her words as she paced, tapping a finger at her chin, to regain her narrative. She seemed a master thespian, nuanced in voice and gesture, the life of the party after all.

"The student loans I've heard you lament are how the young are trapped in debt, graduate to being flogged by that same debt, lured to take on more debt, until at last no longer young they submit to living and working to sustain debt as its addict and slave."

I had always been indebted, I thought, even at home with my foster parents, or at the orphanage. Since college I'd been running on a hamster wheel of money debt, going nowhere.

"In a real economy of democracy you would be paid for the hard work of learning and in the same stroke mothers would be paid for their labors raising children. These, and all laborers, perform the true philanthropic work of our times, not grants made by institutions of guilt."

She paused to study me, then elaborated, musing to herself, confident of my attention.

"Debt is the gateway drug to capitalism and its culture. The question for the young is whether to bind oneself heart and mind to this culture of the loan and never look back for fear of jinxing the investment, or to question the contract at every turn. Should they wrangle to join the ruling class, or save the world from a dictatorship of vanity and privilege," she said, showing one palm up to one side, then the other, as if she were a scale. "Guess which wins."

"You have to wrangle just to stay alive," I affirmed.

"Even so. In the bordello of free markets, the young mind is bound to debt, and put in training to become its whore. Genius is tasked with inventing armaments and advertising. Technology is devised to produce a poisoned diet. From banking and Wall Street, the crown jewels of capitalism, we have feudal indenture, fraud in ever more ingenious forms, usury, war mongering..."

She spoke in her low voice, standing with assurance, level headed and calm.

"We have a culture of fraudulent dualities, an either-or infirmity of the brain, understanding pinged and ponged between two paddles. Take your pick between them: Republican-Democrat, private-public, big or small. Whatever comes to mind will have its bully twin in a prison of either/or. It is a fallacy of thinking so common it is in the Advertiser's Handbook—clean or dirty, new or old, cool or square. What can one hope from such a culture?"

"You could have any culture you wanted, or live happily ever after looking for a better one. You're rich," I threw out at her, sipping some wine and sitting back against the bed.

"It is not difficult to understand rich people as victims as well as the poor," she said, taking the thought on a different tangent and surprising me yet again. "Despite the arrogance of power, their extravagant lifestyles, they too suffer from capitalism gone mad, though to be sure some order of magnitude less. In time the rich themselves may learn to welcome an exchange of power, a chance to shed their leather skin, their three monkey senses. How they must long to socialize other than with the boring wealthy like themselves, as the Old Man does, amusing himself with my father, and yourself."

The flattering notion I might be better company than he had at hand had actually occurred to me before at the range with him, and Keira had once said as much.

"They must long to rejoin the common life of humankind, no longer objects of envy or hatred, unburdened of solitary responsibility for their capital kingdom, relieved of justifying and defending their privileged state atop a massif of need. What a relief to be spared the guilt of creating and feeding on that massif, if they have conscience, or trying to live up to delusions of superiority if they have none, their every blunder amplified by their power."

To be wildly rich, you either had a nagging conscience or delusions of deserving it all, I thought. What else could you think?

"Consider never knowing whether people like you for your money. Consider people fawning over your status, lying and scheming, begging or plucking at you for a charitable cause. Consider never being pitied for the human suffering no human is spared, eyed as a slave master by the people you provide a livelihood or domicile. Consider being unrecognized for doing well, no matter your personal achievement, because you are born to privilege. Consider the temptation to lean on wealth as a crutch for your personal failings. Never growing, never having to."

I'd never thought of being rich in these ways, though this did little to alter its desirability for me. All burdens were eased by wealth in the end, whatever minor trade-offs might be included. In the end, you live to the extent you have money.

"You are not the sum of your bank account," she went on, countering the thought I had not spoken. Was there a way to keep my face from being a billboard in the sky? I wondered.

"It is moral midgets and conniving brutes who best succeed in the jungle of social Darwinism," she continued. "Ethics do not evolve there, but are quelled to near-extinction. Genius is culled to serve reckless appetites and short-sighted bottom lines, hardly the evolutionary impetus of well-reasoned merit and reward. Neither social nor Darwinian, it would be kind to call the notion confused self-serving hogwash."

What if what she said were simply and utterly true? I asked myself in some alarm. What if it all were?

"With what we have," I ventured, "we're better off though, right? Even the trailer towns would look good to much of the world. I went through one once. The worst beggar on the street had some little superfluous thing, a silk scarf, a music player, a fine hat, and a soup kitchen to go to if ends don't meet from panhandling."

"Ha. Would you then have us eat lard soup out of gratitude for not starving as others do in some desperate part of the world? We are as a people entitled to take our rights and well being as far as they may sustainably go, and to pursue them with passion.

"We must get our own house in order before crusading for leadership in the world," she pursued, her head tilted to one side, raising her shoulder and dropping it for effect. "Our GNP does not confer upon the owners of record a right of dominion wherever on earth a desirable resource or new market may appear.

"A globalism worth having is led by national models worth having. The only true leadership, and the only effective ideological export, is our shining example at home."

"We don't shine at home," came out of my mouth unbidden. She paused to take me in.

"Our domestic condition is a misery of financial neurosis for most Americans. Our foreign affairs consist of economic gangsterism and military empire; we export the lie of affluence for the hard working, the lie that power belongs to our people, and the lie that we are free in being able to dissent," she said. "Such idealistic lies are mere jingo markers for the expansion mandate of corporate wealth. We liberate the rich where we conquer, to deepen their entrenchment and power."

She paused, and I could see she was making an effort to simmer down. "These, you see, are words from my own anger and revulsion," she said. "America has no moral grounds for exceptionalism," she added in quiet conclusion.

She returned to the candle for a moment, as if for sustenance, then turned to face me again. The light was behind her now, her form a silhouette, the flame behind her head made her hair seem ablaze. She appeared supernatural for a moment, the impression lingering around her voice.

"We shall never know our talent in a world of need. That's big bad Karl in ten words." She quieted for a moment, stepping out from the fiery halo. I went over her words.

"Eleven," I corrected alertly, and she laughed in assent, "Even so."

"I never heard it put like that," I continued, damping down the swell of pride her laugh occasioned in me. "All I really know are slogans," I confessed, "I don't even bother to vote half the time." Again I had a spell of goose bumps.

"Voting has become ineffectual as a challenge to the status quo," she agreed. "The vote could fade away and not be missed, for all the good it does," she added, pacing and turning to face me. "Indeed, the turnout shows it fading with each cycle. The minority who still trouble to vote, push the button for democracy itself, holding their nose to pick from apologists and liars of the status quo, grateful for an occasionally articulate or charismatic one. There is no essence to issue politics when all issues are framed in capitalism. There is no inspired socialism in counterweight, and no basis for hope from an exclusive democracy, one privately owned by the capitalized few, with a vicious market as its god. Long ago gone, an itch alone remains. Democracy in America is a phantom limb."

She had made my point in spades I thought.

"But no, it does not follow that electoral politics are a waste of time," she corrected, "or that voting and parties must remain as they are. Voting is as dangerous to the status quo as participants may yet fashion it to be, and the governing cannot outlaw such fair opposition as may in time arise without inviting civil war. Voting remains the keenest vulnerability of the big business state, and with well applied resources it can be raised to transformative power."

"Wait, you're not saying you want to make a socialist party are you?" I asked with incredulity. There had been hopeless fringe parties of one kind or another as long as I could remember.

"The word socialist has been wrecked in the American psyche," she replied. "Two centuries of questioning, illumination and insight have been rendered taboo—blanked out of mainstream consciousness with predatory lies. But I fear the making of new parties must await the demise of winner-take-all, with proportional representation established in its place, and undoing the slew of legal strictures erected to smother third parties. These changes, in turn, require the transformation of campaign finance. And yet—none of these goals may themselves prove possible without third-party pressure brought to bear. This is the conundrum of democracy in America—a vicious cycle of pre-requisites for change."

At this she stepped away from the candle in thought, catching a glimmer of light along one side, her cheek bone visible now, the rest of her face in shadow. The curve along her neck and shoulders was distractingly delicious to the eye.

"You are alienated from both sides, Ken, because you are middle class," she said, grabbing my attention back with a verbal slap. "Not to be one of the elite honeycombs your soul, and yet you can no longer sit down to dinner with the unwashed common man you consider yourself superior to and more deserving than. I offer you a chance to mature in your human potential to its fullest. All else is waste of time."

I squirmed at that.

"Democracy is a learning machine. No ism is complete, or sufficient in all times. There can be no forbidden party, even the most noxious side of ourselves we must hear. All barriers must come down. Folly will learn better and fade. True democracy is immune to utopias and final solutions by other name. This discourse between twin capitalist parties, keep-all and tweak-some, is a black tie affair in a museum of democracy."

"Capitalism is set down in the Constitution, isn't it?" I blurted aloud, not entirely sure where I'd read that, or whether this was a stupid question.

"Ha. The ruling roosters strut as if it were so ordained, and sadly you have come to believe it. No ism is ordained or precluded in the Constitution, if you wish to hang your hat on this document. The word 'property' occurs all of four times in the founding statements, and none equate to capitalism or constrain our terms of property to the capitalist version. Yet America makes missions of war, cold and hot, economic and military, against people at home and across the world at the bare suggestion of an alternate ism.

"It is not the document but our mind-set that locks the wheel. We long ago declared the American experiment done, but there is no done, and done should not be wished for. According to the media and our cultural myth, we are living blissful lives of serfdom and consumption, as if the final word for humanity were here and now upon us.

"But the American people are the more deeply unhappy for the abundance dangling out of reach. Look to your own feverish pursuit of affluence."

I was no match for her.

"The progress of the species demands experimentation. Once fair and level elections are put in practice, I'd propose the next amendment ordain a Constitutional convention to be held every third presidential term, and I would ease the amendment process to undo as well as do by direct national referenda. We want our wheel to have good brakes, and a reverse gear, the more to encourage innovation and risk taking. Good ideas are in abundance. We are leaderful, with no scarcity of beautiful minds thinking well among us, many better suited than I for all details. It is for me to mind the big picture."

"Ha," I said, trying out this expression of hers.

"I will have my way with the world. Joined with me or not you shall bear witness, Ken. You will see the news and say, 'That must be Sa at work.'"

She was teasing me with the prospect of missing out, but the thought of us apart did come with some alarm. I would be alone, I realized, back to square one, emptier than I had ever been.

She watched the signal flags moving about my face, but said nothing and went on.

"You suffer an occupation of the soul, as do we all in America. We are a conquered people. I hear the chains clinking, even if the chained do not. I see the scars of wearing them, generation after generation, in every word and nuance, in every face. It is unbearable for me to witness your culture."

She paused, seeking calm.

"I sense a groundswell below consciousness," she said at last. "Can't you feel it? Must there not come a time when the intelligence of a people outstrips its forms and demands the power to change them as a simple point of reason? Toward such time, I make of myself both archer and arrow. That is how I live."

I knew from my own hell what unbearable meant, but I did not sense any groundswell of consciousness at all.

"We do not even know what may come of fair elections and proportional vote," she said with a shrug of amazement. "Imagine political power pried from wealth and severed structurally from it, the playing field finally and for all time leveled. A democracy of ideas made possible."

She was still for a moment, standing now beside the wine bottle, nearly half as high again as she. She stooped to lift the ridged plastic cap I'd provided her as a cup. She paid its bucket size no mind and drank from it. I sat up, one arm clasped around my knees, to lift my glass with her, though I was already well fortified and did not intend to get drunk.

"No one can unmake and remake the minds of people if no one is listening," I observed aloud.

"Each mind must do its own making, but consciousness ready to be born must be midwived. I will be in the birthing business."

"Doing what exactly?"

"I am still formulating startup plans so to speak, but there is scarcely an instrument of capitalism that cannot be turned against it. I favor means that resonate, self-propel, and cascade in effect. The options are endless and grow with each billion in funds. What are your ideas? I invite you."

I had none. I had only a collection of peeves. She explained to me how we had unmade and remade our minds before, that the American Revolution had led the world from one tyranny, bravely and imperfectly, to a less egregious one. A new tyranny had long since hijacked the experiment.

"Corporations and their managers now feed in the place where monarch and aristocracy left off. We the people are as vassals to employer and government alike, each requiring our fealty and owing us none. We have capital kingdoms and corporate empires, princes, duchesses, and lords in an aristocracy of mercantilism and finance. It is a shorter list, what does not smack of king in capitalism."

"Why bother? I mean, why you of all people?" I hazarded.

"Bothering, as you say, is the best job for me. I can't aim for less. Anomaly though I be, I am as American as you are, and I am not proud of it. I am as common as dirt in having no path in this America. I must join the users or the used. These choices are equally repugnant and unacceptable. I face what rebellious Shay faced with his band of farmer-soldiers, what the colonies themselves faced: a wrong with no recourse but bothering."

She paused in thought for a long while, at one point playing with long fingers over her hair as if they were sorting the ideas that ransacked her brain. Every time she held still she seemed classical in the pose under the flattering glow of the candle. I thought I could watch her all night long. She spoke.

"A culture of the Ark is not a moral culture; it is not the culture of Christ which your brother follows. To limit the boarding list and damn the rest, at a vengeful and exclusive God's bidding, is extravagantly dysgenic. What if Noah refused to obey this elitist god and chose rather to include himself among the damned? God was testing Noah, but did he fail?"

I'd been spun around so many times by her words I was beginning to get used to it.

"Systems of scarcity and indenture must be left behind. I have no choice but make it so."

"You have every choice," I argued. "You want to get around incognito? Anyone could help you do that. You could travel, explore. Live. That would be less a waste than this revolution you're talking about. And if you went public you could have or do anything you wanted. The world would pave your way with a golden carpet. Just for being you."

"I can already have or do anything I want." She shrugged and began to stretch herself, twisting her shoulders then rotating them, followed by arching exercises, all manner of feminine eye candy articulated in her movements.

The fact was she excited me without trying. Her voice alone was making me hard. Closing my eyes, I could not ignore the tension. I opened them to find her watching me with a wide grin, which closed into a wry smile and a jut of the chin as if she'd finished with her reading of me. I flushed.

"As public freak of nature," she continued, a secret smile lingering, "I'd command a universal audience, I'll grant you, of a sort, for a while. There is power in my secret I would not forfeit, however. As a practical matter, I am overqualified for the idle stardom job."

She began another series of stretches, this time for her legs and back, while seated on the ledge of the candle holder. She stretched her arms above, her rib cage showing under the tights, small firm breasts jutting braless. She spent a provocative moment undoing and redoing her hair, thighs parting and closing.

She rose and continued to exercise herself luxuriously, with know-how, like an acrobat. It occurred to me all this stretching was needed because of her coiled strength, languishing in the apartment.

"Ha. You're something," I said with admiration and a wink, which she acknowledged with a smile.

"The time may come," she pressed on, standing straight and facing me, "when lives are not a rented expense, when labor is as self-enriching as an art, when the invention of stupefying jobs for extraction efficiencies has gone the way of vampire cults, when artists are no longer capitalized as stars or reduced to economic lepers, when governance is no longer gamed. Then, I may join Big society on its terms."

In the quiet that ensued I wondered aloud, "What would you do then, if you could do what you want on your terms?"

"In a culture that did not punish artists, I would make music, theatre, dance, film, verse, sculpture, and painting. I would make Art. I have studied in each of these forms, have known the joy of freedom in their discipline. Did absurdity not pervade, oppress and prevail, a daily insult to reason, I would use my days to dance and nights to write sonnets, elegies, and haiku.

"The Arts are born this way, as labor that rewards the laborer intrinsically with self-development. They are a beacon of labor that fulfills and rewards of its nature. They are man in pursuit of his divinity, imagination made wise, our species' vanguard. I can imagine a Congress of artists and sages where we have instead professionals of amoral practice."

"Lawyers and corporate shills," I agreed, wondering what a government of mathematicians might be like for that matter.

"Art is a great teacher of labor's meaning and potential. All labor benefits from creative use of the imagination," she continued, reciting someone named Von Humboldt a century before Marx: "...it seems as if all peasants and craftsmen might be elevated into artists; that is, men who love labor for its own sake, improve it by their own plastic genius and inventive skill, and thereby cultivate their intellect, ennoble their character, and exalt and refine their pleasure."

"Instead of strife to survive, imagine a culture of such work ethos," she invited. "Love itself seems a strange breach in this cannibal world," she added quietly.

"Yes," I agreed in a whisper.

"My enterprise is thus prerequisite to any other I would prefer. Mine is the vision of invention, imagination, in a freer, wiser more loving enterprise than profit could ever incentivize."

"Innovation is the name of the game," came out of me defensively. One need only look around.

"Predatory innovation is. The marketing of gizmos that do not even pretend to improve life, more opiate than religion to possess and be possessed by them."

"New technology is synonymous with capitalism," I asserted again, as much to myself as to her. That was written in stone somewhere, wasn't it?

"Unusable junk is rushed to market, let the buyer beware; and markets are themselves dysgenic, efficiently. One need look no further than CycoSoft and Clapple. The worst is exalted and the better is prevented in your vaunted market. The artist is beggared in it, the bean counter is made a god, and all who labor are kenneled in the consciousness of survival. There is a word for this inversion of human development. It is capitalism.

"The root of our ills needs thoughtful digging, and there is no time in the day for such self-examination. We are belabored to keep at maximum activity and minimum reflection. Can one heal one's humanity back in the night, over the weekend, within vacation time?"

The world I knew was taking a beating one cherished notion at a time. I was not, I realized, a good advocate nor even a stalwart believer.

"A just cause, I think, needs no interpreting," she began again, thinking aloud. "Neither sugar coating nor medicinal claims are required to swallow. No clever arguments. No food for misinterpretation. No disguise for our intentions. No twisting to one end. No words. What if we could only act to change the world, instead of 'making words?'"

"Language is what we're stuck with," I said, finally finding my voice.

"Stuck is a good word. Our poor human thoughts chase these little packets of meaning stuck in a row. Thinking itself becomes stuck in language until dogmatic zeal is formed, inciting a defensive opposing zeal in a murderous game of fragments.

"I have made myself at home with paradox. A thing can be articulated from end to opposing end and still not account for its nature. Let us argue deeds with deeds in solemn silence then."

She turned away, crossing her arms under her bosom and stood gazing into the flame, her cheeks flushed in its glow. She let silence gather around her on the stage.

"I think you do want to convert me," I finally said, unsure she wouldn't succeed.

"I shall convert your profits," she said with a tilt of her head and a smile. "Your soul is optional."

A distant thunder sounded. The wind beat floods of rain against the balcony windows. We watched as if behind a windshield propelled through the storm and, turning back at the same moment, found each other's smile.

"Hello, Ken," she said, extending her arm to me, palm forward. I extended the forefinger of my right hand and slowly reached the thick tip of it to the cup of her palm. We exchanged a pressure that ran through my body and tightened my loins again. The dark seemed to buoy the candle's hemisphere of light. I withdrew my finger and rested my hand at my side. She laughed a little at the tremulous care I took in my movements, and her laughter made me laugh.

"I invite your skepticism," she said, returning to her thread. "Be the devil's advocate if you want. You will find I am not easily shaken, and we may each learn something."

"The enormities of power you're up against, you'll go bust in a year," I said. "They'll gang up to crush you."

"Let them gang up. I do not fear those whose malice, guilt or folly makes them my foe. Together they shall make a better target. And if the world be a cuckoo's nest, I shall go bust, but not in a year or years. If there is some reason left, some trace of wisdom among conscious creatures, I shall have a chance and my enterprise will self-extinguish with the rest of capitalism."

"Politics burn me on either side," I confessed, touching my hands over the unbruised parts of my brow and rubbing my eyes gently before facing her. "I can't bear to look at the stuff apart from a factor in the markets," I explained. "I don't think I have a political bone. I can't even say I'm really patriotic. Nations seem a convenience of language and custom, not much more to me. I think I'd make as good a Dane as a citizen of the United States. I'm afraid you're barking up the wrong tree with the American story. You said so yourself democracy was over as soon as it began."

"It is over when we think it is."

"Most everyone thinks it is over now, and by the time you have changed enough minds, you'd have to start all over again."

"Pradeep and I are working out functional requirements for an algorithm of generational shifts and youth empowerment. So much has never been tried."

"People vote like idiots."

"Indeed today they vote against themselves; I confess I despair of humankind to hear a working man declare herself for the Republican party. My thought is for tomorrow."

She wondered aloud whether such workers suffered from a kind of political Stockholm Syndrome, a primitive gratitude and fealty for being allowed to live, in supporting a party against both ethos and interests. "Or is it perhaps, a bond of loyalty in exchange for continued patronage, like the attachment strategy of newborn babes toward the powerful adult?" she asked.

"People who can barely stand their own existence are turned into a drone of slogans for their keepers. Is it madness? Or masochism?" she wondered.

"Everybody is scared of something," I ventured as an answer. "Nobody wants to lose what they have, whatever it is. It seems to me people are happy with their prejudices too," I added, sitting up, my arms around my knees. "Isn't all that effort to have a dialog with mule heads a waste of time?"

"I'd call it basic research in political consciousness. The Democrats may be the more perverse for betraying the rhetoric of democracy. Your Republicans no longer desire such a thing as a free market, if they ever did. It is not enough to blanket all possible patents, for example, big business now owns the patent process itself, with capital and corporate requirements that exclude any individual. They want a controlled market, free for the most powerful exclusively.

"Poor Karl was long in his grave before history's cultural tyrannies," she continued, "and he has been turning over since, no doubt. He left us not a word on a society owned in equal measure by all of its citizens. It can be argued free enterprise is the soul of his post-revolutionary ism. What should a workers' democracy do with their councils and guilds if not pursue a freer enterprise, unshackled from profit? What, if not cultivate the gardens of science, technology, and the arts, no longer beggared by extractive process and consumption fetishes? Those who would pit liberty against equality understand neither to human scale, and scale is a matter I understand uniquely well."

She moved a stray lock of hair from her cheek as she turned to study me for a moment. I was wide-eyed at the sweep of her pronouncements, and looked away to the candle flame. She spoke again.

"Revolution is our birthright. I see a way to bring it about, using capitalism as a weapon against itself. I see ways to ready a people for this change. I have a lifetime to test my hypotheses.

"One may argue we are naturally swine from the premise of our culture," she added seemingly out of the blue. "Do you think we are?"

"Swine?"

"Greedy. Wasteful. Selfish. Crude. Innately," she clarified.

"If you take a look at the norms, the math of consumption, yeah, it does seem so to me."

"Marx dared point out that advanced capitalism makes itself dispensable," she went on. "In spite of the travesties revolution has made of itself in the world, the socialist idea remains the one the capitalist truly fears, the more so in modern, democratic and mixed economy expressions we are seeing now. As in Iraq, Afghanistan, Honduras, Panama, wherever we conquer, the corporate state is used to suppress socialist parties as a matter of course, or ban them outright."

"Because they appeal to the masses?" I half asked, half stated, wondering whether the power of capitalism really feared anything at all.

"They do not appeal as well as conformity though, do they?" she questioned in turn. "No, the powerful fear the validity of its critique and its logic of inevitability, its rebirth in new forms as we see in Vietnam and South America, its adaptability and moral resilience despite Soviet and Chinese failures. Capitalists so fear the socialist idea, it can be said they have endorsed it as their nemesis."

She paused to think, fingers to her chin, elbow resting on the other arm squared across her belly, then observed aloud, shaking her head free, "These isms deserve each other. They are each other's creature. We must look beyond them both or fail in their extremes."

Lightning filled the room for an instant, followed by thunder still a comfortable distance away.

"If we are divine animals, we are animals no less," she said. "Our highest faculties mix with limitations we can scarcely guess. It is guessing that's needed, and in this skill the imagination is more important than facts."

"I've heard that before."

"Al said it. Einstein to you. To me, it is a crime to mystify genius, to place it on a pedestal beyond common reach, so I call him Al. The man was a fount of wisdom outside of physics, which is not widely known.

"Imagine the Old Man deciding the future of mankind. Is he fit to solve even those ills he will admit he causes? No problem is solved at the level of its making. The understanding required must come from a leap of imagination."

She paced for a while in silence, fingers to chin, searching for new words. The gravity of my predicament was dawning on me. As certainly as her being there before my sane eyes was etched in her storm of words, so were misgivings of every other kind. Revolution funded by business? Her enterprise, paid for with mine?

I got shivers from her ramblings. My gut seemed to get what my brain could not quite. You owed fealty, but got none. You owed and owed and owed. I had spent weeks maundering in depressed hysteria at my condition in the ruling ism. In the world according to Sa, we were all donkeys in pursuit of a carrot dangling out of reach.

Her conviction was formidable. No matter how she sliced it though, how could I be kept out of her political handiwork if that's where all the profits went? She'd likely run afoul of the law or come under harassing scrutiny in short order, along with all her business interests, and me with them. At that moment of alarm, in a flash of memory, everything she had said to me in my dreams, in my helpless stupor, in my trembling, half-awake state came crowding back in a tangle. I flushed hot and dizzy.

When the room settled into place, I lay limp, my head back on the bed, passively attending the music of her voice.

"Big capitalism and its subsidiary government are each obliged to keep a welcome mat at their front door. We shall wipe our feet on it and buy Democracy back. How we'll talk about tomorrow, if you like."

"Buy?" It came out as a whispered breath of amazement beginning with B. "You don't mean buy, as in…buy?" I sat up again, the fuzz in my brain beginning to clear at the enormity of her thinking.

"If at first, the idea is not absurd, indeed there is no hope for it. We will buy the most dangerous obstructions to democracy outright, if we can, liberate the most noxious corporations one by one, de-fang them, take them not-for-profit, worker-owned or managed, start up our own social enterprises. And, if we can humanize money machines, we shall run them as such for funding.

"There are many ways to approach buying and I will always be formulating new ways to organize, leverage, and fund. I will groom a new breed of candidates to occupy both of the parties and undo the two-party stranglehold. I will set up revolutionary foundations, leadership colleges, and strike-ready unions. I will found and fund action schools. Pay for badly needed research. Buy out capitalist media and turn it around."

"You would need billions, tens of billions, even more," I said, now recovered from the woozies.

"I have tens of billions. And that is but an egg."

My mouth formed an "o" and stayed open.

"There is no shortage of talent for hire," she informed me, ignoring my shock. "I shall create well-paid careers in revolution to which the best may aspire. Revolution must persist, an expanding institution of disruption and enlightenment, across generations.

"On the business side, you and I will find what works. I'm curious how much profit it is possible to take from the markets, aren't you? As much as the national budget I would reckon, some five trillion or so. Liquid markets alone are a multiple of that."

"No one is that sure-footed," I objected, shaking my head.

"We shall see."

"No one can be that rich."

"But for a democratic will, everyone is already that rich."

"There is no...will," I finally managed to get out. "People are sheep."

"We will transform the sheeple and the wolves. Fire their imagination. If it take a wall of wills, then we shall make a solidarity."

"Everyone is stuck just staying alive. You can't move whole demographics around like chess pieces."

"We will buy people the time to think again." She smiled. "Why not revolutionary scholarships, for young and old alike," she stated more than asked.

Her skin shone with sweat from her performance around the flame, and I guessed, with some relief, that the wine at last was having some sway with her as well.

"It is intoxicating to speak my mind aloud," she said. "Wine and discourse are kissing cousins, no?"

"It still seems to me you're messing up your own happiness," I said, ignoring her footsteps over my unspoken thoughts, "when it's there for the taking. You could have absolutely anything you want, and you want to toss it all to test a wild hunch?"

"An endless joie de vivre is as unnatural a thing as a perpetual rebel scowl. Do you think it is an unhappy thing to leave a better world behind? I am here now, and our ills are in full bloom. As a moral intelligence, revolution is essential to my happiness, not mansions or manners of wealth.

"Yes, it is true enough that generations stewing in mindless consumption and miserable ease make will a hard manufacture, but there is, in any moment, grit enough for revolution, I think. Anger and doubt that forms and fades alone needs only fellowship to ignite to consciousness."

"I doubt it," I said. She pondered this for a moment as if I'd said something remarkable.

"I wonder if, behind the grit of will, is the will to smile at last. Perhaps all will is the will to smile. Maybe that is the power of the Guy Fawkes mask. I shall fashion a revolution of irresistible smiles. A lighthearted revolution."

"Well, I like that," I said. "I also like peace, love, and 'the meek shall inherit the earth.' No one is ever separated from their fortune except at the point of a gun." I knew she was serious, and it seemed prudent to fish in deeper waters for what she had in mind.

"The meek will know their part when time provides," came her reply. "We'll brood and midwife that time. As for the gun, perhaps that is the first thing we should buy. What might we do with controlling interest, say, in Mockheed or Krumman? There may be more imaginative uses, but were we to break them up, sell their parts off one by one to peaceful industries, there may be some profit to our enterprise as well."

"I may be greedy, but I don't want to end up in jail. How do I know you won't land me there?"

"You don't, nor do I know what the future holds. No plan is yet concrete. But I feel certain, Ken, you would break a great many laws were you sufficiently assured you could get away with their breaking.

"Not violence," I amended.

"You attempted self-murder, didn't you?"

I shuttered my eyes. I had lost myself in her torrent completely, and remembering brought a raft of unwelcome emotions. She stood erect, arms at her side, attentive but unsympathetic.

"Everyone is encouraged to be a petty criminal in deed or thought," she offered in meager consolation. "Absurd laws are devised to assure their widespread breaking. Universal infraction keeps a people afraid of the law, fearful of calling attention to themselves, politically isolated if not emotionally as well.

"Will you throw a stone of conscience from your house of glass?" she asked. "Such care for breakage makes action impossible. There are many subtle mechanisms by which you are controlled.

"And where indiscretions and misdeeds do not suffice to keep your profile low," she said, "there is the blunt instrument you know so well, your paycheck, to remind you of your vulnerability. You will have to sort me as we go. I cannot be a force majeure, waiting for others to catch up."

"A force majeure," I repeated. That was still force, I thought.

"Aye, and so is my breath on this candle flame," she huffed, making the flame dance and flicker in the darkened room. "You shall see all I see in time. Time is what I ask of you."

I thought about that. It seemed fair enough, under the circumstances. I could always quit, couldn't I?

She took stock of me. "If only you could see the potential I see in you, Ken. I'm as thankful to know you as to breathe." She was getting tipsy, I thought.

"You are thoughtful and a rather good listener too." She smiled and seemed happy, which made me happy.

"You give more of a damn than you credit yourself," she said at last. "But I do not require your damn-giving."

We shared a laugh at that.

"I'm told I talk funny, but most talk to me seems lazy and weak. I make words work overtime."

We quieted for a while then, and she grew solemn.

"We squander unpromised tomorrows until death calls out our name, and only then does its faint shadow, ignored life long, darken into the bogeyman that takes us.

"We guzzle the earth to extinction in secret fear of death. Children distant in time will be made to pay for our consumption. We diddle the future in a confidence game, a perfect crime in which the culprit is long gone by the time the next generation comes upon the scene. We hide from death, as the dying cannot. We should contrive a mortal scare, the end of the world."

"The end of the world?" I repeated, losing her.

"A deus ex machina or two, wobble some metal sheets for thunder. If imminent death led your royal bankster to rethink, the rented masses to clamor for release, it might be worth the toll. Change is a function of time, the present time is in flux, and in the flux we have a Consciousness Exchange on the pinhead of the moment. What if the future tense were to lose all meaning and leave us just the moment? A singular exchange in the flux of time, the stitch that saves nine?"

I had no real way to know where her earnestness ended and fantasy began.

"Let us imagine the end of the world. We have Death to thank for so much of our propensity. Our towers and monuments are homage to him, our property is clung to in defiance of him, our worship a bribe to forestall him or dilute his power. Yet, in our culture, death's shadow is pale or hidden and comes slowly, to one at a time. What if the shadow of extinction were to get up and speak at once to all humanity?"

"Tell me you're joking."

"IIa. Are you scared? Imagine, the polar caps collapse at once, or a comet brings a shower of meteor bombs or a new virus dines on mankind. What clash and clamor of proclivities in the run up to the end of the world? What antics would we see?

"Our natures would be laid bare, for better and worse, a mirror held up to our individual and species' souls.

"There would be no proper behavior for the occasion. Conditioning would wear poorly, and when denial of death waned away to certainty, discipline would fail. Strife would be pointless, but then, the remaining time would be a heyday of pointlessness.

"How long would government stay on the job? The noble professions? Some bound by oath and conscience would surely try. Doctors, nurses, and the like. Acceptance would come slowly. Resignation slower still."

She went on to paint a world gone mad, where prayer and Hedonism warred in the same soul. Law and order expired, and risk lost its meaning in the same stroke as reward. It was a world of crime and fear. Phantasms of heedless violence erupting, all souls now cornered. To kill and to die would not be far from equal there, and for those made mad, they might well appear interchangeable as nullities.

"All notion of acquisition and bequeathal would be laid bare for the absurdities they are. Facing the end of all, such itches of mortality would trouble us no more. Property for use in the time remaining would be the only meaning of the word.

"Our mortality is at the root of war, of murder, and all art of terror is homage to it," she said. "To live in the present knowing one's death is to ride a beam of joy, or seal the human heart in darkness. But if we knew, all knew openly at once that human life would end with our own in a generation, or a month, or a day, might we not begin to understand how ill we order our lives?

"What would you do, if the world were to end in a month?"

"Hide out with a woman I suppose. There would probably be a lot of them thinking the same thing."

"And if life were handed back to the world at the last minute, what would be learned? Would we pick up the pieces, go back to business as before? Would mankind not have a new thought? That is the question I bring to you, Ken, in your reprieve from death."

"I haven't had a new thought. Have I?" I asked myself as much as her, surprised at the turn.

"I am your new thought," she said. "I might meet the world in person, were each encounter so confluent as mine with you. Or I might meet them all at once on the heels of world reprieve from their certain doom, meet them in a new dawn. Ears would grow very long indeed to hear their little savior, would they not?" she asked provocatively. "I could deliver the word of God to a child-like humankind."

"I think…" I began but stopped, waiting for her to look up from her smiling reverie. "I think you're drunk," I said.

"Ha." She grinned at me deliciously and laughed at herself. "I could be from another galaxy, if you prefer," she said more modestly. "The point is that minds would be open, perhaps as never before. To return to life ordained by mortal itches might actually seem implausible. The overt and covert violence of owner dominion might seem preposterous, the violence of scarcity and excess rejected as a way to live."

Her voice made light of the ponderous, her words resounding in the quiet moment we shared as wind-blown rain swept the window in gusting patters.

"Do you know someone like me? It's not my size I'm talking about."

"I've known some brainiacs who were good traders," I replied, "a banker or two on the investment side. My adoptive brother was mixed up in radical politics for a while. There were protests in college. Even with your abilities, you have to lose on a trade sometime, don't you?"

"I do sometimes, even with a hedge. I have no joy in refining this faculty further. It is, in every sense, a dead end. I calculate in a way that is sub or sur-rational, by kinetic intuition, an imaginative act. I did not trust myself at first. I struggled with this notion, resisted it. But reason has never been as profitable. Why should it be, after all?"

I must have shown my puzzlement for she went on to explain that we all, as a species, have a non-rational way of knowing, what she called a resonant intuition, wherein butterfly and black swan events, or confluences as she called them, are primitively sensed. She allowed this faculty to herself, though she suffered in doubt of its validity always. She explained it was for her a palpable experience, and the exchange trading that so dazzled me was but the lowest grade of its occurrence. She had this sense far more keenly in the fabric of life itself. It had happened to her while sailing down in the chute at the manor well before I arrived at the gate with the guards in tow. It was not her idea to drop in as a snack for their Dobermans, and she was doing all she could to avoid where the wind was carrying her.

"Then I knew something more was happening," she asserted, "more than descent on the breeze and the danger of dogs, I felt the very gust I rode on was a butterfly effect upon the world, and I allowed the wind to take me. In result: another piece fell into place. You. There. Just then."

"Happenstance."

"Yes, but for the unreasoned prescience and compulsion of it." She paused and changed tack.

"Old Man Wellingham understands gain and risk are poorly reasoned. He toys his Illuminati readers with short term trades but holds his bulk in the dullest bonds, and he insures those. He owns quite a stake in the technical infrastructure of government and Wall Street. In a very real sense, they both work for him. Truth be told, the whole world is working for him by a few degrees of separation."

I winced at that.

"His windfalls are few and far between, but for two decades now, there's not been a year he did not net at least ten billion in absolute passivity. He aims to be the first trillionaire in history. Apart from amusing himself with a few modest gambles, which have rarely paid off, he compounds. His betting days ended when his mother died and left her fortune to him."

While bounders like me ante up and go broke, I thought.

"The Old Man never risked more than compounded funds unearned by his great grandparents. There are stories of bounding success in order to sustain the media fiction of the self-made man, but that is what they are, a fiction. No one is self-made, or self-reliant, and 'Risk not thy whole wad' were well advised to you."

I took my medicine without protest, and she went on.

"What capital I do not put to immediate political use must continue to multiply for continued struggle. I will not have you gambling with it. We must have staying power for this work will not be quick."

"I can manage."

"We shall see. If you can, I shall be free to work. We will have incubators and exemplary corporations as well as profit machines. In the short term, you will be busy with what you know, acquisitions and start-ups."

My face, huge in the air, must have worn my enthusiasm. This part of the deal was as good as it got. But could she really pull it off, profits for opposing politics, without landing us both afoul of the powers-that-be?

"I cannot foretell the risks, nor is there a guarantee that money alone can forestall what risk may arise." She paused for a moment, struggling with an unwelcome emotion. "I have no magic tricks, Ken. I am but human, and in truth, I grieve for my work that must make do with so flawed and unworthy an instrument, one so poor in talent, so limited in mind, so full of vice and weakness. I grieve the life I am bound to live in the being I am bound to be. I cannot deserve the work I must do."

I felt the intensity of her inward gaze and wanted to console her. I had just lived through much the same kind of tear up, and nearly died of it. I looked at the enormity of my hands. What could I do for her?

"I have had the advantage of the Old Man's billions to play with along with his tools," she said, using the words to struggle toward composure. "I have my own lab now that is just as good, and yours too will be state of the art.

"No one understands capitalism so poorly as its true believer," she observed, her humor returning, "or is so inept at it. Agnostic opportunists, like yourself, have the advantage in perspective, though I think you will end your long life something rather different, a poet perhaps. You have more imagination than is good for you in your line of work."

That last aroused a welter of raw questions, not least of which was the trustworthiness of my own mind. I was stung with the thought that maybe she was right, and God help me, maybe that explained everything: why I bombed out of the market, twice; why I might yet be dreaming, feverishly; and why I could play my part with her in this surreal dinner date without going stark raving cuckoo.

"You have new work now, where imagination takes precedence over intelligence," she assured me.

"If the Old Man caught you, you'd be treated as a criminal, a spy, a traitor, and terrorist," I recited. "They will hang you."

"I spy to make a virtue of necessity. I spy in every moment. All sentience is a spy."

"For who?"

"That is the question, isn't it?" she said, laughing. "Is it for our ego or for God? Do I spy for truth, for justice, or for what has become of the American Way? One chooses for whom one spies, that's all. As for hanging me, that is unlikely," she said, vaguely amused with the idea. "I am irreplaceable, one of a kind in the world entire, and I dare say I'd be deemed too valuable a specimen to kill."

"You have to spy or come out and show yourself," I stated, then shook my head at her perplexity.

"I have chosen a middle path," she assured me. "I live screen lives on the Net, like any Big. I have friends, business associates. I know inventors, artists, entrepreneurs, technologists, people from all walks of life in America and around the world.

"I will need incubators for some of my cleverer friends. I have an acute need to merge micro electronics with nano circuitry for equipment to scale. I could kill for a Puck that fit in my hand."

She might not be exaggerating, I thought. "Your friends, are they...capitalist anti-capitalists, like you?"

"Some few I have set up are revolutionary, and others are social entrepreneurs or run non-profits. Others still are extractors. I learn from all of them. I am friendly with rampaging pro-capitalists too, frothing neocon ideologues, Creedman-Brandists, who would burn me as a witch if they heard me now. I have learned capitalism from them.

"We must begin at the beginning, however, and *Kaizen*, progress in steps. You will have to train for running what we acquire. I will not ask you to storm the executive citadel unless armed with the necessary skills."

"I can storm the citadel," I asserted.

"In time, you will be chairman on many boards and command an HQ staff that will only grow. In time you shall have to manage some number of surrogate chairmen in multiple industries.

"As an ideology, capitalism is a cat amused with its tail, not the stuff of grown-up men. Leave its unraveling to me."

She returned slowly to the flame of the candle as if to warm herself or draw from its energy. Her body movements had grown more languorous. She was wearing down.

I understood my position in all she had said with dead reckoning, there being no tool to navigate the strange waters in which I found myself. I was not as immune as I thought to her rhetoric. The more they rattled around in my head, the more plausible her words became.

I was not any madder, or less mad, than I had been before she popped up, at least as far as I could tell. I never cared much what a company did with its take anyway, unless I was buying or selling the company. Who knew what sides were served by the dispersal of profits in the end? Why should I care how she blows her billions?

Her dimensions managed to slip my mind for long stretches in her command of my attention. She seemed somehow tethered to my survival in ways I could not guess. She was in the end Sahar, Sa, a rare beauty in miniature, and no one's fool.

I had a choice to make: This creature and her legerdemain of activism, or Hetty and Neil, those creatures, and theirs.

"I shall have a good time of it too," she said, the decisiveness in her voice soothing my indecision, "and I invite you for the ride. You will succeed beyond any man's deserving. You will become untouchable among the elite. While you enjoy your math of extraction, I shall fight fire with fire. There's time yet for you to decide. That old soul lyric 'you can't hurry love' has wisdom for us, though our lifetimes must be time enough."

I said nothing at the end of a long search for words. She smiled with a nod, having read me, I was sure. With a toss of her hand she signaled the finale and slowly set about gathering her gear from the buffalo rug.

From face down in the muck with no options, I now had door number one, getting rich with Neil and company, a dangling maybe, and door two, getting rich with an ineffable wonder, some kind of socialist or anarchist derivative as best I could make out, with good money already paid.

From her side of the equation I had to subtract the possibility of getting my sad sack hauled in for conspiracy somewhere down the line. From Neil's, it was more of the same dog show that made me sick in the first place that I had to subtract.

The system just crapped me out. Didn't I owe the Old Man some payback, and wouldn't this comeback just burn his hide? I looked out toward the darkness, and it occurred to me that Keira would turn up somewhere sooner or later. I might even finagle her back if I put my mind to it, just to spite him.

The scowl faded from my face as I watched her, this weary, slightly tipsy woman Sa. Vengefulness would not wear long in her presence. No, a job was only as good as its boss, and that's where she won hands down.

And what of Neil and Hetty, were they not also going to cross the line, as the Old Man already did, with small arms no less? Who knew where those two ideo-bots would lead me. They meant more of the same, or worse. I'd have to kowtow, and wasn't I sick to death of it?

If that was where sanity lay, I was better off mad.

I regarded her, standing in thought before the flame, elbow propped on the arm across her midriff, her head perched in her hand. She seemed of a density out of reckoning, with a gravitational pull of her own. The miracle of her size faded away in her stark, pensive presence. She stood half in silhouette before the candle, her weapon loosely slung, the hold of her allure beyond my reasoned resistance. Were I to refuse, I wondered, would the next stop actually be Neil, and not the loony bin? Could I ever again be as I was before meeting her? Did I want to be?

"Sleep on it," she stirred from her own reflections to say. "The wine and the day have caught up with me."

She raised her cup in both hands and drank to the bottom. "I will rest soundly tonight," she said, lowering it to the rug.

She brushed a wisp of hair from her face and added, "It's been a fretful week, I can tell you."

* * *

CHAPTER 7

The view from the tower

I stood on the city street yearning in broad daylight for a consciousness more lucid than the glare of the morning sun, but no such cosmic super-clarity was forthcoming.

"Stop kicking," I said.

"I'm trying to get my footing," came the excited voice from the pack hitched high on my back. I could feel her elbows, or perhaps her knees, poking me. She emerged head and shoulders over my right shoulder, standing atop the backpack heedless of being seen. She tossed her loosened hair and smiled completely, deeply at the spectacle of the City scene before her.

"Everything is perfect," she said. By craning my neck around, I could just about look into her eyes.

"Watch where you're going!" demanded a well-appointed middle-aged woman in spectacles whom I bumped walking past. She stood as if slapped, plainly seeing the miniature woman clinging to the strap on my shoulder. Sa laughed aloud, in high spirits at the pained expression on the poor woman's face. I started off at a good pace and with no thought of looking back.

"Are you crazy?" I flung over my shoulder at my burden.

"She's still looking. Ha, now, she's telling someone."

"I get it, okay? No more proof needed."

"See, the one she is telling doesn't believe it, and now the first one's not sure what she saw either. Oops, she's got her Puck out. Hurry up, before she puts the cops on us."

She was reckless in her joy, revealing a girlish side for which I was unprepared. I felt responsible for her.

I slowed my pace and looked back at the woman. She was alternately looking toward me and again at the stranger she had accosted with her tale who'd shrugged her off. She stamped her foot with frustration and talked into the glinting plastic she held in her hand.

Sa swung around my shoulder where I could see her face. Its smallness so near drew me in, made me understand every nuance of face, the phenomenon of face. She knew when she had me. Her expression and eyes grew ever more subtle, holding mine, the both of us exposed, feeding brazenly off the bustle and vitality around us.

"Let's go," she simply said, smiling, old and young, girl and woman. So I did. Half visible above my shoulder as I went, she pointed and yelled in delight at nothing in particular that I could see. She jabbed for my attention and kicked at my off-color remarks. She rode me like a horse, her mouth half open in a wondering smile, sword sheath slung at her back.

"To see I cannot be believed is thrilling, I confess," she explained merrily. "Sorry to put you out."

"I told you," I said, "believed or not, every inch of public space is under video surveillance. If a goon stops me and I refuse to let them search the pack, they'll drag me to the station and do what they want with you."

"With that bump on your head and your fine suit," she teased, "you look like a boxer on his way to a wedding. A very suspicious character, I'm sure." She was jubilant and would let nothing faze her.

I was excited myself at the caper, dangers notwithstanding. I'd come a long way overnight it seemed. The whole idea of her, at once thrilling and terrifying in its possibilities, was growing on me. I foresaw myself becoming a Wunderkind under her tutelage, a celebrity presiding over grey haired corporate boards in her service.

The City seemed brilliant this morning. Feeling so wonderfully alive, sentience itself seemed a shock. Every common thing appeared phenomenal, from the bus on the road to her tiny arms on my shoulder. Light was strangely vibrant, and objects stood each in their own transcendence. Color itself, the arrangement of shapes, my own body, hers, sensation itself, seemed miracles. My last conscious morning seemed a dim age ago; on this day, in this bright sunshine, the world was transfigured.

I remembered every detail. No, I had never remembered before. I never knew what memory was. I had been addled, an amnesiac.

This morning, memory came alive. Scene after scene, every feature in her fluid face, every sentence in her profusion of words, I remembered vividly in a kaleidoscope of wonders.

"What's happening to me?"

"Epiphany," she said.

~

I exited Washington Square heading south, as I had the last time I left my sanctuary. My destination this time was deliberately that self-same place I'd come to dread. She wanted me to walk her downtown to visit the new open air observatory atop the enclosed one at the World Trade Center, which by her reckoning, would be ill-attended on what I discovered was a Monday morning.

She called aloud, slapping me on the shoulder. "I sense a confluence!"

"A what?" I asked, remembering at the same time her prior reference to the word.

"Something is happening, or going to. Give me your Puck."

She clasped the pocket Net with both hands and dropped down into her cache with it. I could hear the unintelligible murmur of her voice behind me. A vagrant thought passed: how typical of a woman to go out and dive into her phone. Keira would do the same.

We crossed over Houston Street and into the narrow shady canyons of Little Italy.

"I see hulks of buildings, shaggy in mantles of green and wintry shrub," came the voice from my shoulder. She faced backward, holding an earphone, its bulk cradled on her shoulder as she called down to the device at her feet in the pocket.

"What?" I said, though I heard her. "Who are you talking to?"

"Papa."

"No, that was to Ken," she said. "He sends his regards. Yes, it is beautiful here. I am fine. The streets are nearly empty. There are no dogs. Papa! There are no dogs anywhere. Ken is looking after me. Yes, he is okay with me. He's more worried his backpack does not match his fine suit. Must say bye now. Yes, we will keep to the plan. Bye, Papa!"

She stepped down to toe the off button and came up again without the earphone.

"Look," I said. "That tower is like terror central with its security. Why don't we take the boat tour around the Island?"

"Their security is no concern to me."

"Your sword will show up in the metal detector."

"I'll take it off and leave it with the pack. You can call it a letter opener. They don't have strip scanners there, do they?"

"Just at international airports, so far. Why are we going there?" I stopped walking to punctuate the question.

"I told you: there's a confluence," she said casually as if she were talking about the intersection of West Broadway and Canal.

"What confluence?!" I nearly shouted just as an elegant silver-haired matriarch emerged from a doorway ahead clad in a striking dress suit of black and gold suede.

"I don't know, but it feels like a big one. We must conquer your fear of this place."

"Get down, will you?" I commanded her in a loud whisper.

The old woman sized me up with shrewd blue eyes. That we were both sharply dressed seemed to make for a glancing bond, despite the flick of her eye as she took in my bruised temple. A glance aside assured me there was no living doll visible at my shoulder.

"Morning," I said with a wan smile as we passed on the sidewalk. She replied in kind. I did not look back.

"I wouldn't want to give her a heart attack," Sa said, popping up at my shoulder.

"You'll give me a heart attack!"

"We'll have brunch afterwards and then you can take me to the Doll House. They are the only shop that uses the right gauge cloth and thread in their fashions, and I need an office wardrobe. Look," she bade me, pointing. "I've never seen one."

It was all-direction utility vehicle that had swung around the corner, its electric engine humming. Then it slid sideways into a spot against the curb. She climbed down my upper arm, calling, "Bend your elbow," as she did.

I made my forearm into a perch for her, and she leaned her head and shoulders back against my armpit as she watched the machine maneuver. She then sniffed, turned to sniff again behind her, then at once buried her face in my armpit. She extracted herself only slowly.

"You have quite an amazing scent, you know." I could feel her nudging her face back into my armpit. She emerged, laughing, with a "Wow!" then ducked her head all the way back in, tickling me.

"Okay, cut it out."

She emerged. "Intoxicating. I would never have imagined such a thing could be body odor. If we could bottle that aroma, we'd make a killing, Big man."

"Well, don't fall off," I said, blushing at her outrageous flattery, which left me with a proud, protective feeling toward her.

"I am quite pleasantly stupefied," she went on.

"You have some kind of thing about living dangerously?"

"Yes, like you, I do. Risk attends potential. Isn't that why you compound risk to trade on margin?"

"Glad we got that out of the way. I'm not sure I like this confluence business at all."

"You'll soon get used to heights."

I plumbed her meanings without speaking.

"It was years before I allowed myself not to simply dismiss this sense of a congruence on the horizon, longer still before I came to recognize its discreet expression in the clutter of consciousness, and only recently have I allowed myself to trust it."

"You have a hunch?"

"If you wish."

"Something will happen. But you don't know what."

"That sums it."

"Great," I opined. "Is it good or bad?"

"*Che sera, sera.*"

I was miserable at the prospect of playing tourist to Tower security with such vulnerable contraband riding in my pocket. I dared not imagine what might happen if we were discovered.

"They won't physically catch me—you can be sure of that. Refuse to admit I exist," she suggested as if I had spoken out loud, and I had no way of knowing whether she was reading or second-guessing me. "Let them sound crazy. I've saved a lawyer's number on your Puck. They can't hold you for anything."

"What if there's no place for you to run or hide? Like in an elevator. What will you do?"

"We will not cross that bridge. You shall see to it."

"Even if you get out of the building. Then what?"

"Hitch a ride in a handbag and have some adventure. Meet you at your place after dark. Trust me, Ken, with imagination and will, there's a way."

"Is that your mantra?"

"One of them."

I would have run from the so-called Freedom Tower were it not for her infectious bravado. She clambered down from my arm perch into an empty side pocket, teasing my apprehension as automatic doors swung open. There was no backing out now.

We reached the checkpoint at the elevator to the observatories. The attendant was a milky freckled young woman in a uniform and cap. Two overweight security guards stood idly by as I fished my pockets self-consciously for the chit card. I could not have possibly looked normal, I thought, but she took the card with a smile, reviewed the ID, credit rating, residence and police records. She checked photo against face with a sly flick of the eye, deducted admission for the open air view, and handed the chit card back.

"Quite the storm last night," I half asked by way of small talk. It rang false, thick with guilty concealment, and my secret sharer signaled her displeasure with a sharp pinch.

"Fine view this morning, sir," the girl replied, nodding toward the multi-detection booth that would scan for metal, certain plastic composites, chemical toxins, and radioactivity. I placed my bag and pocket contents on the conveyor and stepped through the arch as the millisecond scan found no indication of weapon or component on me, and I emerged on the far side as if on a tightrope, steeling myself for the two guards ahead. The attendant's voice called, "Just a minute sir," freezing me in place.

"Don't forget your bag."

"Or course," I said, feeling like an idiot, and retrieved the bag from the x-ray scanner. Evidently they paid no mind to the sword among my pens.

I breezed past the guards and gained the elevator, fishing my handkerchief from a back pocket. We would be under constant surveillance on the way up and on the deck I well knew, and heaved a sigh of resignation as I wiped the sweat from half my brow and patted gingerly over the rest.

The elevator ride was painfully long, unredeemed by the car's vacant public hugeness, the insipid muzak playing and the butterflies in my stomach at the rapid ascent and sickening slow motion stop.

The top deck was nearly empty. There was a young couple, European tourists to judge from the look of them, in drab pastels, cameras out, seeming unusually wholesome. They stood on the far south side so I took up a spot looking north across the grandeur of Empire City. The clarity of the air was remarkable after the night's storm. Blue skies and morning sunshine illumined the east side of the City spires, glinting off structures north and westward as far as the curve of the earth. The western side of buildings cast their shadow in deep blue.

The wind was surprisingly mild. A hint of Spring filled the nostrils. The beetle parade of vehicles and the ant march on the streets were odd and amusing. Across the East River, coming and going, three levels of caterpillars crawled over the monorails. I had never been in a building so high.

"I would never have come on my own to this damned scary place," I confided to her in the right side jacket pocket. It was my third visit to the Tower in as many weeks, the prior two a tangle of painful memories. Aloft I felt trapped, as if haunted by the ghosts of the analysts who had perished in this very airspace so long ago.

She emerged and managed, in a remarkable economy of movements, to exit the side pocket, clamber along my forearm and insinuate herself down into my jacket's inside lapel pocket, from where she held the flap open in front of her to gaze out at the view. With my chin tucked, I could make her out, her free hand shading her eyes.

"Do you want to take pictures too?" I asked.

"Play the tourist and take some pictures for me."

We were surveilled from every vantage point but facing outward at the rail toward the panorama before us, so I put on a show. I removed the Puck and readied the device for photography. She let the jacket flap close over her as I turned to face the surveillance, going through the motions of a tourist, which I realized I was, my secret notwithstanding.

Mission complete, I returned to my spot and leaned casually on my elbows against the rail, the Puck resting on its broad ceramic shelf. The place was jumper proof, I noticed, the drop to the level below a mere ten or twelve feet, while the outer wall from that level was unassailable by anyone looking to take wing.

"Put the news on for me, Ken. You can lean the Puck on its stand."

She was intent in a way that fine-tuned my apprehension. I extended the device's hidden stand, commanded Global News to the small screen, and adjusted the volume up. As I did so, I presented the crook of my left arm in such a way as she had already exploited it before I was aware of her, and leapt atop the waist high shelf, using my body to shield her from the cameras behind me. The morning sun was already high. If anything, it was getting warm. Wind was light and distinctly from the west.

"What are you expecting?" I finally asked.

"I don't know. It may not be here at all, but we should be here, you and I. I cannot say why."

"Is it good or bad?"

"The chances of something particularly wonderful happening are seldom as good as the other."

"Here in the City?" I asked. She did not answer. "Will it affect the markets?"

"I don't know."

"But you have a hunch. Is it worth trading?" I pestered, hoping to salvage an easy bag for the morning's travail. "Why not line up a short and catch the swing real time?"

"I have no heart for it."

"If your hunches are that good, it's a shame to miss the opportunity. Spot me a hundred grand for a stake? I haven't mentioned going nuts, have I?"

"Time enough for that, and part of the deal was to get me home this afternoon. Use what you have, if you must gamble."

She switched the Puck over to Empire City News, which was hosting a live roundtable on the crisis in US financial markets. I was sharply tried not to grab the Puck and place a trade.

"Oh, go ahead, take it. Purge yourself," she said, chidingly. She sat down cross legged and gazed out upon the phenomenon of the City.

In a flurry of commands I replenished my trading account and grabbed a fistful of near put options on a triple leveraged index ETF, no hedge. Relieved, but now soul-bound to the news, I returned the Puck to its perch and she resumed the City broadcast.

"Why don't you take advantage, if it's profits you want?" I ventured to ask. "You could make a killing if you're right."

"No reason," she said, as if she had something other than a reason. "Do you mean to suggest I am being irresponsible to my mission?"

I could see it that way, and I said as much with raised eyebrows and a few nods. She looked at me and did not elaborate, turning back to the vista before us.

"I guess, for you, being up here is something wonderful, but it gives me the creeps." I got a shiver from the intense spectacle before me near and far.

Now was now and here was surely, sharply here, I assured my-self, closing my eyes against a bout of vertigo.

I opened them to find her turned around, standing now, looking back up at me with solicitude.

"You really are scared, aren't you?" she asked, scanning me.

"Just got a little woozy. I'm okay now," I assured her, lessening my grip on the banister.

She looked back over her shoulder to the east, shielding her eyes as she took in the view. The late-shift cargo barges and freight trains were still moving across the East River, along with tiers of passenger monorails. The 12-hour supply and removal opera-tions would cease before noon. The river was no longer a water-way but a system of ingestion and excretion for the City. Cargo trucks were banned from Empire Island, and they queued by the hundreds in Brooklyn, a line that would not diminish until long after the last barge was still.

Not far from the depots on the Brooklyn side began a gradient of residence and business high rises, ranging from affluent to super affluent. The City view from across the river in Brooklyn occa-sioned generous private parks, malls, and promenades in front of and in between the prime real estate. To the southwest was a very different matter. The industrial Jersey side remained an eyesore. though residential inroads were being made.

To the northwest, the Palisades Park abruptly took over the river shore, stretching away along the Hudson River beyond the GW Bridge, the bridge and park under lease to Empire City Corpo-ration. To the south was the City bay and the Statue of Liberty. The length of Empire City Island reached away before us to the north. All around, residence, business, and industrial properties stretched away in a patchwork to the edge of the earth.

The expanse seemed almost quieting after a while, as I watched with her standing hand over her brow as if in salute. The grandeur was undeniable under the resplendent morning sun.

"Civilization seems forlorn," she said at last. "I must wonder at such density." She was quiet for a while again.

"All, it seems, or something in the all, wonders back at me," she continued mysteriously. "The unsayable becomes a surge, until some time-bound word-thought is made articulate." She turned to me from facing west. "It will be something awful."

"Here?" I asked in alarm, reckoning anew the ground zero site on which we stood. Impulsively, I scanned the skies for incoming jetliners. Surely not here, not twice. "Don't tell me…"

"I brought you here in the broad light of day to stand with me on the stage of the world, nothing more or less. We will not die today."

There was a long silence in which she stood gazing out from the ledge, arms crossed beneath her bosom.

"You'll let me know when it comes to you, right? Look, we've had our view, let's just get the hell out of here."

"We shall bear witness. I wish it were not so."

"Great."

"I am not wearing my sword, and I stand on the ledge of a fatal fall some four meters to the stone below. A sweep of your arm and I am out of your life. You can go back to who you were, or try to do so. They will pickle my remains in a jar. I need to know I can trust you with my life. I need you to trust me with your life and your future. I cannot use a halfway man."

I glared at her and did not speak. What was this all about now, I wondered.

"Ours is no easy deal," she continued. "The world is in the balance. I can feel it now. I need to be certain of you. I need you bound to me, to my goals and my will."

"What are you saying?" She was changing the terms on me, I thought. I groped for words. "'Til death do us part?" I didn't like where she was going with this.

"Just so. For better or worse, 'til death do us part. Ours must be a union more binding than marriage; cheating and divorce are not options with your nine inch bride. The enterprise we have at hand is greater than my life or yours. We will need a blood bond; and our partnership must have a soul."

"You expect me to agree to that?" I was getting nervous fast.

"You will know better by the time the day is done. Give us time."

"You're just being metaphorical, right? About marrying, I mean." I tried not to sound as nervous as she was making me.

"The metaphor is not lightly made, but rest easy, Ken. What I ask, in time you will gladly give. An official arrangement might be useful though," she mused, her mood lightening as she toyed with the idea and finally laughed. "Mrs. McCavity who is never there. It seems a shame to deprive you of all the wonderful excuses you would have to invent for my absences. But no, a Big man needs a Big woman, and I doubt I could manage loving just one person. Ask me again sometime," she added, turning away and scanning eastward. "I may have a different answer."

I regarded her solemn figure against the wide Big world. "You're not a secret I'd want to try out on anybody," I volunteered, fidgeting. Nothing seemed easier to me than to speak of her to no one. I could only humiliate myself.

"Is that a promise?"

"Yes."

"You will break it before the week is out." I shook my head and found her eyes. "I know you, Ken," she smiled inwardly. "I'm fond of you anyway," she said with laughing eyes that turned sad. She scanned westward. "Bear witness with me. In time you will have all the clarity you need."

"The sooner we're out of here the better, Sahar." The words came out jittery, her name strange to my mouth.

"Just call me Sa," she advised.

If she was not worried by her ominous hunch, why should I worry, I reasoned in an attempt to calm myself. I breathed her full name again.

"Better. By the clock, we will not be here much longer." She did not explain.

She returned to the Puck, touching the controls expertly. A pre-roll jingle began, signaling the start of the discussion roundtable. Below ran a ticker news feed:

> *Markets began the morning with gains on expectations congress would quickly resolve the latest in a series of nuclear waste disposal scandals in the industry, with Mil-Con leading the indexes to a .7% gain. The Dow Industrial Index has declined an additional 7.8% in the past two weeks. Carbon credits fell nearly 2% in early trading...*

She raised the volume as the talk show began.

"Good Monday morning to you all, the day after one of the worst Northeaster's to hit the Empire City area in many years and three weeks into the storm that has unsettled world markets. I'm Dan Prescott. Welcome to The Empire Financial Roundtable. Joining me this morning from Los Angeles is Nathan Keenespan, former Treasury Secretary under the Kagan Administration, and now senior fellow at the Freedom Institute, a Washington think tank. Nat, welcome back. Good to see you again."

"Always a pleasure, Dan."

"From the University of Virginia, we have Professor Noel Vromsky, author of the prophetic best seller 'Free Market Free Fall.'"

"And joining us live in our Empire City studio is none other than the world's wealthiest man, investor par excellence, Avery Wellingham, President and Chairman of Wellingham Enterprises, the Illuminati International Bank, Green Con, Lebensraum Financial, and Chairman of the Board of Empire City Corporation. I hope you'll forgive me if I've left a few things out."

"Quite alright," the Old Man said. I flushed with anger at the sight and sound of him.

At the bottom of the screen the scrolling news text read:

> *Unemployment rose a point to 10.9% according to the weekly Dept. of Labor report, inflated by job losses in the financial sector...*

"Thank you, sir, for coming back to the show."

"Water under the bridge," the Old Man said, trying to appear pleasant. "It looks like your producers have finally got their act together. What was it you wanted to ask me?"

"Where are you right now, in cash or what sectors are you looking at?"

"I was in cash, as it happened, before the recent turmoil. I am not in cash at the moment."

"He's lying," Sa commented without rancor. "He was short."

"We saw credit default vehicles melt down last week, along with their derivatives, joining in the general rout. Do you expect a rebound?"

"I do. And across the board. What isn't in is ready to go in. I'm not going to be more specific than that."

The scroll across the bottom read:

Washington Standard became the sixth investment bank to fail in the wake of credit contractions in technology and finance. It will be taken over by private equity giant Resource International, a subsidiary of the Illuminati International Bank, for an undisclosed amount. The deal was brokered by the Treasury Department in the latest government effort to stem the tide of bank failures...

"And recession?" the show's host pressed Wellingham.

"We're in for a mini-recession, not a bad one, and I believe it will be short-lived. A few dominos have yet to fall in stocks, but not many."

"Do you agree with the government taking partnership interests to bail out the too big to fail?"

"Where's that camera girl who used to be here?" asked the Old Man with no concern for the propriety or relevance of the question, a tick of his to remind underlings of his unassailable lack of obligation to them. Sa and I exchanged a glance.

"We've had a few layoffs ourselves in recent weeks," the host explained awkwardly.

"Sorry to hear that," replied the Old Man with pointed insincerity.

"Now to Nat Keenespan, former Treasury Secretary and acclaimed financial author. Do you see a bottom forming?"

"The dollar is benefitting from this downturn, which will provide counterweight to any recession. The downturn is deep but narrowly confined, and I also believe it will be short-lived. The circuit breaker in credit markets is a natural defensive reaction and will pass once the corner is turned."

Shares of Solar Wind (SWI) drop 23% on news of Congressman Green's indictment for bribery over turbine acreage in West Texas. SWI was a heavy contributor to the TX Republican's re-election with high stakes in the acreage...

"Now to Professor of Economics at Virginia U and noted author, Noel Vromsky. What do you think will get us to that corner?"

"A steady stream of pundits on commercial media oozing confidence back into a terrified market."

"Well, professor, there was never anything proven against the Total Security Theorem. There still has never been a breach. The failures were vendor implementation."

"That's all it took to spook the derivatives market and expose the institutional domination of financial markets for what it is, a confidence game. The TST sideshow only serves to draw the curtain open on new rounds of laissez faire recklessness and gaming in abstract financial instruments. If I may, I've heard more than one insider suggest Mr. Wellingham was not in cash but shorted the market just in time."

"Who is this guy?" Wellingham butted in.

We shared a grin as the Old Man's nastiness emerged on-air.

"Mr. Secretary, can you suggest how long this market turn might last?" the host asked.

"I must agree that the subject is not Mr. Wellingham's anticipations three weeks ago but his actions now. And my projection is that the financial sector may remain crippled for some time, but the larger market will show greater resilience. I expect we'll see the first foray up from here by summer's end, some six to seven months from now."

"Mr. Wellingham, six to seven?"

"Less. We'll see the first bounce in an early summer rally."

"The Total Security Theorem scare will hang over markets as long as TST is a private club run by the most powerful corporations," inserted the Professor.

POTUS Wong, suffering a further setback in Wallup polls, announced a State Department trip to Beijing, China later this month in ongoing efforts to shore up US Treasuries...

"Did you have a comment, Mr. Secretary?"

"Academic socialism always takes the pessimistic view."

...and avert global recession in the wake of market turmoil and mounting liquidity pressures. The meeting paves the way for the April G20 session of financial leaders...

"Last word to you Mr. Wellingham, before our station break."

"Pessimism, hogwash. That's the disinformation of a communist traitor. I know people at Virginia U, professor."

"Sir, if I were a communist, it would be my democratic right to such beliefs. There is no capitalist duopoly ordained in the United States Constitution."

"We'll be back after this word from our sponsor."

"I may have a job for this fearless professor," Sa noted, smiling.

The psy-mercial took over the device, the tiny screen displaying a montage of symbolic images invoking financial security, order, strength, growth, and innovation as a series of carefully modulated voices intoned these words, all to the greater glory of Empire City. It was a seductive relief from just about anything, including Empire City.

The news scrolled on:

Venezuela has been placed on the list of countries whose residents require additional airline passenger pre-screening as part of a policy to pressure and isolate President Morales...

"I can't watch Wellingham without burning up," I said. She stroked my left forefinger with her hand.

"Come on. What are we doing up here?" I pleaded like a little boy.

"Oooh," she moaned softly as if in a faint, then stumbled backward toward the precipice, one arm groping the air, the other across her body. My heart seized up, then beat again as she swung a leg around and let herself fall on her rump facing outward to the north, hugging her knees in a ball at the very edge. She grimaced and was trembling.

A boom, muffled in the wind, came to us from the northwest long after an eruption of orange flame drew our eyes to the distant GW Bridge. The ball tapered away, leaving a small fire near the Jersey side, smoke trailing silently eastward on the breeze toward the City.

A small plane emerged from the superstructure, a white blur flying close to the car traffic, and disappeared from view on the north side. Neither of us spoke.

The plane re-emerged only to vanish again from our view as a yellow light streaked westward toward it, exploding on the bridge superstructure in an orange ball like the first. The plane emerged from under the bridge at the Island end and made its way low along the West Side Highway, flying just yards above the car traffic.

"What just happened?" I blurted out.

"What we are here to see."

"It's an attack?"

"I'm sure of it."

She rose from her huddle, and stepped awkwardly to the Puck. She poked out a text message. "Execute E-3, D-1, F-3."

"You're taking a stake?" I was surprised.

"For a future without this kind of hatred, damn us all."

The air began to fill with the sound of helicopters, as if a swarm of locusts had arisen from the ground. Attack helicopters converged toward the west while passenger machines dispersed in every other direction.

"I don't believe it."

The plane looked like a World War I relic with its double set of wings, one stacked above the other as it emerged in plain view, its escort of helicopters slowly banking southward in pursuit. The biplane swung onto Canal Street along the south side of the Archway Towers we had traversed not an hour before. It seemed to crawl across the air, turning north along Broadway.

Breaking News ran across the screen, followed by Koki Madeira, the network's well known Chinese-Hispanic anchor.

"CEO Boomberg has announced that a drill of the Empire City Defense System is taking place this morning that will involve helicopter tactics for a simulated small plane attack. Residents are requested to proceed to the nearest subway station or building lobby until the exercise is concluded. The maneuvers are the first of their kind since the Emergency Preparedness Initiative began two years ago, and one of the many ongoing security operations on behalf of Empire City."

"It's a drill."

"They're trying to head off panic," she said.

"How can you be sure?"

"The City fired their defensive missiles and missed." She searched the Net for Empire City attack.

The device produced over a million results from every conceivable source, but a handful at the top glared out at us:

Alt Media blanketed with terrorist statement...

> *Pilot declares he is carrying vapor enhanced Sarin nerve gas, radioactive dust, and anthrax in dispersal containers that will detonate if punctured or the dead man switch in his hand is released...*

Terror Pilot issues Death Threat to Empire City...

Mystery plane identified by eyewitness as a Laser 370, a modern, two seat propeller driven biplane designed for high performance air circus aerobatics. Limited cargo space makes terror claims unlikely...

New Jersey pilot found dead in hanger moments after an irregular take-off from Teterboro Airport and failure to respond to tower...

Terror flight evades Empire City's Auto Response Defenses in high speed dash over car rooftops on the GW Bridge...

Fire drill? Authorities try to head off panic while assessing threat...

Serial numbers indicate attack craft registered to Douglas Parrel of Elizabeth, New Jersey. Family report him missing since Saturday...

Rogue aircraft at large on Manhattan's West Side...

Sa commanded the Puck to refresh. The screen renewed its results and the alarms quintupled.

I looked around. The couple had gone. We were alone on the observatory.

"Let's get out of here! Before it's too late!" I shouted aloud in the mounting din of rotor engines from the Lower West Side Heliport.

"We're safer above than below if the pilot is going to disperse poisons."

"I'll bet the Old Man is already on one of those choppers out of here."

"Bear with me," she said.

The deadly white bird had banked and was now plainly visible travelling lazily uptown in the canyon of Fifth Avenue, an escort of angry insects on all sides. The surge in civilian flights had dwindled as suddenly as they appeared, but the air was soon shaking with the staccato of police and military helicopters arriving from every direction to hover at intervals the width and length of the Island and beyond. In the avenues, pedestrians stood still, nearly everyone with a handheld in front of their face or against their ear, the plastic glinting where the morning sun penetrated. Below us traffic began to snarl as those in the know sought escape and those who didn't obstructed their progress. Accidents proliferated up and down the avenues, and a crescendo of honking from below joined the racket of machinery in the air.

In minutes the City had become utterly surreal. Or did I lack credentials to call anything surreal, given the little woman standing before me on the ledge of a world gone mad? She peered out below the shade of her hand, unruffled at the fantastical present, it seemed, and intent on its dim future.

To me it was as if a Sopwith Camel had materialized to challenge all modernity, though the double-winged ancestry of the invading plane belied its powerful engine and air circus design. Midtown, at what I guessed would be 57th Street, the aircraft lowered its right wing and vanished around the corner, emerging a moment later in a steep bank that swung the craft onto Sixth Avenue. It was heading downtown directly toward us. As it roared above the street at fourth floor level, pedestrians surged back against the walls or fell prostrate on the sidewalk.

Police and ambulance sirens joined the melee of sound as first responders attempted to secure subway stations amid the pan-

icked pedestrians and those who had abandoned vehicles to immobile snarls of bewildered traffic.

The plane accelerated through Chelsea and flipped on its side to
squeeze between two of the New Houston Street Towers, leveled
out over the Noho rooftops, veered again eastward, and dipped
back down into the Broadway canyon out of sight.

"What the hell is he doing?!" I yelled.

"Playing with them," she called back over the racket of helicopters.

She was standing upright, her legs firmly planted and arms folded across her bosom. The adrenalin seemed to be catching up
with her too.

"Playing?!"

"If he wanted to detonate or if they wanted him down, he'd be
dead already."

"Then what does he want?!"

"To force them to explode his poisons."

She refreshed the search adding "terrorist statement" to the key
words.

"You think he really has them?!"

"Look!"

The plane slipped in and out of sight as it porpoised high and
low above Broadway until directly across from us. As it rushed
past, we could see the pilot plainly for a moment along with an
odd silver shape strapped in the rear cockpit. The engine revved
angrily as the plane accelerated, dropping down to disappear
and then re-emerge beyond Wall Street climbing steeply, almost
vertically. The plane began a loop just above the level of the
buildings that made the canyon wall.

A police chopper above the plane was surprised by the maneuver and veered desperately to the west to avoid a collision. The helicopter nearest to it veered away but not quickly enough and the two collided in an explosion of flaming wreckage that dropped against a building and spilled noisily down its side, vanishing from our view to the street below. Sounds of the wreckage on the ground reached our ears a second later, our eyes already back on the plane as it rotated to fly right side up in the opposite direction, uptown along Broadway.

"Jesus Christ!" was all I could say at the simultaneous stunt and disaster that came and went in a matter of seconds.

All across the City, rooftops were filling with spectators, film crews mounting cameras, and police and military deploying an array of surveillance devices and laser pulse weapons.

The plane dropped low again into the canyon, heading along the diagonal path Broadway cut across the grid of City streets, coming into view intermittently as it went.

> *Pilot identifies himself as 'falcon of Allah' in a live broadcast to 37 alternate media organizations in an unprecedented open communique. Terrorist claims to be fourth generation Al Qaeda...*

Sa followed the link to an illegal Netcast in progress from an apartment that could have been anywhere in the City. A young man, whose composure had long frayed, spoke in a wavering voice, his eyes nervous and wet.

"Two of the pursuit helicopters collided seconds ago near Wall Street. No possibility of survivors among the crew. According to the search I've just run, there would normally be a complement of four service personnel on each T-64 attack helicopter. There is still no word from the City since they announced exercises twenty minutes ago. We return to our replay of the audio statement from the 'Soldier of Shari'ah,' as this flying dead man calls himself. Stay with me for feeds as they come in."

The terror message was calm and chilling in certitude, the sound of his engine and the rush of air audible in the speaker of the Puck.

"By now you are wondering why your money lords have not shot me down," came a hard, insolent voice thick with accent. "It is because I carry dispersal weapons that cannot fail to detonate if I am killed. Americans are going to die, and your technology cannot stop this chastisement. Your deaths today are blood on the hands of the evil ones you have elected. *La ilaha illallah, Muhammadun Rasul Allah*. I am privileged to deliver this message to you in martyr's blood.

"Your leaders deceive you. We are here to open your eyes. Your military aggressions and crusades of culture in the nations of Islam are revisited on you. We bring you another taste of your imperial wars.

"Your economy of *riba* and filth is reviled in Islam. Your greed is as the wolf, your consumption as the pig, and your culture a plague of locusts on the children of Allah. Shari'ah is our law, and we gather for the good of his children, their wellbeing, all wealth is in trust for the children of Allah.

"You invade our countries, and now we invoke ancestral jihad and invade yours. You corrupt and empower governments that oppress us, and now we make you impotent. You infiltrate our economies, and now yours shall fall. You poison us, and now we poison you. Smite me with all your weapons that I may have Allah's reward."

The young Netcaster returned. "We have some background for this statement from Dr. Hamad Sharif, a neighbor of mine. Doctor?" An elderly Muslim appeared in casual clothes.

"It is central to Islamic economic philosophy that capital be used for the good of the community, that it be invested in the first place for the common wellbeing. The owner of wealth is a custodian of the value it represents on behalf of the people, not its

dictator. Interest on loans is forbidden as usury. Fundamental-
ism is at war with Western capitalism from a social as well as a
religious premise, which for them is inseparable..."

The weak unsanctioned signal was overwhelmed by the City
Emergency Broadcast, its symbol taking over the Puck monitor
at the same moment Sahar keeled over again, dropping to her
knees on the ledge as if smitten. She lowered herself onto her
haunches, drew her arms to her chest, and bowed forward as if a
supplicant in prayer.

My rage was cancelled by helplessness, dwarfed by the mad thun-
dering of helicopters hovering around us at eye level all around
the Freedom Tower spire. It occurred to me that anyone in those
helicopters could make her out with a pair of binoculars. They
could certainly see me as plainly as I saw them as they hovered
some few hundred yards out in the churning air manning their
guns. I assumed they mistook me for someone who belonged in
that privileged place at this moment in time. Or perhaps, in the
event, no one gave my presence there a second thought.

Watching the helicopters was disorienting, and I leaned to the
wall, cupping my arms around Sa in protective concealment
while searching for the plane far uptown. If true to form, he
would head down again, choosing his avenue by the largest
crowds, as many people rushing out of buildings as were mass-
ing outside to get into them. Subway entrances were queued for
blocks. A pandemonium of mixed messages and conflicting survival mechanisms reigned.

"People of Empire City," a voice message began from CEO
Boomberg, the nominal mayor.

"Authorities are assessing the threat. The cargo capacity of the
hijacked plane is extremely limited, and the circumstances of its
seizure suggest there was no opportunity to equip the craft with
weapons of any kind. As a precaution, we are asking the people
of Empire City to stay indoors or to get indoors if not there now,

whether into a building or subway tunnel. Local train service is halted and Empire City Police and first responders are in place to assist you with shelter in the tunnels. Express trains will conduct what emergency evacuations are required for medical reasons only.

"If you are in a vehicle, stay in it. Do not wait in lines at subway or building entrances. Police have been dispatched to regulate movement throughout the City. Seek immediate shelter in-doors but do not stand to wait in long lines outside, seek alternate shelter where you can find it. All building security personnel city-wide are required to open their lobbies to the public and building maintenance personnel must immediately engage chemical attack filters in their ventilation systems. Please keep order. Together we will get through this."

On the streets below countless heads were bowed to their handhelds as the sonorous voice pronounced his appeal with grave paternal authority. The moment he finished pedestrians began hastening in every direction, like a film in fast forward. Car traffic awakened with new urgency, collisions compounding the hullabaloo of belligerent horns.

No matter who knew what specifically, the whole City knew something was deathly wrong and no place was safer than another. Fear and outrage cycled in me in turn.

The deadly showman arose above the buildings and angled east over midtown. He appeared again heading back downtown along still-crowded Fifth Avenue. Instead of running at its approach, astonishingly, people surged as it passed, hurling a scarcely human sound at the low flying plane along with every manner of thing that might be tossed in frustration at it. No matter the improbability of reaching the bird, shoes were being yanked and flung in symbolic fury. Taking a cue from the block uptown, a chain reaction of animal rage roared down Fifth Avenue with the plane. The white monster clung to their fury as if buoyed by it, accelerating but rising not an inch.

Sa turned to face me, her arms still clasped over her knees. I leaned my ear in toward her.

"I know what he will do," she said calmly. "Look over there, to Brooklyn." I followed her extended arm and gaze, shrouding the sun from my eyes as she did.

The far shore of the East River in Brooklyn was a living organism. Throngs exiting subways, monorails, buses, occupants of every business, residence and means of transportation were massed along the streets, parks, malls, and depots north and south of the Brooklyn Bridge. Those already on the river shoreline were trapped by mounting walls of spectators and first responders behind and on all sides, the tableau of a besieged Empire City before them.

A curious tinkling sound wafted up from below us and seemed to reverberate in a muffled echo from the far shore, where countless thousands of handhelds rang, buzzed, chimed, and played a faint cacophony, glinting en masse in the March sunshine as individual Emergency Broadcast calls rippled through the devices.

"The City can't decide where to shoot down the plane. The pilot is waiting them out. When he sees the size of that crowd, he'll go for it."

The plane passed through the Canal Street Towers and banked violently east over to Broadway again, diving into its canyon. Helicopters along its path began to rise in unison as if clearing the way south and east. The plane emerged into view at City Hall Gardens where it veered sharply east toward the Brooklyn Bridge. Gathering speed as it traversed the bridge access road lined with captive cars, the plane then shot upward at full throttle above the Bridge's first tower to an apogee, only to drop straight down over it in a deliberate stall. The plane climbed briefly again, and dove, climbed and dove toward the second tower, like a porpoise at play. It moved away from us toward the teeming shore, an armada of faster helicopters already over and around it on all sides.

The plane climbed again and kept going up as it passed midway and approached the second bridge tower. Two thin plumes of smoke trailed in the blue toward the receding plane at the apex of its near vertical climb, where it stalled and dropped nose down, the missiles passing where it had stood in the air a split second ago. A sound arose from the Brooklyn shore, the inhuman roar of human terror as it wafted on the breeze.

In a full-throttle dive at the far shore, the pilot forced their hand. A trail of tracers streaked from multiple gunships and intersected his path. A faint beat like a distant snare drum followed in the slow air. The plane became a blackened orange flame in a silent instant, wreckage falling through the glowering shroud of smoke. A muted boom followed belatedly.

An ominous smoke cloud mushroomed outward in a ball and overtook the fire within it, holding a dense round form as the current of air carried the death it bore eastward across the water. It moved as a sphere in an agony of slowness slowly lowering and expanding, obscuring a patch of the Brooklyn shore.

"Let's go, Ken," she called out, but I was riveted to the scene and could not budge. "They'll be resuming VIP flights. The heliport is nearby." I saw her sullenly through wet eyes. "I have to get back," she insisted.

I turned again to watch the killing mist.

"The wind has shifted," she stated as a matter of fact without looking back toward the imperiled shore.

I faced her then, finding her eyes, clear and dry, her expression alert and calculating.

"I brought you here to witness with me the sweep of the world in the naked glare of day. And so we have. Our murders revisit our shores in clouds of hate. Whether by omission or by commission, we are none of us innocent.

"We must leave now." She tugged at my sleeve. "You are a target for the authorities up here alone. There is nothing more to see. It's over."

With that, she leapt to my jacket lapel and clutching it, swung herself inside and back into my vest pocket as deftly as if born to it. "Go," she said.

I was in a new dimension of real altogether. My head seemed to be exploding with reality. It seemed I stretched beyond my skin and, looking out to the river, filled the vast space within my vision. There was no mistaking this kind of real.

I could feel the wind coming around from the east. The death cloud was indeed breaking up. It was being blown back, losing form, until it stretched in a long trail of mist toward the northwest low to the water. I could see the far side clearly. Adrenalin began to slip away as I beheld the feckless miracle of wind. I was weak with relief and wonder.

"It's over, Ken," she said again, holding the lapel open.

"Keep your Puck on speaker and tuned to Empire City news," she said. I had to tear my eyes from the dissipating cloud to look at her. "Give it to security if they ask for it. Have your ticket and ID in your other hand. Be yourself, a shocked City denizen," she advised as I hoisted my pack to one shoulder and crossed over to the terrace door with an inflamed idea of the possible, of this creature and her mind, of this terror and a fickle wind.

Puck in hand tuned to the official news, I could no more account for her timing of this visit than for fate itself. The elevator was quick in coming, and its doors silently opened on two armed security guards. They looked at the talking Puck, then each other, then back at me.

"Have you heard? The wind changed. It's dissipating," I volunteered, holding up the news on my Puck. "It's a miracle. The gas cloud is dispersing in the wind," came a voice through the tiny speakers as if on cue.

They looked at each other. "Okay," one said, and that was all. I stepped into the elevator, conscious only of the lump resting against my thumping heartbeat.

They escorted me down to the counter where I'd entered.

"Your ID?" The crew-cut requested when we got there.

I was handing it over to the agent, or guard, or whatever he was, when it was snatched, scanned, and handed back to me with unconcealed hostility.

"Take him to the mob scene in the lobby," said the one who had not yet spoken. His tone was nearly civil but meant hurry up, get rid of me.

I followed him to the mezzanine door, which he opened for me. Before me lay every emotion in a communal din, a bedlam of shouting, weeping, and cheering. A throng filled every visible nook, in every stage of vocalization, from sullen silence and open weeping to commands yelled through bullhorns. All exit from the mezzanine was choked, and no one in the vexed and nearly immobile crowd wanted to be there another moment. There was a mass edging movement in the direction of the exits but little more.

"Chit him a grand for another way out," came her whispered voice from my jacket.

"You say something?" inquired the guard.

"A thousand for another way out?" was out of my mouth before I had a thought.

The guard glowered for a moment. "Wait here," he said and discussed the matter with his partner in arms. He held up three fingers with a grin.

"That's outrageous," I said, ever the thrifty New Englander. A pinch to my nipple reminded me of her will and I informed the older suit with a wave of my chit card. He showed me his. "Once we're out," I stipulated.

He extended his arm to invite me back the way we came. From there he walked me through a series of doors and corridors, and finally we took a flight of stairs that led outside through a service door. We were facing Vesey Street, and I chit him the money, thinking it was a bargain after all. Up the block, Broadway was now mobbed, but the side street here was nearly empty.

"There's a walkway bridge over the highway around the corner south of us," I informed Sa, walking briskly, just short of a jog. There were a few runners to be seen, but most now were trudging, Puck in hand, resigned to walking the Island to get home or to an interminable wait at crowded stations to return to their Borough.

The walkway was thronged but moving. Outside I could see the length of the West Side Highway stretching away to the north. Those who had abandoned their cars were coming back from all points as efforts to undo miles of gridlock began. Banality returned as communal shock gave way to discreet weariness, re-crimination, resentment, and sorrow.

We found the heliport entrance and made our way in through small groups assembled at the news walls. As we approached the confirmation counter a common cheer went up as first the news and then the PA system announced the ban on flights was lifted.

Crowds remained in front of the news walls, which were reporting that contamination was contained to the East River while evacuation operations were proceeding smoothly and no reports so far of fatalities from the cloud. Dead were the eight servicemen in the helicopters, and twelve deaths were attributed to stampeding. Three people succumbed to heart attacks, and there were two homicides in road rage incidents. The range of injuries needing medical attention numbered in the thousands.

"I have a VIP reservation in your name," Sa said from the shadow of my lapel. "Just show your City ID."

Passengers began to queue. At my turn I learned the price of the ticket I had in my name had been jacked up to twenty times usual, down from thirty times usual. They were honoring reservations and gouging us blind. No one refused to pay.

"That stunt, climbing up, stopping in the air, dropping like a stone. You used that with the Old Man."

"Climbing stall, vertical dive," she said in a low voice. "It is a risky evasive maneuver when someone is taking aim at you. You give them the shot in the stall, but then drop like a stone out of the zone of fire. But to time it so well against guided rockets, no, that was dumb luck or a trick of Allah."

"They'll catch hell for not taking him out over the City," I said.

"There will be heat enough to go around. I'll rest in your satchel during the trip. This alters my thinking. All of my canvasses must be retouched in this light. I will meditate. We will be in Albany in an hour and have privacy in the limo to Blackhead. Rest yourself until then."

I presented the backpack and she dropped into her favored pocket. I came to the boarding gate, consented to the extortion rate, and was cordially welcomed aboard, a very important person.

I had never flown in a helicopter. It was cramped for all the faded trappings of luxury. The engine whined overhead, prop whooping, and I feared I would be sick. I refused the flight assistant's suggestion I secure my backpack in the overhead compartment and kept my precious cargo on the floor cradled between my legs.

The window seat beside me was occupied by a stout man in his fifties with a shock of white hair and a pin-striped suit, shirt open at the collar, his tie removed and half stuffed in a pocket. He breathed heavily and was sweating through his jacket armpits. He was drunk. A patch of grey dust on his shoulder and a smudge of soot on his face made him look like he'd been mugged. We had all been mugged, I thought, over and over again.

Across the aisle from me sat an attractive middle-aged woman in a black pantsuit, data case on her lap, listening with earphones to her Puck and staring intently at its screen, where spokesmen and women reveled in the morning's madness. No one in the cabin spoke above a whisper, and few whispers reached my ear as I eased the seat back modestly and allowed my back to meld into it. It was barely eleven o'clock. What worse can a day have in store?

Phantasm had become fact, I thought, as the machinery rose from the earth and set off above the Hudson in a surge of air. The West Side Highway remained a calamity of cars, though passengers were mostly standing outside their vehicles in the general relief. The GW Bridge was charred where the missiles had struck. Military and police choppers stood ominous sentinel all over the Island. I was Sa's enchanted hostage but with no regrets, relieved without reservation to get out.

She was so deft in the ways of the world; yet I thought how bitterly alone she must be in her small steps, unable to stride among us, challenged by all creation, hardened from overcoming. I could do nothing for her. She seemed to me far more miracle than the rest of us, no matter what she said.

We were heading back toward another in my store of baleful memories, I remembered. At least I'd be spared the estate and any encounter with the Old Man himself. Her father would meet us in town to pick her up. Someday I'd spit in the Old Man's eye, I imagined with no strength left for rancor.

Exhausted in the adrenal meltdown, I finally dozed.

~

I fairly jogged through the small Albany terminal and out its front door, glad to be free of confinement and other people. It was as brazenly sunny a winter day as the day's events were dark. It was sharply colder here though, and I clutched at my lapel as the wind picked up. A middle-aged brown-skinned man approached with a sign bearing my name.

"You are taking me to Blackhead?"

"Yes, at your service, sir. Do you have no other baggage?" he said with an East Indian accent, offering to take the pack.

"No. I'll keep this with me."

He opened the door to the stretch limousine and I leaned inside, placing the bag securely on the floor, before sliding in after it. The door closed solidly behind me. Once on our way, I moved up the luxuriously large compartment to the partition.

"There's a nice tip in this for you if you get us there for 2:00 PM, and I'll need privacy to work on some recordings and notes. You know the way?"

"Oh, yes, sir. It is maybe one third of our service is to Blackhead," he said in his sing-song accent.

"Figures. Let me know ten minutes before we get there. It's about an hour?"

"Maybe longer by fifteen minutes," he said, "but we will make it by 2:00. Please enjoy the ride."

"Thank you."

"I shall close the partition for you. You will have complete privacy."

"Yes, please."

"The switch to open the partition, if you need it, is just below your elbow."

I nodded thanks and turned to face the rear. The interior darkened as the shaded partition slid silently shut, and the cabin lit up warmly with a series of small lights, the dim interspersed by sunlight shining through breaks in the side window curtains. Soft upholstered seating surrounded the cabin on three sides, and one long side held a bar, a refrigerator, a small sink and mirror, and a Netbox with swivel-mounted screen. A bouquet of fresh flowers imparted its scent.

When my eyes grew accustomed I saw her standing on the far rear seat beside the bag, and I slid over to her. We regarded each other gently.

Finally she said, "Thank you, Ken."

She stretched. "For me, a productive meditation," she said. "How about you?"

"I'm okay, considering. Got a few winks of shuteye anyway."

"We have to cover some ground between us in this time. There is a table here. Is that it?" she said, pointing.

A table, ingeniously hidden, slid out of the bar. I negotiated its extension, making sure it was solid.

"Let's try something," she said, smiling with a wisp of playfulness.

I want you to hold out your palm right there. I'm going to step onto it. Let's see if you can convey me to the table without making me lose my balance.

"Okay, I'm game," I said, holding out a stiff hand, which she stepped onto and looked up at me.

"Slowly now," she said, and I did as she bade, transporting her in slow motion with rigid hand and arm to the table level, where she stepped off solemnly.

"Thank you," she said. "I rather enjoyed that."

"Anytime."

"I may hold you to it," she said. "Do you want to talk about what happened?"

"No, let's talk business," I said, hoping to ward off the involuntary replay of the scene in my head.

"Very well, then. I mentioned my priority is micro tech. You'll need to pull a team together for miniaturization of all standard electronic communication devices. Our first order of business is to get a Puck at least down to the size of a backpack for me, with full functionality. The list of things I need in micro is long. We'll need to develop a research team. You can call it a secret contract under deadline, or whatever it takes to expedite. I expect you to start due diligence while you're resting up."

"Resting up?"

"I believe President Wong will be in holding pattern until he hears from Old Man Wellingham and his gang of thieves. I'm sending you on a working vacation. How do the British Virgin Islands sound?"

"Great. Why there?"

"I want you to finalize our offshore holding company. I've made preliminary arrangements for a segregated portfolio investment corporation. There's an account waiting, and a corporate brief. Just contact the financial services center in Road Town on Tortola. They'll be expecting you. This holding company is to be above board and transparent, but owned by Krypt Corporation, a dummy through which ultimate ownership is nicely lost in a circle of corporate legerdemain. In the name John Salt, on behalf of Krypt, you will appoint yourself, Ken Loehner, sole officer and CEO."

"John Salt?"

"You will have a chit card in this name, which you are to use for all living and business expenses. As a matter of discretion, you will have to be two people for a brief while, a corporate fiction when you are spending money traceably and then yourself when setting up the company once you are in charge. As far as the world is concerned, you have been hired to run a legitimate business. Corporate law will insulate us both.

"I have much work to do for the Old Man's board meeting in two weeks. I have bugs on order from a boutique in London, and I must make up for lost time planting them. These meetings are nothing if not a ceremony of secrets and a treasure of discovery."

"Last night I wanted to know what you're up to," I said. "Now I think you're right: I don't have to know. Let's talk compensation."

"The situation changed today, Ken. You will return to the moneymaking side of operations, but for a while at least I need you to act as my dedicated agent, a stitch in time among the Big."

I was about to protest yet again her changing of the terms but again she overrode me.

"A deathly stake was let loose in the world today. I would rather not see America inciting further attacks with the opportunism we pursue in the wake of this one. I'm afraid America will punch itself in the face with another war abroad, this time directly in the Pakistani territories."

"So what? We've been knocking around there on and off since who-knows-when."

"Wellingham will have his eyes on prospective war profits and mineral claims. Talk will be plentiful at the manor. I need a man in the Big world to act upon what I learn."

My face must have shown my discomfiture.

"There is no way to connect you with me unless it comes from your own mouth," she reminded me. "I don't technically exist."

I demurred without speaking, and she studied my face. "Do you feel guilty knowing what I am about?"

"No. I don't think anyone would take you seriously if you told them you were out to pull the plug on capitalism," I managed to say in earnest. "And no one would take me seriously if I told them my boss was all of nine inches tall and prowling the Wellingham Estate with imported bugs. I don't feel guilty; that's the problem. The Old Man is a warmonger, and though I am personally indifferent to Pakistan, I see your point about meddling there, and making another mess.

"And you're my big break," I finally stated, blushing with the honesty of my admission. "Besides, it's not like you're going to start knocking them off one by one."

I said this facetiously and she answered alike. "I make no promises for a future I cannot foresee."

But I had other concerns, like my own skin, that needed plain saying.

"Even if they never catch you, and I never talk, I might still be traced to you. If they can't prove what they believe, I'll just get renditioned off to never-was or meet with a fatal accident."

"You exaggerate, and I remind you it is still dangerous to cross the street. Our communications will be effectively untraceable. My technology is tailored to defeat the Old Man's surveillance, which I know intimately, and I can turn his systems against him at will."

"Nothing is foolproof."

"Then you understand the risk of the endeavor, unlike the myriad other possible dangers that may blind-side us at any moment. I should think you've seen enough of those recently. Today alone..." She shrugged.

I was long past going back to nabob-Neil and hell-face-Hetty, if they would even have me, much less going back to pound the pavement to restart my life apart from this little jewel. She wanted me in the know and a co-conspirator. I had to eat the risks.

"Three million," I said. "For three months, and then we renegotiate."

"Very well, then. Three million for three months. But the timespan will not be consecutive. Only days you are put at special risk will count, and I can't anticipate what or when or how I may need you."

"You'll pay me by the day?" I asked, figuring I might not live to spend it otherwise.

"If you prefer."

"And this is on top of salary, right?"

"Yes. I'll start you at a quarter mil base and one percent of profits."

"One?"

"One percent of a billion is ten million. With patents I have in development I expect to see tens of billions annually long before you have a single gray hair."

I mulled the numbers. "Okay then. It looks like capitalism has met its match."

"Care to make a wager," she intoned seductively, "as long as you're gambling?"

"Wager what?"

"Before the year is out, you will prefer to lose this wager and work for me of your own conscience, without any pay, rather than leave my cause. Say, a hundred large? You can afford to lose that."

"Not a chance," I said. "I don't roll dice with oracles." I felt I'd won a prize to see her smile. "But I don't know any politics worth going to jail for," I said forthrightly.

"It would take years to unravel my funding sources, if it can be done at all," she assured. "The greater part of my undertakings will be legal and aboveboard anyway. In due course, we'll have you in the news as a business leader, which will be useful to us and further serve to protect you," she went on. "We'll work on getting you into high society, with some well-placed media attention to start. You'll become a tuxedo socialite beyond reproach or suspicion."

"Sounds bearable." I laughed, genuinely flattered.

"There are tens of thousands, hundreds of thousands, sometimes millions of lives blighted in each Mil-Con war," she added thinking out loud, "American lives as well as lives native to the lands we subvert and conquer. I am sorry to spring a trial by fire on you this way. And I would rather this were not happening on the heels of your recovery. But who can say? It may be just as well for us as we shall each have proof of the other's mettle.

"You will need healing time yet, and I prescribe work and leisure in new surroundings. Set up our umbrella as described in the brief, find us our first acquisitions, and be generous to yourself while you are there. With a few installations to your Puck, and each Netbox you use, we can meet securely whenever needed, day or night."

"There's no such thing as secure."

"We will be speaking via random IPs double blind, at the server and local end. The John Salt identity is a necessary fiction for this transaction, and later not being tracked by your chits may prove useful. You will need to lose some of your respect for law to find respect for justice."

I wondered how much.

"It is hard for me to be sympathetic," she explained. "I have slight regard for your law. It was, I believe, the father of scientific method who said, 'When plunder becomes a way of life for a group of men living together in society, they create for themselves in the course of time a legal system that authorizes it and a moral code that glorifies it.'

"Capitalist law, like its charity," she continued, "regulates the symptom to authorize the disease, so its law must be broken for justice's sake. If not sooner, then later."

"Okay, okay," I capitulated. I was no cherry to feeling above the law. I was just scared.

"The day will come when I will have thousands of agents trained and ready for greater risks than I shall ever ask of you. There is no one else at hand who can do this now, however. Can I count on you?"

"That depends on what these special services turn out to be," I said. "I can't say, carte blanche."

"You may refuse an assignment if you wish, but rest assured I will not allow a risk to you that I can assume or prevent. I think you well know how corporate law and the naked power of wealth will insulate you. I repeat, you cannot be connected to me or my doings except by your own admission. You need only keep our secret."

"I can watch my mouth well enough."

"Time is all I've bargained for. Do you imagine the Old Man and his ilk interrupt their thinking with the illegality of anything they want to do?"

So the ends justify the means, I wondered in resignation, but she seemed to reach inside and pluck the thought out.

"Why do the Big dawdle over linguistic sophistries of the human condition?" she fairly wailed. "Language is of necessity selective and selectively fragments the truth. It takes poetry and storytelling to make truth whole. We had better a discourse of poetry than such contentious fractions as ends and means and their justifications. Mine is a good and just fight is all. My means are moral intuition."

"I wouldn't mind a whack at the bastard, I'll grant you that," I said, intending the Old Man. Silence ensued.

What we had lived through just hours ago bound us like kin, I thought. I was still vibrating in its aftershocks, giddy with life for surviving its tribulation. And she was asking me to risk jail, at least, for a pile of loot, all of her good arguments notwithstanding.

"If I end up in jail as an accomplice of 'person unknown,' are you going to break me out?" I said with a straight face.

She wasn't sure if I was joking, but I knew with these facetious words there was no turning back for me. She finally smiled.

"Cross my heart and hope to die," she added playfully. "I will look after you as my own self and soul, I promise you. Do you promise to look after me? I want this to be the true essence of our pact."

"Yes," I said, nodding. Every minute with her seemed to empower me. I am in love with the boss, I thought. But then, looking her over, I underwent the same hot spell of grossness and shame as when we'd first met, feeling my hugeness compared to her, my bestiality, my every breath and gesture a storm of air, thick, slow, clumsy, odorous; while she seemed to have the natural elegance and frailty of a butterfly.

"Pedro knows how you feel," she said studying me. "To myself, I am slow and clumsy."

Though it made me wince, I was getting used to her seeming to peek inside my head.

"You will spend the night at the monastery in Vermont with your brother?" she inquired.

I nodded. "Open invitation. I'll ring him on the way over."

"Good. I should have Tortola arrangements and a compensation escrow completed by the morning. Spare nothing to ferret out the best that can be acquired, preferably under one roof, but a merger will do. I want them to start work as soon as the ink is dry. The list of acquisitions will grow long. Let's see how well you handle this one."

"A piece of cake."

"We'll see. Your solemn word, then: will you be my accomplice? Three monkeys to your silent partner's political crimes?"

I did not share the fire that fueled her, but I was almost glad of the stakes, which removed failure as an option. I admired and felt for her. I could not deny it. I was buoyed in her presence to be a far better Ken, and I was grateful for that; and she was mine alone in the wide universe. There was no turning away from a privilege beyond my deserving.

"Partners, Sa. My solemn word," I said with a secret prayer to what gods may be.

"Very well, then," she said, glad of what she read in my face. "I invite you to the blood bond I spoke of on the Tower." She held out her arm, palm forward, and I extended my forefinger toward it. With a fingernail she'd nicked me before I knew it, then cut her palm minutely.

I mouthed a silent ouch and moved my finger with its tiny bead of blood into her palm, pressing to find her resistance, eyes fathoming hers for a moment. I tingled from the roots of my hair to the end of my toes as together we broke off contact, as if by silent agreement, sharing wondrous smiles.

"Well, partner," she said. "We will have the good life of it too. Let's make a toast. I requested a rare port for the ride. There, on the shelf. I've had it before in the afternoon at the manor, and it leaves a most wonderful glow. Just one glass though. You can get happy on the trip back if you like. It will be a several hours drive."

I placed the bottle and liqueur glasses on the table, my wounded forefinger extended to preserve her precious blood commingled with mine.

"Here you are," I said, pouring a few drops of the deep purple liquid into her glass and filling mine.

"More than one milestone has been passed," she said, then extended her hands around the delicate glass and hefted it slowly. "To us then, you and I, our partnership, and long fulfilling lives," she said filling her mouth as I did mine. Her smile turned wry as she caught my eyes in an embarrassment of tenderness. I wondered again what my heart was doing.

"I should get a text off to my father now. It were best he is not seen with you in town. The Old Man may hear of it, and there'll be questions my father cannot answer. He does not understand that I am thirty-four and my life's work has begun. The time will soon come that I can no longer live on the estate.

"One day, we'll have a spire in the City for the company you will charter in Road Town, but I'll have a place in Blackhead for us to meet by the time you get back. I can sail down to the valley and motor back up to the estate when I have a new plane."

She was awakening me to the fact that we would not see each other for some weeks at least, that we would only meet on the

Net, and this time in the car was all we had left to us until then, a fleeting honeymoon of sorts before we parted.

"I don't think I'll be missing my apartment anytime soon," I said. "It seems a shame to waste the rent though, after all that misery over it. Ah, I can ask Robbie to move in from Canarsie. He'll love that, and he can help with due diligence from my Level 7 there."

"Good. I'm thinking a townhouse in the City for business and residence by the end of the year. You can use the top floor for living and reserve a room for me. Stay at your apartment while you see to its equipment and furnishing, if you wish. Hereabouts I already know a few spreads that will be soon be foreclosed and serve the turn nicely."

"How do you know about them before they're in hock?"

"The staff at the manor gossip, and Pedro hears everything. Some of the Old Man's cronies have getaways up here and have paid the devil his due in the recent crash.

"Small businesses are also going under. Whatever doesn't depend on the estate hurts badly in a downturn. There's an election for mayor coming up and I intend to influence its outcome, the more since the Old Man troubles himself to do so."

"You're involved in local politics?"

"Does that surprise you? I'm a local girl, if you will, and as country as they come, more country than my country-men. Though I have travelled widely in the Old Man's stereovision, I had not ventured outside Greene county before I landed in your car. I have had neither desire nor purpose to do so. I cannot ignore the estate's overbearing influence locally."

She paused for a moment, then added mysteriously, "There is much wonder in our meeting, Ken, more than you or I shall ever know." She hoisted her glass. "To serendipity."

"I'll drink to that," I said, tasting the heavy wine.

"At the last Board meeting, the IIB planned to extend its tentacles to the more volatile regions of the world. The Old Man has declared the IIB for influence over national economies even if it dampens short term margins, gambling there will be windfalls in war and long term gains in their aftermath. There are also rumors of new mineral and oil discoveries. The précis of these meetings at the manor informs US foreign policy. This mad bomber's attack presents new opportunities for his investors and their government both. I have my work cut out."

An incoming message chimed. "There," she said turning to the monitor and keyboard. "There's his reply already. We'll meet at the Villager restaurant as planned. Shall we see what the media is up to?"

"Might as well," I said reluctantly, jealous of the intrusion but curious myself.

"The monstrous has been my fare from birth, Ken," she confided, opening a news channel. "I seldom know the world otherwise."

We were greeted by a street level view of Fifth Avenue thronged with enraged City denizens as the plane approached low. The living mass marked the air machine's passing with raging fists and a roar of animal fury in rolling unison.

The scene shifted to the Brooklyn shore, a montage of stampeding terror as people fell beneath the onslaught of blind panic from behind, the death cloud visibly menacing on the river.

She engaged audio command. "Empire City government," she said. We were both startled to see the Old Man in his role as Chairman of the Board for Empire City flanked by its CEO, Lionel Boomberg, and its Security Chief, the scar-faced Rudolf Haar. The FBI Director and a National Security Agency officer rounded out the speakers at a cluster of podiums. We listened attentively, waiting for the Old Man's temper to find its way out of his solemn and officious facade.

"If they take questions, he'll lose it, ten to one," I said.

"I'll take those odds, but keep your money. If there are questions, they will be sugared ones from his plants among the journalists."

The Old Man introduced the Deputy Director of the FBI, Mr. Charlton Ayre, as the camera shifted to him adjusting the outdoor microphone, the noise of nearby helicopters carried over the airways.

"As the NSA spokesman has noted, intelligence is being analyzed as we speak. We ask for your patience while our investigators do their work. There is every indication that a support cell does exist within US borders, but we have no indication that other attacks have been planned. The President has declared Homeland Code Red, and we are deployed accordingly. We are of course constrained in what we can share with the public while investigations are underway."

"Thank you," said the Old Man, nodding his head to let a lock of grey hair spill boyishly forward. "We'll now hear from Security Chief Haar."

"I'd first like to dispel some of the rumors I've heard going around. The missile defense system did not malfunction. It was deactivated after the second missile struck the bridge and the nature of the threat was known. The pilot was flying full throttle at car level and was across the river in less than a minute. The light anti-aircraft missiles that struck the GW Bridge caused no structural damage and only minor indirect injury to motorists at the scene. The wind at the time was blowing from the west, and we halted the automatic response system on the assumption that the pilot's claims of chemical and biological weapons were true. Our response plan for a small plane threat was activated before the aircraft reached the West Side. There was no option to force it down or destroy it without detonating its deadly cargo. No order was given to crowd the pilot out over the East River, though once he took that course we seized the earliest opportunity to kill the pilot before he reached Brooklyn. The City's private defense force acted quickly and professionally and saved countless lives. We mourn the tragic loss of life of two brave helicopter crews, eight brave men who gave their lives for us today. Their families' grief and our own is shared by a grateful City."

"In recognition of their heroic service," the Old Man stepped in, "and as Chairman of the Board of that grateful City, I am setting up a trust on behalf of the families of these brave soldiers. Their survivors shall not want."

"Look at him," she said without moving her eyes from the screen. "He's really shaken up."

"The vicious twinkle is missing," I added. "I'm afraid you were right."

"He is gritting his teeth as he does in his sleep."

"Questions?!" he barked, as if to shake himself from a spell that had taken hold of him.

The reporters clamored in their bid for his attention. The Old Man pointed to a young pup from Box News, but a nearby correspondent brazenly called out his question instead.

"Mr. Chairman, what do you say to the persistent reports of an even greater number of fatalities on the Brooklyn side of the river? Seventeen have been reported dead and several hundred severely injured."

The Old Man was obviously caught off guard by the question, which was evidently not in the script.

"Brooklyn's handling of the situation at the shore is hardly comparable."

The Brooklyn Borough President could be seen to bristle at the snarling rebuke in the Old Man's voice.

"You win after all," Sa admitted.

He was arrested in his distemper by the Empire City Security Chief. "If I may, Mr. Chairman. I have the facts from my counterpart in Brooklyn. There have been fatalities along the river despite our early warning to keep crowds from the shore. There was simply not enough time, by official accounts. All of the reported fatalities and injuries were from stampeding and reckless disorder after the bomb detonated. The perpetrator had a clear path to exit south to the harbor, but he saw the crowd and went for them. We have it on video. He knew the wind direction as well as anyone. If he had not bolted over the East River, our helicopters would not have collided. They were in a blocking pattern to prevent that from happening and the pilots and crews sacrificed their lives protecting Brooklyn."

We looked to each other. That was not what we had witnessed from our high perch. "The choppers went down long well before he turned to Brooklyn," I said.

"They went up in unison and gave him the option of the crowd, and then the bomber took it," she recalled.

"Mr. Chairman," resounded the chorus of supplicants. The Old Man again pointed and nodded to a reporter, a mature woman from the Wall Street Times, which the Old Man owned.

"Mr. Chairman, how long before the City is back on its feet?"

"Thank you, Margaret," the Old Man responded, obviously grateful for the canned question. "We intend to declare a market holiday tomorrow in deference to our fallen, but all City services will resume the minute it is humanly possible to do so. We encourage all businesses to remain open, and we urge everyone to show their mettle by going to work as usual. It is the only way to defeat these madmen."

"Follow up," the newswoman declared, and the Old Man nodded.

"What effect do you foresee on the City economy?"

"Life must go on; there is no stopping us. We do have reason to conclude, though I cannot disclose the details at this time, that this was an isolated attack. These are dangerous times, as you know, and none of us has a crystal ball. We are always vulnerable to suicide attack. No defense is foolproof."

The litany of platitudes did not stop there, but ever mindful of business, he refined them somewhat as he continued.

"As to the economy, this comes on the heels of a retrenchment in the market, risk aversion in banking and capital management, and flight to safety. I expect the City to rebound with courage, a brief disruption in tourism the only real economic consequence specific to the attack. This may well be the best buying opportunity for Empire City stock in a generation."

"Mr. Chairman!" burst the shouts.

"Last question," he commanded, pointing to a reporter in the back row.

"Sir, is there any indication those responsible were aided by a rogue nation state, as real estate magnate Arnold Krump has publicly stated?"

"Arnold is entitled to his private opinion, but I'll let Homeland Security answer that for the record." The view shifted to the Homeland Security Director.

"The shape of the particle and gas explosion indicates a high level of technical sophistication to produce the device. We are still running tests, but we see all the hallmarks of the Al Qaeda network, which as you know is tolerated in certain technologically advanced nations around the world."

The Old Man spoke and the frame cut over to him. "The City's Security Director will be holding updates through the evening, and the City newsroom will be netcasting as events unfold. That's all for now."

Security agents ushered the speakers from the podium and the scene cut to a newsroom, but not before a general groan was heard from the ignored and frustrated reporters on the scene.

Sa commanded an alt-news venue. Two young men and an older woman appeared seated at a round table in casual dress. "Take a look at these two clips. The first is from a roof along Broadway," the woman said, cueing a video feed.

The pilot of the stunt plane hurtled out of the Broadway canyon and looped over, causing two choppers above him to take desperate evasive action, which brought them into collision. The choppers exploded on impact as the plane flew upside down before righting itself, heading in the opposite direction, north.

The next clip showed a point of view from the Brooklyn shore just north of the bridge as the swarm of helicopters rose in unison along the east side of Empire City from the vicinity of the Brooklyn Bridge down to the south end of the island, clearing those directions. The white plane was heading south now along Broadway and rolled eastward toward the Bridge easily, with nothing to block its way. The footage was damning to the assertion we'd just heard which conflated these separate events and confirmed what Sa and I had witnessed, though I could make no sense of the barefaced lie.

The bomber went through his see-saw maneuvers clinging to the bridge, and a rocket streaked by, barely missing. As he began his dive, tracer fire crossed his path and the plane exploded in a ball of flame, which was followed by another explosion that concealed the flaming wreck in an expanding sphere of smoke. The sinister cloud drifted ever nearer and lower until it seemed it must consume the shore, but then the wind miraculously changed and the still cohesive, much expanded ball of particulate drifted back over the water before our eyes, losing form as it went.

"Apart from the near universal expression that the change in wind direction was a miracle, which is understandable, how does this fit with the story we've just heard from the City desk?" the older woman asked. "You first, Tom."

The next speaker was about as clean-cut and all American as the freckles on his face.

"Well, it's pretty clear the helicopters were opening the way and the bomber took advantage of the opening. It looked to me as if they wanted him out, east or south. I've heard reports that Broadway was nearly empty at the point where he veered off, which might indicate he thought a detonation then and there would not inflict enough casualties. He may have noticed the size of the crowd massed on the far shore and so turned eastward."

"Do you think we will ever know the truth, Chris?" the woman asked of the other young man, a lanky blond with long hair tied behind.

"I'd have to say the truth of the matter isn't the question. It's what will people believe. Empire City News is likely checking and editing all its video as we speak. There'll be a war of videos, and people will believe what they want to believe."

"I'd have to agree," said the first. "It's unlikely we'll ever know the orders or intentions. In the end, the official version will prevail, despite this video and the protests gathering in Brooklyn."

"That Empire City sought to dump its terror on Brooklyn to save its own inhabitants is clear to me," the lanky blonde added, "but as long as they put out news to the contrary, the nation on the whole will choose to believe it."

"Is that what it comes to, then? No investigation, no charges. Believe what you like?" the moderator asked.

The others both seemed to agree, but the freckled youth wondered aloud, "Why not dump it on Brooklyn or Queens? From an objective point of view, if Americans have to die, why blame Empire City for not wanting it to be them? It may not be admirable behavior, so they're fibbing about it, but it's understandable."

"This from one so young," Sa lamented, shaking her head.

"What do we know about the bomber?" the woman prompted.

"We know he was one hell of a pilot," the freckled boy chimed back in. "That much even Box News is granting. It seems he was well educated, to judge from his speech. He was obviously a religious fanatic, as they all have been."

"The guy must have had nerves of steel," the thin blonde man opined, "to fly aerobatic stunts in a confined space while reciting a murderous speech, then force them to pull the trigger on your bomb. This was a highly trained pilot and a hardened militant, not some crazy man looking forward to a harem of virgins."

"Are we facing a new breed of terrorism then?" the moderator asked.

"Enough," Sahar said, turning off the Netcast. "We are facing a new breed of capitalism. I suspect the Old Man was not himself because some guilty knowledge is humbling him. Few things cause him such discomfiture as humility."

"He was definitely out of sorts. It couldn't just be the shock of it all?"

"I don't think so, not entirely. Subtract the public hypocrisy from the emotion he could not conceal and there is something amiss, unknown to him beforehand. Maybe the FBI has something on him, or his friends at the CIA. Or he could have conspired to produce this as theatre for political ends and is queasy now that he has blood on his hands."

"You really think he would do that?" I asked incredulously.

"No. What I think is that, for a hundred billion in war profits, he would write down a billion or two in tourist trade. We shall have a dozen conspiracy theories before the week is out. I will leave speculation to others."

"War profits?"

"Back to the Pakistani frontier is my guess, what with the mineral finds there. He'll want to secure the area for his multinational clients with or without Pakistani cooperation."

"You think they'll talk about that at this board meeting?"

"They will surely seek to capitalize on the event, as they would any other. Their grey operations they speak of openly; the black are reserved for private conversations among the Quorum."

We were quiet for a moment. Sa walked to the window and drew a curtain. "We will be there shortly."

"Ten minutes, sir," came from the driver on the heels of her remark.

I moved up front to activate the intercom. "We'll be stopping at the Villager restaurant. Do you know it?"

"Yes, sir. I am there most often."

I slid back over to Sa, who was sitting lotus on the table. "Will you play my suitor?" she asked.

"Suitor?"

"Just don't ask about Kiera, he knows no more than I do, and look at me as you always look at me. Nothing should be explained. Leave him to understand for himself."

"How do I look at you?"

"Like you like what you see," she said, smiling and ignoring my blush. "Let's also try to keep off the subject of the attack if we can. We don't actually know more than anyone watching the news. Ask him about the west slope he will be landscaping this Spring if you like."

I nodded agreement, getting more nervous by the millisecond.

"Few know what a genius my father is," she went on. "I don't use the word lightly," rising to stand and stretch herself a little. "He is like a Picasso who has been condemned to menial labor. He has been chased from himself all his life, condemned to survive on one finger of his talent so he cannot get to the other nine. It makes me as mad as Ahab to see one such soul so wasted.

"Capitalism exhausts our hopes, and strips the soul desolate. Toiling for *el cáncer parasitario* has so eaten my father away that his life seems worth no more than his pay, a trifle to squander. He understands how this poison works well enough, but he cannot help himself now. The conditioning is deep, and he will not let me ease his way to greatness. He is resigned to the solace of Jesus and Marx and the pleasure of his handiwork on my behalf. He says I am his great work of art. He has a good answer always, for everything. We would have an earthly paradise in a world of such men as my father."

She was quiet for a while, but I could see anxiety in her eyes. "I expect this will be brief," she finally said. "Once we get him into the limo, he will not want to stay long. He claims luxury burns his skin."

"It's hard to say good-bye. I'm afraid I won't see you again."

"No good-byes. Until we meet again," she replied automatically, then considered for a moment. "We've made a good start, haven't we?" she asked.

I dared not speak for emotion and nodded a lot.

"Events have not been kind to us, Ken, and yet we've done well. There is some binding to this happenstance. From the moment you arrived at the estate, all that has occurred may have been of one confluence for all I know. The very pattern of the shot that hit my plane may have had a part. The gust that carried me to your car. Your despair. The sky of hate this morning. The change of wind they call a miracle. If only I could see the whole of its entwining sense.

"We're here," she added as if suddenly sensing her location, and as if at her command, the car slowed and turned lazily, tires crunching over the snow as it bounced into a driveway.

I drew back a curtain from the side window and looked about the parking area and the restaurant beyond, a clapboard house with a low porch on two sides. Pedro's pale blue pickup truck was by the front entrance, but he was nowhere in sight. We rolled smoothly to a stop.

"I'll get squared with the driver and find Pedro," I volunteered.

"No, ask the driver to go inside and order for both of you. When Pedro sees the driver, he'll come out to the porch to check. Wave him over. We don't want you seen together by customers, the restaurant help, or the driver for that matter, if we can help it. No one is anonymous in this town."

"Sir, we have arrived already at the restaurant," came over the intercom. She walked behind the wine bottle as I slid over to the sound proof partition and opened it with a smile. "Thank you. That was a remarkably smooth ride with all the snow."

"It is very little left on the highway, and so the road was covered in snow just these last few miles. A few weeks more and it will all be gone."

"I have someone to meet here in the car briefly. It's very important but will not take long. And then I go back the way we came. Do they have takeout?"

"Oh yes, sir. They make the tastiest sandwiches to go. Many drivers make a stop here to get something," he said, his Indian singsong making me smile.

"Would you mind getting us a few sandwiches?"

"Yes, sir. It was my intention to suggest this for yourself, sir."

"Take whatever break you need. It will be a long drive to Vermont."

"What will I order for you?"

"You know their sandwiches. I'll have what you have."

"They charge quite a lot, but there is nothing to complain of in the making of their sandwiches. I like the hot pastrami, but the roast beef is also very good, as is also the roast turkey with bacon."

"My treat. I'll chit you a hundred. Get me a pastrami for now. We can stop for something on the way back. There's plenty here to drink, so that's it for me. Keep the change."

"Most generous, sir." I tapped the amount into my card and my card to his. The transaction displayed.

"Would you not like to stretch your legs, sir, or use the facilities?"

"In a few minutes, thanks."

"Very well, sir. I'll go in now and make the order for us."

"Take your time," I managed to add belatedly as he left the car and headed for the front entrance. I shut the black partition, then turned back the side curtain to watch his progress. He no sooner gained the porch than Pedro appeared in the doorway, plainly sizing up our driver. He glanced over in our direction and headed out as the driver entered the building. They exchanged a brief acknowledgement as they moved past each other.

He did not come directly to the limo, but instead went to his truck and retrieved a bulging brown paper bag. Cradling this in one arm, he came over to us with an earnest intensity that I understood all at once was more suited to the occasion than any pretense of nonchalance I was contemplating. I saw him in a new light, as never before. He seemed now, as she said, a formidable man. His pleasant features were darkened over now, his eyes wide, alert, emotional, and intelligent under the shade of his cap. He was in a way as intense as Sahar.

Whatever I may have known from prior meetings with fathers of women, whatever enabled me to get through them, the circumstance of this particular father-meeting played havoc with all balance, proportion, convention, and propriety. I was utterly at a loss where I stood and felt helplessly unready for the encounter.

"Slide over to the back where he can see you." I slid over to the right rear door and drew down the window. He recognized me and I waved. "Give me your palm and take me to the seat," she said with some excitement of her own. She stepped off my palm to the seat on my left.

"If we keep calm, Ken, he will too. You are the key. You have to show us calm. Get him to smile. Open the door. You can do it."

I focused on my breathing to steady myself and opened the door. Suddenly it came to me. The bag was full of... "Apples?" I exclaimed to him, involuntarily smiling with a nod toward the bag tucked in his arm.

He seemed surprised and regarded the bag as if he'd forgotten it were there. Then he smiled back and said, "*Si*, they are *dorado delicioso*, winter apples from the devil's sun house."

I took the bag from him and he caught sight of Sahar standing beyond me on the backseat.

"Come inside, Papa," she said. There was a sorrowful moment between them, the man's eyes wet, the woman's wide and tender. What did I really know about either of these two?

"Let me just put these on the table over here," I said as I moved back to the side seat, leaving the rear to the two of them.

I reached the ice bowl to the table and poured apples into it as Pedro slid onto the seat, half in and half out of the limo.

"Close the door and let me kiss you," Sa said.

He slid over bringing the door closed, and leaned down to her, closing his eyes as she pressed her brow to his forehead, kissed each of his eyelids, and then his hands. When he opened his eyes, they were brimming, as were hers.

She leapt up and laid her head on his heart, clutching the wool of his jacket. He stroked her back with two fingers.

"Papa, Papa. Do not be sad. Look, here is Ken," she said, swinging her arm out to direct his attention.

"*Gracias*, Ken. You have brought her back to me. You cannot know what worry she brings me."

"Close the curtain, Papa," she said sliding down to the seat again.

"*Si*," he said. "So, you are ready now to come home, or no?" he asked her soberly, one adult to another.

"Yes, Papa. I have come home, to you and all my happiness. Ken will be getting a place outside of town and another place in the City for our new business."

"You will live here in the village?" he said to me. "What new business?" he said to her. "You are going to join them to make philanthropy?" She did not answer and made a face.

The them to which he referred, I realized was me, a creature, as far as he knew, of Wall Street and the Old Man's granddaughter.

I was no longer his sometimes friend but an outsider stealing his precious gift from under his very nose.

"She is going to make the philanthropy," I volunteered. "I am going to make the money. Is that about right?"

"My father is teasing me," she explained. "He detests the lie of philanthropy as much as I do. For the time being, let us call it revolutionary social enterprise."

"You think you can do something alone, no? How is this not philanthropy? This isolation is where you will hurt yourself. The real *filántropo* is the worker, suffering his wage to make goods."

"We are all hurt, Papa. I see all victims, including *los capitalistas*. And I am not alone anymore. Ken has agreed to be my partner. In time, our argument will have critical mass with a life of its own. You saw today what madness we provoke in the world."

"*Mi angel, mi mariposa, en solidaridad las personas son oídas.*"

"*La solidaridad necesita empujar,*" she said. A jump start," she translated for me.

It seemed they had revived a familiar argument and were resigned to disagree.

"Ken, ayeee," he said as if seeing me there for the first time, and then he laughed nervously. "I can almost not believe you are there, that I am here present with other eyes seeing her," he said, gesturing.

"How can I trust you with her?" he shot at me in sudden earnestness. "She can be beaten to death by a rainstorm."

I stammered, my breath taken away at the reality he had just suggested. "I think it's her that you can trust with me. She's the boss."

"You see, Papa? Trust me. I trust him. Soon you will too. You know the shadow is long, the time has come for me to be about my business."

"What is this business?"

"A holding company to start," I replied in response to her cue for me to answer.

"That is a business?"

"The starting point for acquiring or incubating any number of businesses."

"Do you call yourself a capitalist to your friends?"

"Papa!"

"Well, yes, Pedro. You know me." I squirmed.

"*Si*. It is the money and the women with you."

"Don't forget the fast cars," I added, guilty as charged. "I have had two days with her and my life has...let's just say I am still finding 'up' where 'down' was."

"*Si*. She does the same to me, *mi mariposa capitalista*, after thirty-five years. It does not get better with time," he confided to me, his tone softening. "But why do you say two days? She is three weeks with you."

"I was observing, Papa. To prepare him, I spoke in his dreams."

"For so long?" Neither she nor I answered, and he went on. "Sasita, he is two days old, two days in the world with you, and you trust him?!"

"Yes, Papa. Is this how you speak of my partner and the man who brought me home to you? He is earning my trust with his open mind, and we are earning his. So, enough of this. You know you like each other. You and I are the same as three weeks ago, but Ken is facing many difficult changes, and rather bravely."

"*El leopardo no cambia su piel,*" he said.

"You must be patient, Papa."

"I apologize, Ken. She is my blood, *y milagro de mi vida.*"

"I am not a miracle, Papa."

I took a cue from hunger, wondering about the driver's return, and picked up an apple. I took a loud bite.

"God, these are good," I fairly grunted, surprised. My taste buds tingled with its citric sweetness. My whole mouth came alive. "Umnh," I grunted aloud. It seemed the first apple of my life. How could such an apple be an accident in the cosmic scheme of things, I wondered. "Wow. Mystic apple. Want some?" I offered Sahar.

"Yes," she said, and the fruit was no sooner extended to her reach than her sword appeared and sliced out a piece in two strokes, the wedge of apple still rocking on the table with the blade restored its sheath. She raised it in both hands and took a bite.

"She likes to show off *con la espada,*" Pedro said, taking an apple himself and biting in with a popping sound. The three of us munched on the exquisite moment without words.

"I will welcome the woods in the moonlight tonight," she said, breaking the silence. "Did you find where my plane crashed, Papa?"

"*Si.* It is not worth repairing. I have most of the new parts, and the new one will be ready soon."

"*Su corazón es mi casa,*" she said.

"*Suyo es mío también,*" he replied. "*Ahora,* before you tell me we must hurry up and go, what are all these packages I am picking up at the post office? What are you up to?"

"It is a surprise," she said evasively. Evidently Pedro didn't know what she had planned for the Quorum at the manor house.

"There is more trouble from the guards than I have seen. *Es la conferencia de criminales, no*? There is more danger now. More security, new cameras for this board meeting. I had to let them inspect our house."

At this Sa's expression showed alarm.

"*Si*. I took care to hide all your equipment where we agreed. You must check they did not put some device to hear or see in the house. It is no time to be going to the mansion, Sasita," he warned, shaking his head somberly. "There is much tension. And the snow is deep, we have five inches new from last night."

"I shall use skis," she said, despite the worry on her face at the picture he was sketching. She was unwilling to compromise.

"It is damp snow and will freeze tonight."

"The snowmobile then. It was an electric toy before Papa adapted it for me," she explained for my benefit. "Is the battery charged, Papa?" she asked, her tone unaffected by the dark concern written on Pedro's brow. She seemed to me too confident, and it was my turn to worry about her perilous plans at Fortress Wellingham.

"I have much to do. Papa, we should go before the driver comes."

"He can say to the driver I sell him apples."

"Ken's brother expects him in Vermont," she chided. "He has a long ride back the way we came."

I took my cue and confirmed by nodding.

And with that she climbed onto Pedro's thigh and made her way up to his jacket zipper, which she pulled, peeling back the cloth to reveal its fleece lining and inner pocket. She lowered herself into it.

"I'll be warm by your heart, Papa. Ken, I will text you a link for your security downloads, and instructions how to reach me. Let's confer at least once a day. I can arrange a secure channel, but the caller must page the other to call back in order to complete the connection. The details will be in the brief. You will have your expense account tonight, and they are expecting you in Road Town within the week. Go when it suits you. Happy hunting. Yes?"

I could feel myself beginning to panic at the impending loss, the moment so quickly at hand, her safety so uncertain. She blushed a little and hustled her father along.

"Come, Papa. Hand on the door. We have to go now. We will have many happy visits with our new neighbor to look forward to."

Pedro put his hand on the latch and reluctantly pulled, releasing the door with a clunk, then pushed it open. I felt I too would vanish at her departure so precipitously upon me. It was all I could do not to call out to her, to beseech her not to leave me alone with myself. I could not tell if her eyes were wet for mine were awash.

"We'll be together soon, Ken. Soldier up," she teased me. "You have weeks of sun and surf ahead of you, but get me my engineers. We will see each other soon on the vid. Keep to the world as you did before Sa," she said firmly.

"*Vaya con dios.* We talk when you come back," Pedro said with resignation, sliding out with our precious cargo.

I nodded and managed a sound of affirmation that was not quite a word. Then the door clunked solidly shut. I drew the curtain to watch him strike off toward his truck, Sa's head and shoulder poking up above his lapel as she looked back at me. She waved gently, then ducked away at the sound of the restaurant door.

She was gone, and I found my heart pounding, certain some crucial thing was left unsaid.

~ E N D ~